———••——⬥——••———

On the periphery of his awareness, Zeth noticed Owen come in and fall to his knees in horror over Del's body. Del's body! Dad killed!

That agony hit Zeth just at the moment when Rimon drained his secondary system and was ripping away at the natural barrier, making Zeth flinch away in self-preservation as his father's life ebbed away beneath his tentacles.

No—I won't kill. Ever!

He willed his system to flip over into primary mode and let his father drain and drain him. His body convulsed, ripping loose the contact points just as pain ceased in blackness. It was beyond his endurance. He could have held it no longer, even to save his father's life, and Fort Freedom's dream. . . .

"The authors quickly summarize earlier events so a newcomer to the series will not feel lost. Lorrah and Litchtenberg, both of whom have also long been active in *Star Trek* fandom, have created a rich world peopled with believable characters. The Sime/Gen relationship establishes the thematic undercurrent of the interdependency of all mankind. Moreover, these books have spawned three fanzines to handle comments on and contributions to the series background and to advise the authors about future projects."

—*Science Fiction & Fantasy Book Review*

CHANNEL'S DESTINY

A Sime/Gen Novel

by
JEAN LORRAH
and
JACQUELINE LICHTENBERG

DAW BOOKS, INC.
DONALD A. WOLLHEIM, PUBLISHER

1633 Broadway, New York, N.Y. 10019

FIRST PRINTING, DECEMBER 1983

1 2 3 4 5 6 7 8 9

DAW TRADEMARK REGISTERED
U.S. PAT. OFF. MARCA
REGISTRADA. HECHO EN U.S.A.

PRINTED IN U.S.A.

ACKNOWLEDGMENTS

To the economy, but for which this book would have been somewhat longer, and might have covered the actual founding of the House of Zeor.

Also to all the Sime/Gen fans who have read and commented on this book in manuscript and kept up the dialogue on the series background in the three Sime/Gen fanzines. (For information on the fanzines, send a self-addressed stamped envelope to AMBROV ZEOR, Box 290, Monsey, NY 10952.)

Thanks to Anne Golar for helpful medical research, and to Katie Filipowicz for many thankless tasks in putting this book together.

And to all our readers—if you would like to comment on this book or the Sime/Gen series, you may write to us in care of the publisher, or through the AMBROV ZEOR address, above.

Jean Lorrah   Jacqueline Lichtenberg
Murray, Kentucky   Spring Valley, New York

Chapter 1

"No matter what happens," said Zeth Farris, trembling with an emotion he could not name, "when I grow up, I'm never going to kill."

"You can't say that for sure," challenged Jana Lodge Erick, tossing her braids back over her shoulders.

Her older brother Owen said, "Zeth's going to be a channel, like his father. And channels don't have to kill."

The three children were walking along behind their dogs, herding sheep into a sheltered pasture. Zeth, the youngest of the three, had to stretch to keep up. As he caught them, he saw a stern glare pass from Jana to Owen, the same kind of glare grownups used to swerve conversations away from topics not for children.

"No matter what your father says, there's no way to know if you'll be Sime or Gen," said Jana.

"It doesn't matter," replied Zeth, with the belligerence Jana always seemed to wake in him. "Even if I'm only a Sime, not a channel, I still won't kill. It's too hard to stop once you start."

"That's why I want to be a channel," said Owen. "To heal people. I want to be a healer."

Zeth had heard this argument many times, and knew there was nothing Jana could say to deter Owen. But Jana snorted at her brother's ambition. "I'd rather be Gen. A Sime is either a channel or he isn't. But a Gen can learn—"

"Hey, listen!" Zeth interrupted. "Is that the bell?"

"Can't be," said Owen. "Can't hear it from here!"

But the wind was carrying faint echoes. "Let's go see," said Jana. Instructing the dogs to mind the sheep, the children scrambled back along the trail toward the stockade of Old

Fort Freedom. As they emerged onto a rise of ground over-looking the neat community, the pealing of the bell became clearer and clearer—until the alarm pattern sounded *danger* across the landscape.

As far as the children could see, the land was part of the township of Fort Freedom. The original religious community still stood on one side of the creek, but on the other was a growing secular community, loosely incorporated with them and sharing their ideals.

In the far distance, the hilly land on which Owen and Jana's father raised the finest horses in the Territory sloped down to join the New Farris Homestead. There, at his own home, Zeth spotted a column of black smoke. "It's a fire!" he shouted. "Come on!"

The three children ran pell-mell down the trail and across the newly sprouted fields just in time to catch the last riders from the Old Fort. Dan Whelan, the blacksmith, slowed his horse to catch Zeth up in front of him. "Hang on!"

"I'm all right," Zeth panted. "What's going on?"

"Raid. You kids get out of the way. I'll drop you, and you run on up to Mr. Erick's."

"But Dad and Mama—" started Zeth.

"They'll want you *safe!*"

Zeth was safe enough for the moment, Mr. Whelan holding one arm about the boy's waist, the other hand on the reins, handling tentacles out to steady them. His laterals lay quietly sheathed amid the rippling musculature of the smith's forearms.

After one glance at those calm laterals, Zeth let his fear well up. His child's nager could not irritate Mr. Whelan.

"Dan!" called one of the other men. "Are they Freeband Raiders?" Such outlaw bands descended like locusts, stealing, looting, killing Gens, murdering Simes—but Fort Freedom had not seen a band of them in years.

Zeth had one clear memory of a group of Gens—his mother, Hank and Anni Steers, some others—advancing on the aston-ished Raiders, sending the scarecrow forms scurrying to their horses. Had he seen it, or been told about it? He recalled the nightmare image of a tattered, skeletal Raider grasping his mother, trying to kill her the way Simes used to kill Gens, by draining her life energy.

But Kadi Farris could not be killed. Her red hair was a halo of flame, her body surrounded by a glowing nimbus that drew her attacker helplessly, hands and tentacles grasping her smooth, untentacled arms, lips pressed to hers—

And then a blinding flash, deafening thunder, and the Sime attacker lay dead at his mother's feet.

Zeth could not have seen it like that. He was a child; he couldn't zlin fields. He wasn't sure he had seen it at all, or if it was his father's vivid account engraved on his mind. The raid when he was four was the last Fort Freedom had seen of Freeband Raiders, because they'd developed a superstitious fear of Gens who could kill.

As they drew near, Zeth saw one of the barns burning. Mr. Whelan and the riders who had picked up Owen and Jana swerved off toward the hills, where Del Erick's land lay.

"You kids get on up to your father's place—Zeth, you stay with them till someone comes for you," Mr. Whelan instructed. "Head around to the east!" he called to the other riders. "Shen! Who'd have thought they'd attack Farris?"

"I'm going home!" Zeth said to the older children.

"But Mr. Whelan said—" Owen began.

"Zeth," interrupted Jana, "you come on home with us now."

"I don't have to listen to you! That's my house down there! Your pa's down there," added Zeth. "You know he would've gone to help."

"That's right!" Jana said. "We'll all go!"

The children scuttled down the hillside, through a stand of evergreens, to the edge of the fields. The attackers were not Freeband Raiders, but in-Territory Simes, farmers, sheep ranchers, tradespeople—a posse, not militia.

Nor did Zeth see any badge of authority. Vigilantes, then— but why attack the Farris Homestead? All they'd ever done was good!

Zeth couldn't see his father or mother. They'd be in the house, according to the attack plan. That plan had come out of the raid when Zeth was four, when Liz Carson, a Gen Companion, died not in the kill, but from a Raider's dagger. The loss of a companion was grave indeed, but the precarious balance of their lifestyle could be overturned by the loss of a channel. They had only three: three precious lives between Fort Freedom and the kill.

A cordon of Simes protected the main house. The channels would be inside, and all Fort Freedom's Gens. No—not all. Zeth saw Hank Steers gallop up, steady as any Sime, bursting through the line of attackers as their horses reared and plunged. Zeth wished he could zlin. Mr. Steers must have hit the attacking Simes with a nageric shock. Steers, meanwhile, rode straight to the house, stood up on his saddle, and vaulted onto the porch roof. A window opened, and eager hands pulled him inside.

The torches thrown at the house could not catch in the slate roof or stone walls. People from the Old Fort and the town outnumbered the attackers, so the gang left their assault on the main house, throwing their torches at outbuildings. The three children crouched behind a wagon—until one of the attackers threw his torch onto the wooden bed. When Zeth thought the man had turned away, he jumped up to snatch the burning brand.

The man must have zlinned him, for he wheeled his horse and lunged at Zeth. Zeth tried to parry with the torch, but a ten-year-old boy was no match for a Sime. Zeth was caught up and held dangling as his captor shouted, "Shendi! Kora—hey, look what I caught!"

A woman clutching one whip in her tentacles and another in her fingers came to see. Her face was twisted with fear and hatred as she said, "Slaughter the brat! He'll grow up into one o' them perverts. Gut him, Trev!"

Zeth squirmed and kicked, but was firmly held as the man pulled his knife—not a Raider's dagger, but a farmer's sharp utility blade. Helplessly, he watched his death approach—

"No!" Owen and Jana appeared from under the wagon, Jana grabbing the horse's reins, Owen lunging for the man's knife hand. Owen's weight dragged the man off his horse and Zeth was flung aside, the breath knocked out of him.

For a moment he blacked out. When his vision cleared he saw the woman holding the squirming, kicking Jana before her on her horse. On the ground, the man hit Owen, knocking the boy down. Zeth scrabbled to his knees. His midsection hurt violently, every tiny breath torture.

"Shen!" screamed the Sime woman, and flung Jana away, nursing a hand that bled where Jana had bitten her. Jana jumped at the man beating her brother, but was thrown back against the wagon. She gave a sharp yelp of pain, and her face went white as she fell, her arm bent at an impossible angle. She tried to rise, gasped, "My arm!" and wilted, unconscious.

A child's pain might not have the penetrating effect of an

adult's, but Zeth knew pain pervaded the whole atmosphere, impinging from all sides on the two Simes. Like a harpy, the woman screamed, "Their arms! Cut off their arms, Trev! They'll die in changeover!"

Jana was unconscious, Owen helpless before the man now wielding his knife, licking his lips, eyes flaming with unholy zeal as the woman goaded him on. Zeth tried to force his rubbery legs to work, trapped in a nightmare in which his body would not obey his will.

When the Sime bent to slash at Owen, the boy tried to roll away, and the blade glanced off his shoulder, sending more pain into the atmosphere. The Sime grasped Owen's left wrist with his left hand and tentacles, and with augmented strength brought the knife slashing viciously through Owen's upper arm. Zeth clearly heard the crack of bone as, too late, he heaved himself at the man's legs.

He was kicked away, stunned, and then the attacker was looming over him, bloody knife in hand, reaching for his arm.

Behind the man the thunder of hoofbeats rose. A shower of mud cascaded over Zeth. White hair flying, Abel Veritt loomed astride his horse, wielding his whip with the skill of a Freeband Raider. The whip wrapped around the waist of Zeth's attacker, and he was caught up and flung toward another rider.

It was Del Erick, Owen and Jana's father. There was a crunch louder than the hoofbeats as Erick broke the man's neck and dropped him, not even looking back as he leaped from his horse and ran to where his children lay.

Veritt was there already, kneeling beside Owen. "Jana's arm is broken," he said. "It's not serious. But Owen—"

"Dear God!" Erick whispered—and Zeth knew it was hopeless, for Mr. Erick, like his father, would not pray unless there were nothing else a man could do.

Mr. Veritt, though, was saying, "Here—stop the bleeding. Somebody get Rimon!"

Relieved of having to try to move, Zeth watched Del Erick wrap handling tentacles to stop the bright blood spurting with every beat of Owen's heart.

Veritt took off his jacket and put it carefully over Jana. Then he turned to Zeth. "Are you all right, son?"

"I'm not hurt," Zeth lied.

"Just knocked breathless, eh?" Veritt's eyes unfocused as he zlinned the boy. Then he nodded. "You'll be all right."

"But Owen—Jana—" Tears choked Zeth's words. "Mr. Veritt, they said to cut off our arms so we'd die in changeover!"

Pure pain enveloped the old man's face. "They don't understand, Zeth. Killing is so much their way of life that it frightens them that some people have learned to live without it." He sighed. "Fear is our real enemy, not the people whom it possesses."

"But—what will happen to Owen?"

"I don't know, Zeth. It is in God's hands."

"*Will* he die in changeover?" Zeth insisted. "That man cut his arm off. I saw. I couldn't st-stop him!" Zeth fought down a dizzy nausea.

Veritt hugged him close, letting him cry, saying, "You tried. All God asks of us is to try our best, Zeth."

"But Owen's gonna die!"

Perhaps. Perhaps not. Pray for him, Zeth. That's all we can do—pray and await God's will."

But Rimon Farris did more than that when he arrived on the scene, his wife at his side. Veritt had gone back to kneel beside Del Erick and Owen, while Zeth sat watching.

Farris began directing the people with him. "Take Jana to the house—brace that arm. It's a clean fracture. Jord can set it. If she wakes up, give her fosebine. Zeth, have Uel or Jord check you over. What were you kids doing here?"

"I only meant to help," said Zeth.

"Never mind," Farris replied. He was already kneeling beside Owen. "Shen and shid!" he swore as he zlinned the boy, then looked into Del Erick's anguished eyes. "Del, he's alive. You kept him from bleeding to death, but—"

Grimly, Erick said, "If you save his life, he'll die in changeover."

Abel Veritt gently urged Del to release his grip on his son, remaining with one arm about Erick's shoulders as Zeth's father took over. The support Veritt gave was more than physical—often Zeth sensed something the older man gave to those who were troubled, whether Sime, Gen, or child.

Zeth's mother took her place beside his father. When Mr. Veritt spoke of angels, Zeth envisioned his mother as she was now, her flaming hair a halo, her hands steady on his father's shoulders as both concentrated on healing.

Blood spurted again from Owen's wound, but Farris quickly clasped the boy's arm with his own tentacles, holding and slowly releasing, in a kind of trance, untll finally he let go, and the bleeding did not start again.

When he sat back on his heels and opened his eyes, Del Erick asked, "Will he live?"

"I don't know," Farris replied. "I'm almost certain I could save a Gen with that wound—or a Sime if it were not an arm injury. But it's so hard to influence a child's fields, Del."

"Try, Rimon!"

Zeth's father said, "Del, I'll do all I can for Owen, but I can't save his arm. If he lives, it could be for only a few weeks or months. If he goes into changeover—"

"Then he's got to be Gen!" said Erick.

"Del," Abel Veritt said, "we will all pray for that, but with both parents Sime—"

"He has to be Gen," Erick insisted. "Rimon, save him!"

Zeth's father gripped Erick's shoulder, years of intense friendship in the gesture. Then his mother said, "It's damp and chilly out here. Let's get Owen into the house."

By this time, Zeth could walk. He hung back, feeling terrible guilt. It was his fault Owen was hurt—he had taunted him into coming to the New Homestead, and then Owen had gotten into the fight to save Zeth. *I'm the one they meant to hurt.*

But he couldn't say it to anyone—his father and mother had to concentrate on healing Owen, and the other three people Zeth could confide in were Owen, Del Erick, and Abel Veritt.

He arrived home deeply troubled. Patches came running to him, whimpering. Zeth saw that someone had wrapped a bandage around the dog's ribs. "What happened to Patches?" he cried.

"He's all right." It was Ann Steers, the Gen who was Hank Steers's wife. "Patches and Biggie helped drive off the attackers. Patches got some whip cuts, but poor Biggie has a broken leg."

Zeth's dog and Hank's were littermates, and Hank had helped Zeth train Patches. Now Biggie hobbled after Ann, one leg splinted. Anni bore bruises on her face and arms, but she was carefully controlled.

Upstairs, Uel Whelan and Hank Steers, who always worked with the youngest channel, were just coming out of Zeth's room. Uel said to Del Erick, "I've just checked on Jana. It's not serious, Del. She'll heal as good as new."

"Thanks, Uel," said Del. "I'll stop in to see her."

"She'll sleep till morning. You can see her then." He paused to zlin Owen as he was carried into the big bedroom Zeth's parents shared. "Rimon, can I help? Spell you?"

"Maybe later," Farris replied. "I'm in need. That may give me the sensitivity to heal Owen. How's everyone here?"

"Fine. No one was hurt as badly as the kids, except . . . they killed Teri Layton."

"I must comfort her parents," Abel Veritt said at once. But he paused, looking around. "Where is Jord?" Veritt's son was the third channel in Fort Freedom, although he wasn't as capable as either Uel Whelan or Rimon Farris. Zeth didn't understand Jord's problems, but knew they had increased after his wife died. He couldn't seem to find another Companion.

"Jord took the Laytons home," said Hank Steers. "Let him pray with them. It will help him, too—and you should rest, Abel."

Something unspoken hung in the air between the old Sime and the young Gen. Zeth knew there were things he could not comprehend because he was still a child. Today, however, he glanced at Uel Whelan and saw a peculiar mixture of compassion and revulsion on the young channel's face. He knew it was difficult for a channel to give up transfer from his Companion, even for one month. Hank gave transfer to Mr. Veritt every few months; Zeth had heard his father say it was good that Hank and Uel didn't have so strong a dependency. Still, there was something more in Uel's expression he could not fathom. *If only I could zlin!*

His parents were installing Owen in their bed. Trying to be inconspicuous, Zeth hovered just inside the door until his mother came over to him and said, "Zeth, go downstairs and eat supper."

"But Owen—"

"He's alive, Zeth," said his father. He studied Zeth, his black eyes, deep-set with strain, almost unreadable. His mouth set in lines of grim determination as he added, "You're old enough to understand. Owen isn't going to bleed to death, but his body could just give up and die of shock. I can try to save him—but I mustn't be disturbed. Kadi, go with Zeth."

"But, Rimon—you're in need."

"That's all that let me stop the bleeding. Kadi, I had to have you for that, but now . . . let me try something. With no Gen in the room, I think I can get Owen's fields to respond."

"But—"

"Let me *try*, Kadi!"

At the ragged edge in his voice, she backed off. She tucked the blanket around Owen's still form, then took Zeth's hand and left the room, closing the door behind them.

He let his mother lead him down to the kitchen, where Trina Morgan was making a huge pot of vegetable stew while Abel Veritt's wife poured trin tea. Mrs. Veritt came over to Kadi at once. "What's wrong? Why aren't you with Rimon?"

"He's trying to bring Owen out of shock. Where's Uel?"

"Making one more round. Hank will make him stop soon."

Mrs. Veritt poured tea for all of them, and sat down across from Kadi, her hands wrapped about her tea glass. Zeth, seeing her tentacles move restlessly within their sheaths, knew she was gaining strength from his mother's field. Zeth could not interrupt their rapport to talk about his own guilt.

He stared at Mrs. Veritt's arms, wondering what it would be like to have tentacles. He rubbed his forearms, raising gooseflesh as he thought, *It could have been my arm cut off, not Owen's*. A Sime died horribly if even one lateral tentacle were badly injured. The loss of an arm meant complete loss of two laterals—and death by attrition.

Zeth had learned about the Sime/Gen symbiosis in school. Simes and Gens were both human, born of the Ancients who had ruled the world before they split into Simes and Gens. Now, though, everyone was either Sime or Gen—and no child knew for certain which he would be, for all that Zeth's father insisted Zeth would be Sime.

At adolescence, a Gen began to produce selyn, the biologic energy of life. Mr. Veritt and others from Gen Territory said Gens never even knew it, although Kadi Farris, Hank Steers, and other Gens said there was a definite feeling of change.

A Gen's establishment, however, was nothing to the dramatic changeover of a Sime. As the new Sime's metabolism shifted from the caloric base of a Gen or child to the selyn base, the external change that captured the imagination of Gens and children was the development of tentacles sheathed along the forearm to emerge at the wrists. The four handling tentacles, called dorsals and ventrals, served as extra fingers or hands. The smaller laterals, however, seldom emerged except to perform their primary function: the drawing of selyn.

But the major change from child to Sime was not tentacles; it was the need for selyn, with the attendant ability to locate it, absorb it, and use it. Rimon Farris said the incredible developments in the nervous system were the true drama—and trauma—of changeover. A Sime could not produce selyn at all—yet had to have it to live. A Gen produced a huge amount beyond any imperceptible quantity he might consume. Clearly, Simes were meant to obtain selyn from Gens.

Life ought to be that simple. Zeth had grown up in a community where Simes and Gens lived together in cooperation and harmony, yet his home was legally classed as a Genfarm—a breeding farm for Gens destined to be killed by Simes stripping them of selyn. To the Simes who had attacked today, they were doing evil by avoiding the kill.

Fear is our real enemy, not the people whom it possesses.

Zeth was the first child born of one Sime and one Gen parent. Only ten years old, all his life he had heard the story of how his father, only a year before he was born, had become the first Sime to take selyn from a Gen without killing. That Gen had become Rimon's wife, Zeth's mother.

It wasn't simple. Teri Layton had been killed today—not died, been killed. Teri had established selyn production only two months ago, and had not yet given transfer. Zeth knew what had happened: the one flaw in the Sime/Gen mutation.

Once each month a Sime had to receive selyn, or die of attrition. To locate selyn, he had the ability to sense—zlin—a Gen's field. The dirty trick nature had played on the human race was to make Gen pain and fear devastatingly attractive to a Sime in need.

Thus when a Sime grasped a Gen and began to draw selyn, the feeling of selyn movement startled the Gen. Resisting the flow caused pain, feeding the Sime's need. The Sime reveled in the Gen's pain and fear, drawing against the resistance until he burned out the Gen's nervous system, killing the Gen and giving the Sime an emotional high known as killbliss.

When Zeth had begun changeover training, he had been told all this—but until today he had not been able to imagine taking pleasure in pain. Those people—Trev and Kora—would he ever forget their eyes as they attacked helpless children? *That must be killbliss,* he thought with a shudder.

It was addictive. Once a Sime killed, he sought the same

sensation every time he took selyn. When Abel Veritt told the changeover class last winter, Zeth had found it impossible to believe that Mr. Veritt could have been addicted to the kill. Yet he would never lie about it.

And every new Sime was vulnerable.

Zeth remembered the lessons, drilled over and over. Never to be alone until either changeover or establishment. Never to remain alone with a friend in changeover, but to go for a channel as soon as the victim could be left. "And especially if you are Gen," Rimon Farris reiterated, "no heroics! You may have no fear for yourself—but your fear for your friend in changeover may kill you, and at the same time addict your friend to the kill. Come for me, Uel Whelan, or Jord Veritt."

If Zeth inherited his father's capacity for selyn storage, he would also inherit his voracious need—beyond the capacity of any Companion except Kadi Farris. "That means you could kill even a Companion, Zeth," his father had warned him grimly. "Not burning out his system drawing against fear, but draining him totally. I will give you your first transfer, and you'll have transfer with Gens only after you've learned control."

That was the role of the channel: to stand between the Sime and the kill. The channels, like Rimon Farris, had a dual selyn system—one like any other Sime's and a secondary storage system which they could control. Rimon Farris was the first channel to learn that control, to draw selyn slowly from even a frightened Gen, without hurting him, and then transfer that selyn to another Sime, so he could live without killing.

Zeth was willing to do anything to learn to channel. To be like his father—the best channel—*no, Owen won't die, not with Dad there!*

"Zeth. Zeth!"

He looked up as his mother's voice penetrated. "Yes, Mama?"

She put her hand to his forehead. "Are you all right?"

"Yeah. It's just—Mama, Owen won't really die, will he?"

She hugged him tightly, and Zeth realized she knew full well that he could have been the one lying upstairs, mutilated. "Not if your father has anything to say about it! Now go find Uel Whelan, all right? Ask him to zlin you to be sure you don't have some hidden injury, and then ask him . . . to check on your father. He can do that without disturbing him."

Glad to do anything that might contribute to Owen's recovery,

Zeth went out into the yard. The setting sun cast a golden glow. A sour smell came from the smoking ruin of the hay barn. No one had yet begun to work on the trampled kitchen garden, but the fires in the other outbuildings had been doused, and the corral fence repaired.

In the long rays of the setting sun, the raiders' path sliced across the newly sprouted fields. People were shooing the dairy cows out of the field. Among them were Hank and Uel—along with Slina, who ran the pen in town. Slina wasn't "Mrs." like the women of Fort Freedom. She was Slina to everybody, and her little girl was simply Mona.

Slina was another adult mystery to Zeth. A killer with no intention of trying to stop, she always came to help when there was trouble. Even Rimon Farris and Mr. Veritt respected her. She sent Mona to school in Fort Freedom, too.

"Hi, Slina!" he called.

"Well, hi there, Zeth. Come help us move this stubborn cow."

Slina had, as usual, been in the thick of the fight. Her hair was coming loose, her boots were muddy, her shirt torn—no, slashed by a whip. He could see the cuts on her shoulder and neck. Her dagger, stuck through her belt to be cleaned before being sheathed, showed by the stains on its blade that she'd given as good as she got.

"Come on, Slina," Uel was saying, "let the others chase the cows while I treat your injuries."

She laughed. "What—these coupla cuts? I've had worse from the bite of a stubborn Gen."

"You want to contend with *this* stubborn Gen?" Hank threatened cheerfully.

"All right, all right—but there's nothing wrong with me that soap and water and a little sleep won't cure."

They walked back to the house, where Slina let Mrs. Veritt clean her wounds as Uel turned to Zeth. "How about you? Feeling achy?"

"Yeah. Mama wants you to zlin me."

"All right—let's do a thorough job. Hank—" Zeth watched as Uel's Companion moved to the precise spot where his field would cancel the Sime fields around them, allowing Uel to read Zeth's childish nager.

Slina shook her head and asked Hank, "How do you do that?"

He chuckled, "Gen secret."

Uel laid his hands gently on Zeth's forearms, wrapping his handling tentacles about the boy's arms. When his grip was secure, but not tight, the hot, moist laterals emerged to touch Zeth—a tinglingly pleasant feeling. Dismantling his grip, Uel said, "Nasty muscular strain, Zeth. Take a hot bath and get ready for bed. I'll give you some fosebine and help you heal in your sleep."

Zeth's lip curled at the thought of fosebine, but he couldn't argue with a channel. "All right—but . . . Mama wants you to check on Dad."

"I intend to," Uel assured him.

"And Owen. Uel, I don't want to be asleep if he—if he—" Tears threatened to break through.

Uel said, "I'll wake you, Zeth. I promise—whatever happens. And, Zeth—Owen is alive if your father is still in there. The longer he stays alive, the more likely his recovery."

Zeth managed a watery smile. "Thanks," he said. When he returned, though, clean and wrapped in a borrowed robe, he explained, "I don't know where I'm sleeping. Jana's in my room."

There were pallets already prepared in the upstairs hall, they found. Del Erick was sitting on a bench beside Kadi Farris, just staring at the door behind which Rimon Farris fought for his son's life.

Kadi gave Uel a welcoming smile, but no one spoke. Zeth accepted the fosebine Uel gave him, trying to drink the vile stuff down so fast his taste buds wouldn't notice it.

He didn't expect to fall asleep right away, but the next thing he knew he was in the strange state of knowing he was dreaming. Bright afternoon sun poured down as Trev and Kora tossed him aside, then grasped Owen and began to hack him to pieces. Zeth could rescue him, but his legs were a dead weight. Endlessly, Zeth tried to move, while the attackers cut off Owen's arms, his legs, his head—

The dream shifted. Rimon Farris bent over Owen, miraculously putting his body back together. The parts all joined neatly, even his clothes—but Owen was still . . . *dead*.

Del Erick was suddenly there, saying, "Save him, Rimon."

Farris looked up. "He can't live as a Sime."

"Then he has to be Gen!" said Erick desperately. "He's got to be Gen, Rimon!"

Zeth chimed in the growing chorus, "He's got to be Gen!"

"—to be Gen."

"—be Gen."

"—Gen!"

Zeth woke, disoriented to find himself on the hall floor. Dawn was breaking—but what had wakened him was the sound of a door opening. His father stood in the doorway to the master bedroom, looking unutterably weary. Del Erick sprang to his feet, his whole bearing one fearful unasked question.

"It's all right!" Farris said at once. "Owen's alive, Del, and out of shock. He's sleeping."

As Erick started forward, Farris gripped him hard by both shoulders. "Del, I almost lost him. But then, a couple of hours ago, his field shifted and suddenly I could get a grip on him. He's started selyn production—he's established, Del. He's going to live. He's going to be all right."

As his father kept talking while Del Erick slowly assimilated the news, Zeth felt a warm glow of security. *My dad can do anything, even bring a person to be Gen if he has to.*

It was only hours later that he recalled the conversation of the afternoon, and realized that Owen probably wouldn't remember anything from the time he was grabbed by the attacker until he woke up in bed, one arm missing—to be told he was Gen.

He wanted so much to be a channel. Now what?

Chapter 2

It was afternoon before Zeth was allowed to see Owen. His friend lay in the middle of the big bed, looking very pale. The blanket was pulled up over his left shoulder, hiding the stump of his missing arm. He didn't look at Zeth.

Zeth approached, his mind a confusion of guilt, curiosity, and desire to do something—anything—to help. Suddenly they were strangers. His mind fixed on the pattern of the blanket, woven from Fort Freedom's wool in bright colors, an endlessly intertwining pattern he could follow until his eye muscles jumped, and he realized the silence was dragging out as endlessly as the pattern.

Finally, Zeth blurted out the formula greeting to someone who had just become adult, Sime or Gen: "Congratulations, Owen."

Owen's eyes flashed, and fixed on Zeth's. "For what?" he demanded. "For staying alive to be a useless cripple?"

"I'm sorry!" Zeth cried, hit right upon his gullt. "It's my fault, Owen. I'm so sorry!"

Owen rolled his head away, and said through gritted teeth, "It wasn't your fault."

"I tried to stop them," said Zeth. "I couldn't move."

Owen looked at him now. "You were hurt?"

"I'm just stiff and sore, but you and Jana—"

"Jana?" Suddenly Owen was interested. "They did the same thing—?" He tried to sit up, but pain dropped him on the pillow.

"No! She'll be fine! They broke her arm. It'll heal—really! I saw her this morning."

Owen's eyes closed. "Good. Pa will have someone to help him." He put his right hand over the stump of his left arm, and grimaced.

21

"Owen, does it hurt? Should I get a channel?"

"It hurts all the way down to my fingers, and I know they're not there. No," he added as Zeth moved, "don't get a channel. They'd put me to sleep again. I'm going to sleep enough of my life away . . . as a Gen."

There was bitter self-loathing in the word "Gen." "You had to be Gen to live," Zeth pleaded. "Now you can be like Mama—like Hank Steers—"

"Don't lie to me! How can a one-armed Gen be a Companion?"

Zeth choked back his words. How could a one-armed Gen offer transfer with the crucial contact points gone?

"That's enough!" Both boys jumped at Abel Veritt's stern tones. Veritt flinched at Owen's pain, and then came steadfastly to his side, zlinning him critically. "The fosebine is wearing off. I'll get Rimon to check you over and give you more."

"What for?" Owen asked dully. "Maybe I should just die."

Veritt said, "Zeth, you're tiring Owen. Find your father, and ask him to come up here."

"He's with Mama," said Zeth. "They're having transfer."

"By now he should be—oh. Well, find Uel or Jord, then."

"Yes, sir."

"No—don't, Zeth," said Owen. "I don't want to sleep."

"What do you want, son?" Veritt asked gently.

"I want to die."

"No," said the old man. "God made you Gen to preserve your life. Do not question His wisdom."

"I don't think God cares," Owen said flatly.

In the same reasonable tone he used to teach the older children, Veritt said, "You are not thinking, Owen. You have grown up in a community blessed with constant proof of God's caring. I, too, questioned His wisdom many times when I first became Sime. Yet I've lived to see His plan unfold. We are building a world where such brutality as you've suffered can never happen again."

The grim set of Owen's features relaxed under Veritt's care, and tears began to slide down the boy's cheeks. "That's right," Veritt said, pushing Owen's bright blond hair back off his forehead. "Tears are good. Let them cleanse your grief away so you can find God's plan for you. Pray for guidance, son. There's a reason for what happened to you. I don't know what it is, but I have faith it is a part of God's plan."

Owen drifted to sleep under the spell of Mr. Veritt's words. Then the old Sime guided Zeth from the room. "How did you put him to sleep?" Zeth asked. "You're not a channel."

"Did you think I'd never noticed you boys nodding off during my sermons?"

Not believing he had heard right, Zeth looked up to find the old man's eyes twinkling. Abel Veritt joking with him? He felt suddenly grown up, admitted to the adult world . . . but he didn't deserve it.

"Zeth," Mr. Veritt said seriously, "Owen's injury is *not* your fault. You were hurt yourself, son."

The aching guilt exploded. "We shouldn't have been there! Mr. Whelan told us to go up to Mr. Erick's place, but I couldn't. I made Owen and Jana come with me."

"Let's talk about it," said Mr. Veritt, leading Zeth to the bench in the hall. "Tell me, how did you make them come with you?"

"I told them their pa would be there."

"But was your purpose wrong, Zeth? Did you intend to harm your friends, or profit at their expense?"

". . . No. I was just scared to come alone," Zeth admitted.

"So," said Mr. Veritt, "you disobeyed Mr. Whelan, and you enticed your friends into disobedience."

As it was not disobedience that bothered Zeth's conscience, he brushed that aside with "Yeah, I guess so."

"However, Owen and Jana were under no constraint to follow your example. They also chose to disobey. Zeth, you are blaming yourself for the wrong thing."

"But I'm responsible!" Zeth insisted, looking up to find Mr. Veritt half smiling at him.

"Yes, Zeth, you are responsible. Not guilty, but responsible. Like your father, you accept the consequences of your actions, whether you intended them or not. That's a very grown-up attitude for such a young boy."

The words warmed Zeth, but they couldn't remove the hollow feeling when he thought of Owen. Mr. Veritt studied him. "I wish I could assign you a penance, Zeth, to atone for your disobedience. But your parents have never fully accepted my beliefs, and I will not impose them on their son."

"Assign it, Abel."

Zeth looked up to see his father at the head of the stairs.

"Don't call it a penance," said Rimon Farris, "call it a punishment. I trust you to know what's right for Zeth."

"Don't you want to know—?" Veritt began.

"It wasn't me he confessed to. Want to tell me what you did, Zeth?" Farris was calm and relaxed now, glowing with repletion of selyn.

"I didn't go up to Mr. Erick's yesterday," said Zeth, "so neither did Owen and Jana. That's how they got hurt."

"I see," said Farris. "You feel responsible." He turned to Abel. "What would you have him do about it?"

Mr. Veritt said, "I think two problems can be solved at once. Owen will require a great deal of help in the next weeks and months. He'll be awkward, and others will feel embarrassed around him. Some will avoid him, while others will find it easier to do for him than to teach him to do for himself. Zeth, I'm assigning you the job of making Owen independent."

". . . What?" Zeth asked in puzzlement.

"He doesn't have to be helpless. Take care of him until he can care for himself. Figure out how he can feed himself, dress himself, bathe himself. As soon as he's strong enough, get him on a horse. If you require apparatus, get Dan Whelan or Tom Carson to help you make it. Ask the women to design clothes Owen can get in and out of by himself. You see, Zeth—your penance is over when Owen can get along perfectly well without you."

Zeth was stunned. It was the worst punishment he could imagine. It was impossible. *He won't even talk to me!*

Rimon Farris smiled warmly. "Pefect!" he said. "Abel, I wish I'd thought of it."

Soon Zeth decided his punishment would destroy his friendship with Owen forever. The more he tried to be gentle, the more sullen and stubborn Owen became. The first day he wouldn't eat at all. The second, as his pain receded, his growing Gen appetite caught up with him.

Owen's sister, her arm in a sling, was temporarily suffering the inconvenience Owen would face for the rest of his life, but she wasn't much help to her brother. When Zeth brought the lunch trays up, Jana told Owen, "Trina made us soup in mugs, see? That way we can drink it."

"I'm not hungry," said Owen.

"You didn't have any breakfast," Zeth said softly. "You've

got to eat something.'' Owen had been defeated by the bowl
of cereal that slid around on the tray when he tried to spoon it
up. By the time Zeth thought to brace the bowl with a rolled
napkin, Owen was too frustrated to eat.

Firmly now, Jana said, ''To produce selyn, Gens have to
eat even more than children.''

''And what am I producing it for?'' Owen flashed.

''To stay alive, dummy,'' said Jana. ''I didn't know they
cut off your brains with your arm!''

Owen was infuriated. ''If you had the brains you were born
with, you'd know I'd be better off dead!''

''Nobody's better off dead!'' Jana snapped. ''You know
how Pa feels when—'' She broke off with a glance at Zeth.
''Only cowards give up. I never thought my brother was a
coward!''

Owen leaned back against the pillows, fighting tears of
frustration. Zeth said, ''Jana, that's not fair. If you can't keep
a civil tongue, you'd better leave.''

''He's my brother—and I'm not going to have a helpless
coward in the family!''

''Owen's no coward! You're the one that can't take it,
Jana! Get out and don't come back until you can be nice.''

Zeth took a threatening step toward her, a little surprised at
himself. All at once, Jana turned and stalked out of the room,
pausing only to close the door with exaggerated care.

Zeth turned to Owen, who was staring at him wide-eyed,
tears brimming his eyes, but awe in his expression. ''Zeth,
that was *Jana* you just threw out of here.''

''Yea-ah,'' Zeth said slowly. It was the first time he'd ever
faced her down. The two boys stared silently at one another
until Owen said, ''That soup does smell kinda good. Be a
shame to let it get cold.'' Once started, Owen ate more than
Zeth.

The next day, they moved Owen into Zeth's room. Still
weak, leaning heavily on Zeth, he insisted on walking. ''If I
can't be useful, at least I won't be a burden.''

But by the time they got him settled he was almost as pale
as when they had brought him in unconscious. Rimon Farris
said, ''No harm done. You're still healing, Owen.''

''But why does my arm hurt?'' Owen asked. ''I mean the
whole arm, Mr. Farris. It hurts all the way down.''

''The shock was to your nerves, as well as flesh and bone.

When they heal, the pain will stop. You're doing fine, Owen. Your field is climbing normally in spite of your injury.''

Owen's soaring field soon proved the greatest nuisance on the New Homestead. When he met frustration, the emotional intensity of his nager irritated every Sime past turnover—the point in the monthly cycle at which the Sime had used up half the selyn from his last transfer, and began to move toward need.

His clumsiness infuriated Owen. All Gens were clumsy compared to Simes, but Owen could not even walk right at first, the loss of his arm having changed his balance. He went at everything bullishly, forcing his way to victory over inanimate objects, careless of how often he fell, or cut or bruised himself—or the shock of each such event to nearby Simes. Zeth was reminded of the two dogs, Patches and Biggie, who had never quite grown up to the size of their feet.

Owen's normal sunny good nature had disappeared. Grim determination was now his most positive mood. After a while, only Zeth, Del Erick, and Jana spent much time with him; Zeth because he was determined not to fail, Erick because he wanted desperately to help his son, and Jana . . . Zeth decided she really loved her brother underneath the bickering. Things went better when Zeth finally gave up trying not to lose Owen's friendship. Owen was not able to be friends with anyone at the moment.

One day, after Owen had upset every Sime in the house, Zeth found him in the barn currying his horse, which was now stabled at the Farris Homestead because, as a Gen, Owen could not go back home to live.

Zeth started to call out, then paused. As he stroked the horse's flank one-handedly, Owen was crying. A shaft of sun caught his good right arm, and Zeth could see the bulge of Gen muscle that had developed over the last few weeks of savagely forced exercise. He backed up and called from outside the barn doors, "Owen?"

"Go away!" Owen called back.

But Zeth went in. "Hey, that's a good idea. The horses could use a good grooming. I'll help you."

"No!"

"What's gotten into you?"

"I don't like being your punishment!"

"Who told you that!"

"Jana." He paused. "It's true, isn't it?"

Picking up a pair of brushes, Zeth went to work on the other side of the horse. "Owen, honest, it used to be I did it 'cause Mr. Veritt said I had to. But not anymore. You can be as nasty to me as you want because it's made you learn. When you can ride again, it will all be over."

"Ha! I'll never be able to ride again!"

Owen had attempted, prematurely, to mount his horse, fallen off, and reopened his wound. The pain disrupted a transfer that Zeth's father had been giving at the moment. Owen had been strictly forbidden to attempt it again until Rimon gave permission. The reopening of the wound had been followed by infection, the delay only worsening Owen's temper.

"Jana can already ride again," said Zeth.

"Jana still has her arm."

From the doorway, Del Erick called, "Oh! There you are, Owen!" As Zeth leaned out to say hello he couldn't help noticing that Erick was in need.

"Hello there, Zeth. Dan Whelan sent these over for you." He held out a handful of buckles.

"Did he find a way to make them work?" asked Zeth, who had asked Whelan to design a one-handed buckle.

"I think so, with a little practice." He held them out to Owen, who glanced over his shoulder and then turned back to currying his horse. Zeth reached for the bundle of straps.

"I'll see if I can figure it out," he said.

"I don't know why you keep pretending—" Owen's voice cracked perversely at just the wrong moment.

Del stepped back, and Zeth could see him taking a deep breath, striving for control. Owen, wrapped up in his own miseries, hadn't noticed. But in a moment, Erick seemed calm again, as he said, "I figured out a way for you to mount that horse, Owen, but if you're not interested—"

Owen turned, and Zeth could sense the hope that was more pain than anything else.

"Saddle up, then, and come outside. I'll show you."

Before Owen could turn sullen again, Zeth quickly helped him saddle Flash, letting Owen do most of the work.

Outside, Del took the reins in his right hand, tentacles retracted. "I've been working to get Flash to accept my weight from the right. It may take some practice, but watch. You take the saddle horn in your right hand, step with your right leg, and—"

In one leap he was mounted. "I didn't augment to do that. You're tall enough, there's no reason you can't learn it."

With a pained expression of defeat Owen turned away. Zeth picked up the reins he dropped, and said, "I wonder if I can do it."

But when Zeth tried the right-hand mount, the horse shied. Desperate now, he said, "Well, it will take some practice."

That wakened Owen's spirit. "I've trained Flash since he was a colt. He'll let me do it."

"Well, let's start with a slower mount," said Del. "Come over here by the fence and go on from the railing."

Owen became wrapped up in the project, until he tried to scale the horse's side, right foot in the right stirrup. The horse sidestepped, and he went up one side and down the other to land with a thump.

Erick stiffened against the pain while Zeth rushed to his friend's side. But Owen was on his feet, his expression savage. He rammed his boot into the stirrup, and in a moment was seated atop his horse for the first time in weeks. A grin split his face and with a yell and a whoop he let out the reins. Before anyone could stop him, he was galloping down the road toward town.

Erick leaped for his own horse and raced after his son, gaining gradually. As he caught up, Owen pulled the horse into a sharp turn, seemed almost to lose his balance for a moment as Zeth held his breath, and then was racing back to the yard gate.

When the two horses pulled up, blowing hard, Erick said harshly, "What made you pull that fool stunt? Where did you think you were going?"

Owen slid to the ground and met his father's eyes on a level. "There's nothing for me to be afraid of in town. If I can't donate, I can't be killed!"

Erick was trembling, his tentacles restless with need. "But you can certainly make a Sime *want* to kill!"

Ready to snap back at his father, Owen stopped. It was as if he saw beyond his own anguish for the first time since the raid. "Oh, Pa, I'm sorry!" His arm went about his father's waist, and Zeth noticed that although they were the same height, Owen was already a larger man than Erick, who was thin even for a Sime. He seemed suddenly frail, leaning on his son, and Zeth, knowing that he was about the same age as his own parents, wanted to deny the sight. *He looks almost as old as Mr. Veritt.*

Erick's face smoothed, his tension relaxing under his son's touch. It took long months of Companion's training to learn that. Owen had no training.

Del Erick spoke slowly, carefully. "Owen, now don't be afraid, son—but you've got to stop that."

"What am I doing?" Owen asked blankly.

"Offering me selyn. I mustn't fix on you. Think about something else. Zeth, go get your father."

But Rimon Farris was already running from the house, Kadi Farris behind him. Immediately, Rimon fell into his channel's stance, voice soothing as he said, "Easy, now. Nobody's going to be hurt. Del, I'm here. Zlin me."

"I—I can't—"

"Kadi," said Rimon, pointing. As she moved into position, Erick pulled his eyes from his son to look at Rimon. Rimon held out his arms. "Owen, let him go now, gently—you're not denying. It's just the wrong time. Come, Del, you don't need Owen, not now. That's it. Excellent."

Rimon put his arm around the man's shoulders and sheltered him from Owen's nager. "Rimon," Erick said with infinite sadness, "I don't dare touch my own son."

"It's all right, Del. Nobody got hurt," said Rimon.

Erick raised his head. "Owen never did that before!"

"I know—" said Rimon, looking toward Owen. "Shen! What a Companion you'd make!"

"Well, why *can't* I be?"

Zeth saw his father flinch at Owen's frustration, even with his mother standing between Owen and the Simes.

"Dad, you've got to find a way! You've said yourself our community can't afford to waste selyn."

"Rimon," said his mother. "You could take his field down using a shoulder contact, for example."

"What?" said Erick.

"It's something Kadi and I worked out," said Rimon. "I saw it done by Freeband Raiders once. Any symmetrical contact for the laterals will work, you know."

Erick's gaze went again to his son. "Yes—of course."

"Then I can do it—I can become a Companion!"

"No," said Rimon gently. "Using secondary positions, you can never have that kind of control. But at least I can take your field down, and perhaps with a little training and discipline, you'll stop disrupting every Sime you come near."

"Then I could still help you, Pa! I can ride! I can help herd the horses." But Owen was more subdued now, desperately clinging to the day's gains.

"Del, come on inside, and I'll give you your transfer now. Then—Owen, I've got two more people waiting, and then you and I have some work to do together."

Owen and Zeth were left alone. Owen turned away from Zeth, crying with renewed frustration.

"Owen, nobody got hurt." Zeth tried to reassure his friend. "You can learn—"

Owen turned on him furiously. "You couldn't feel it. It was beautiful. I was doing something not just useful, but . . . there aren't any words!" He took a deep breath and tried again. "Pa was in need. I wanted to help—and I *could*! Zeth—I could have given him transfer, I know I could."

Over the next few days, Zeth's father worked with Owen until finally one afternoon he did take Owen's field down. When Owen came back to their room, Zeth said, "How did it feel?"

"I didn't feel a thing," said Owen disgustedly. "Now he wants me to work with Uel Whelan, learning not to affect Simes. But you know what? I'm going to prove I can give a real transfer!"

"But why? You're donating now—"

"Zeth, when I'm near someone in need, I want to ease that need so bad my whole body goes weak inside! And all they want me to do is turn myself off!"

This was a side of Owen Zeth had never seen before. It seemed to be a healthy side, and as Owen took hold of his life again, Zeth thought his punishment was over.

One bright early-summer day, Owen was working beside Zeth, the other children, and several of the community's Gens, picking strawberries. He tucked a basket into a sling Jana had rigged for him, and picked berries almost as fast as Zeth and Jana. It was a glorious day, with fluffy white clouds high in the brilliant blue sky. The smell of berries was intoxicating, and the children ate almost as many as they put into their baskets.

Zeth moved along in pursuit of the biggest, reddest berries, and suddenly looked up to find that he had drifted away from Owen and Jana, to where Kadi Farris and Trina Morgan were sorting through the berries, choosing the largest, sweetest ones to be eaten fresh, and putting the others aside for jam-making.

Strawberry season was a time for Gens and children. The luscious berries were poisonous to Simes, who stayed away from the kitchen these few days.

As Zeth emptied his overflowing basket into his mother's tray, Trina was saying, "They're guarding us again. Look— Tom Carson's up on top of the hill."

"Well, we do have all these Gens running around free and acting like people."

"We *are* people!" Trina said.

"Not by law," said Kadi. "Our petition to count Gens as citizens scares people. Slina says that's why we were raided."

"You think we should stop petitioning?"

"If it were only myself, I'd be tempted to stop," Zeth's mother replied. "It's never made any difference between Rimon and me that by law I'm his property. But what about Zeth?" She reached out and gave him a little squeeze. "My son will probably be Sime, but suppose he's Gen? I want him to have full legal protection."

Zeth worked his way back to where the children were picking strawberries and singing while Owen, whose voice was changing, whistled a merry accompaniment. He sounded so happy that Zeth joined in the song, off key as usual. Owen was soon laughing so he couldn't whistle, and told Zeth, "Hush! You'll sour the strawberries!"

"You're in a good mood," Zeth observed.

"Why shouldn't I be?" Owen glanced around, making sure no one else could hear over the singing. "You know what, Zeth? It's a whole lot better to be Gen than to be Sime."

"Owen, it doesn't matter—"

"But it does! Oh, Simes can zlin, but Gens can use it against them. I can make a Sime laugh or cry, make him feel wonderful or terrible. Channels are only a little harder. I almost got Uel Whelan into a transfer this morning."

"Owen! Even if you can, you shouldn't. Mama wouldn't do anything like that, or any of the other Companions."

"Well, I've got to prove I can *be* a Companion. They're not going to let me—" He looked past Zeth and said, "Uh-oh."

Zeth turned and saw Abel Veritt coming across the strawberry field, headed straight for Owen.

When he arrived, he asked conversationally, "Are the berries good this year?"

"Very good, sir," replied Zeth.

"I remember picking strawberries when I was a boy. Owen, you're getting along well, I see."

"Yes, sir."

"I've come to talk to you about something very serious, Owen. Are you happy here?"

"Well—yes, sir."

"You want to stay?"

"Yes, sir." Owen was getting nervous.

"Mr. Farris and Mr. Whelan have asked me to talk to you. Every Sime in Fort Freedom knows the mischief new Gens cause when they discover their effect on Simes. We also expect this to be a phase that passes quickly."

"I didn't mean any harm, sir—I'm sorry for the headache I gave Jord, and the time I made Mrs. Veritt laugh so hard."

"It seems you don't know your own strength. Only Mrs. Farris has a higher field than yours, but her field is always carefully controlled. Uel Whelan tells me he had to work with his Companion for almost an hour this morning before he could go on with his duties—after you raised his intil. You did that on purpose?"

Owen hung his head. "Yes, sir. I would have followed through if he'd asked me to serve him. I wanted him to—you don't know what it's like—"

Veritt smiled grimly. "I have a fair idea, Owen. But if you're not—satisfied—here, if you can't adhere to our standards of good manners, I'll arrange a Farewell Ceremony and send you into Gen Territory. You know the language. You can make a good life for yourself."

"No!" Owen cried, and Mr. Veritt moved back a step, wincing. Owen immediately calmed. "This is home," he said. "Pa—Jana—everyone I care about is here. I'll behave— honest. Don't send me away, Mr. Veritt!"

In the past, Fort Freedom's Gens had been sent to a town built by other Gens from Fort Freedom, across the border in Gen Territory. But for years now, most of the Gens had stayed to donate selyn.

"Very well, Owen—but my offer remains open. If life here doesn't suit you—we'll see you safely across the border."

As he left, both boys knew he meant that life was hard

enough for Simes without a Gen who made a child's game of enticing them.

"It's not fair," said Owen.

Zeth ached for his friend—cut off from the experience they had all dreamed about. *How would I feel in his place?* And he knew his job was not over.

Chapter 3

Midsummer brought plans for two celebrations. In Zeth's family, it was his eleventh birthday—a Gen tradition, the celebration of birthdays, but Fort Freedom deliberately maintained both Sime and Gen customs just as it maintained both languages.

The other celebration was a community-wide conspiracy: a fiftieth birthday celebration for Abel Veritt. In Gen Territory that might not be a particularly long life, but Zeth's father speculated that Mr. Veritt might be the oldest Sime who ever lived.

Three days before his birthday, Zeth was doing his morning chores when Mr. Veritt rode up to the New Homestead. By the time Zeth went in to breakfast, Mr. Veritt was seated at the table with Zeth's parents, drinking tea. Rimon said, "You don't have to put yourself through this again, Abel."

"No, Rimon. I've told all the others, and I'll tell Zeth. It's my duty until there is nothing left to tell." He smiled. "Perhaps not long now. I managed seven months this time— and then transfer with Hank two days ago. This time—" He broke off, but Zeth understood.

The Simes who had killed for years, before Rimon Farris found a way for them to stop, had to have direct Gen transfer every so often. Hank Steers always provided transfer for Abel Veritt, for he had lived with the Veritts when he first came to Fort Freedom, and was like another son to them.

Now Mr. Veritt said, "Zeth, I'm going to take you away from your chores today. One more lesson, and your changeover training will be complete."

"Yes, sir," said Zeth. He had known it was coming. Eleven natal years was the youngest changeover his father had ever heard of; therefore every child in Fort Freedom was

thoroughly trained before his eleventh birthday. Whatever he
was to learn today was very adult and very sobering. He
remembered Owen, and later Jana, returning from the final
lesson with solemn, still faces.

They rode through town, and out beyond the Old Homestead.
Mr. Veritt reined in atop the hill that overlooked Gen Territory.
"It is many years," he said as they got down from their
horses, "since we sent one of our children down that trail in a
Farewell Ceremony. But you must know, Zeth, that if you are
Gen, if you choose, we will send you across with our
blessings."

"I won't be Gen," said Zeth. "I'll change over before
autumn."

"Zeth!" Mr. Veritt said reprovingly. "You don't know
that."

"Yes I do!" the boy protested, for somehow he *did* know.

"You must not presume. Your father *thinks* you will be
Sime and a channel. Indeed, we pray for it, as we must have
more channels. But no one can know God's will before the
event."

Zeth had never been more certain of anything, but he
decided not to argue further. "If I *am* Gen, Mr. Veritt, I'll
stay and be a Companion like Mama."

Mr. Veritt nodded. "I'm sure you would. However, you
must know that the choice is open. Zeth—you are unique.
You're the only child in Fort Freedom of your age. I have
always brought three or four children here before. It is a bitter
secret I must confess to you, Zeth Farris."

". . . Confess?"

They sat down on a shady rock, the horses wandering away
to crop the dry grass. It was a still day, the only sounds the
movement of the horses and some insect noises. Zeth stared
down the trail, where some distance down the hill was the
border between Sime and Gen Territories.

Mr. Veritt seemed to read Zeth's thought. "Do you know
what marks the border between the Territories?" he asked.

"Fear," Zeth replied. "If we could remove fear between
Simes and Gens, there'd be no borders."

"Yes," said Mr. Veritt, "that's right. However, I meant
the question literally. The border crossing on that trail before
you is marked by a grave—the grave of a martyr."

"I know," said Zeth. "Jon Forester." He had seen the
name on the Monument in the chapel to all who had died to

make it possible for Simes and Gens to live together. The most recent name was Teri Layton's.

Jon Forester had died the same way Teri had: a Gen still learning to be a Companion, not yet able to avoid panicking when touched by a killer Sime. Jon Forester, though, had not been killed by some raiding stranger, but by Abel Veritt's own son, Jord.

"You know the story," said Mr. Veritt, "and you know what we learned from Jon Forester's death."

"The test," said Zeth. "If a Sime has killed, even once, like the ones who come to us from Gen Territory, they can go a few months without killing, but then they reach a crisis. They want to kill. It seems they *need* to kill, that transfer from a channel or Companion isn't enough."

Mr. Veritt nodded. "You've learned your lessons well."

"That one? I've heard it every day of my life. Dad's really scared I'll kill. He thinks I'll be like him, but there won't be a Gen like Mama to give me transfer. He's making me watch Bekka Trent." Bekka had changed over in Gen Territory, and killed in First Need, but her desperate flight had brought her across the border at Ardo Pass, where Del Erick had found her and brought her to Fort Freedom less than a month ago. Such Simes were welcomed at Fort Freedom, as they were willing to go through almost anything never to kill again.

"The young ones," said Abel. "Yes, they go through agonies and come out purified, the kill burned forever from their souls."

"Well, I'm not going through that," said Zeth with a shudder. "I'll do whatever Dad tells me." He studied Mr. Veritt. "Is that what this is about? I know I've disobeyed sometimes, but I'm sure not gonna take the chance I might kill someone!"

Sadly, Mr. Veritt said, "No, Zeth. What I must tell you concerns those of us who had been killing every month for years, before your father learned to be the channel of life force between Sime and Gen. I was the first, Zeth. To save my life, Rimon Farris first transferred selyn to a Sime."

"I know," Zeth whispered. He remembered being brought in afterward—the crowded room, the atmosphere of rejoicing, his vow to be a channel. The first time he had vowed it, a very small boy caught up in a moment that changed history. "I was there," he said. "I remember the way you looked—I guess I'll never forget. When I was a little kid, and used to picture God like a person . . . I pictured you, except sort of mixed up with my dad.''

Fleeting pain played over Mr. Veritt's features. "We set ourselves up for that, we who take on the spiritual leadership of a community. I felt the same way about my father. He was the minister of our church, many years ago.''

Zeth knew that Mr. Veritt had come from Gen Territory, fleeing across the border just as Bekka Trent had—but back then there was no Fort Freedom to welcome him, and in his despair he had fallen in with Freeband Raiders. But instead of launching into the familiar tale, Mr. Veritt said softly, "I killed my father, Zeth.''

The boy jumped, shocked.

Veritt drew his gaze from the horizon. "To him I had become an abomination, for the Church of the Purity teaches that all Simes are evil demons. I believed that, even more when I realized what I had done. It took me years to find my way back to God, and many years more to stop distorting His truth with my own prideful theories. Your parents taught me that, Zeth. I no longer pretend to interpret God's will.

"Yet some things I know. My entire life is evidence of God's mercy. He has a way of bringing together the right people to implement His plans. While I was building Fort Freedom, your father was undergoing his own changeover and suffering terrible guilt because in First Need he, too, killed someone dear to him. You bear the name of the man he killed.''

"I know,'' said Zeth, for that was another familiar story.

"Throughout your father's sufferings, there was your mother, a woman of courage and devotion.''

That story was Zeth's favorite: how Rimon Farris and Kadi Morcot had grown up together. How Kadi, still a child, had helped Rimon survive the tragedy of his First Kill—not a Gen, but a Sime, his cousin and best friend. How Kadi had established and been taken by Gen traders to be sold at the Reloc Bazaar as a Choice Kill, and how Rimon had rescued her.

Rimon, in need, had meant to escort Kadi to the border and send her safely into Gen Territory, controlling his own desires in the face of Kadi's soaring field. Then they had encountered a Gen raiding party, torturing to death a Sime they had captured.

Rimon intended to release the prisoner, and send Kadi

safely across the border with the Gens. Neither Rimon nor
Kadi spoke the Gen language nor understood that a party of
bounty hunters was no safe escort. When Kadi ran to them,
pretending to flee for her life, they took her in all right—and
began fighting over who would have her.

Rimon had to rescue Kadi again. The Sime captive of the
bounty hunters, he saw, was a member of the Border Patrol.
It didn't take him long to find the rest of the Patrol and lead
them to attack the Gens. In the melee of battle, he was
releasing the Sime captive when she died in his arms, driving
him from need to intil—the helpless urge to kill. Instinctively,
he turned on the nearest Gen: Kadi.

Somehow through hard need, Rimon Farris recognized her,
and when he should have killed to renew his own life—he
stopped. Shenned, ripped from the source of satisfaction through
an act of pure will, he fell unconscious. Now Kadi faced a
life-or-death decision—and decided to give her life for Rimon's.
Taking him in kill position, she gave selyn, expecting to die.
But because she did not fear, she did not die.

Zeth shivered as Abel Veritt retold the story. It was a
perfect legend, each lover willing to die to save the other.
Mr. Veritt continued, "When your mother and father could
find no acceptance in their own home, God led them to us.
Here they learned all that Sime and Gen can do together—and
here your father found his destiny. Your heritage, Zeth. You
may be the channel we so desperately need. We have not
found another since Uel Whelan, nine years ago. You are our
hope, along with Uel's children. In your father's family,
changeover comes early, usually by twelve. Soon you may
face a great responsibility."

"It's what I want," said Zeth. "I vowed I'd be a channel
before I even understood what a channel was!"

Mr. Veritt looked down at his arms, extending his tentacles
in an uncharacteristic gesture. "It is not always easy to keep a
vow, no matter how heartfelt."

The hollow despair behind the softly spoken words made
Zeth put his hands over Mr. Veritt's. The old man twined his
tentacles over the boy's hands, squeezing gently. "You have
a channel's instincts, Zeth—or a Companion's. But you may
not wish to touch me when you know that I have not yet kept
the most important vow of my life."

Zeth had heard that vow repeated at every year's turning
ceremony. Slowly, the tone had changed from triumph to

determination to something close to desperation, and the older Simes wept when Abel Veritt declared, "As God is my witness, I shall not die a killer!"

Horror-struck, Zeth whispered, "No! Oh, no, you can't mean—"

"Zeth . . . my last kill was not nine years ago. It was seven months ago."

Veritt had retracted his tentacles, but Zeth still clung while he fought conflicting emotions. "But . . . *why*?" he whispered. "We've got channels, and I know Mr. Steers gives you transfer. *Why!*" he cried, backing off with a sudden angry urge to throw the frail old man who had betrayed his trust down the rocky hillside.

"I pray constantly for an answer to that question," Mr. Veritt replied softly. "Thus far, there is no answer . . . that I can accept. Perhaps I must pay for the presumption of my vow . . . and yet I cannot comprehend a judgment against me paid with the lives of others."

"What . . . what does Dad say?" asked Zeth. Rimon Farris surely knew everything about Simes.

"There is a change in the nager of a Sime who has killed, when once he passes the crisis and is separated from the kill. That change takes place only in the young—those Simes still in First Year, when they have the great flexibility required to adjust to being Sime. If they don't stop killing in First Year . . . your father thinks they never can."

"No," said Zeth. "Dad killed for four years before—" Total panic overtook him. "No! No, he doesn't! He can't!"

"No, Zeth," Mr. Veritt said firmly. "Your father does not kill, ever."

"Then why—?"

"I don't know. Your father passed his crisis the first time the test came upon him—for others, it may simply take longer." Mr. Veritt looked over into Gen Territory again. "I'm a very old man, Zeth. I never expected to live so long. But it is my fervent hope that God is allowing me time to fulfill my vow. As the years pass, the crisis comes on me less frequently—but with greater power."

"When you were so sick last winter—?" Zeth realized.

"It was not illness," Mr. Veritt confirmed. "I was determined to pass the crisis. The first month, your father forced transfer on me, but I remained debilitated. The second month—I can't even remember. I've been told I shenned Uel, Hank, and then your father. I would have died of attrition.''

"What happened?" Zeth asked.

"Slina." He sighed. "She doesn't understand us, but she is a good woman in her own way. She brought one of her Gens right into the house. I . . . responded—demanded it, your father tells me. I was not in my right mind—but your father is a healer. I suppose he could not help weighing my life against the life of that poor drugged creature who had never had the chance to become a person. All I remember is coming to with that dead Gen a burden in my arms.''

Zeth's head was whirling. If Mr. Veritt could not stop killing, what about the other people he loved? Mrs. Veritt was another mother to him, Del Erick had taught him to ride—and all the others who had raised him—killers all? Hypocrites?

"Everybody . . . ?" He couldn't even ask.

"Everybody beyond First Year when your father gave me transfer that day, when you were two years old. We have found that one of our Companions can meet the crisis sometimes, and prevent a kill. With Hank's help, I have gone eleven months. Now it has been seven months—and this time I shall pass the crisis. I cannot go on taking a life every year—and someone must prove it is possible to stop killing even at my age.''

"Everybody," Zeth repeated. "I thought we were different!"

"*You* are different, Zeth. In nine years, no Sime who has changed over in Fort Freedom has killed. We have set our children free of the kill. Now you must carry on—you must do what we could not.''

As Zeth tried to absorb the enormity of what he had learned, he no longer felt anger toward Mr. Veritt. He wasn't sure what he felt.

Zeth had never seen a kill. Transfer, yes; both Sime/Gen transfer and channel's transfer were demonstrated in the chapel, and every once in a while a channel gave public transfer to someone so desperate that he could not wait for privacy.

But the kill . . . that was the enemy kept at bay on the other side of the creek. Or, he realized with a shock, imprisoned within the walls of the Old Fort. Except for Del Erick, all those Simes Mr. Veritt said could not put the kill behind lived in the Old Fort. Only a few young Simes, who had never killed, lived at the New Farris Homestead, where all the newly established Gens came to live while they learned to be Companions who could walk safely among all Simes.

All their customs were designed to protect the new Gens. Zeth found it impossible to imagine anyone requiring protection from Abel Veritt, or any of the older Simes. He remembered Del Erick, in hard need, holding Owen steady that day when his son accidentally provoked him. He had resisted what everyone said was the most tempting field since Kadi Farris. But Owen was his son, and Rimon Farris had come to extricate him—

Zeth could not imagine Mr. Erick killing, or Abel Veritt taking a human life merely for some strange satisfaction. Any channel or Companion could provide the life force to satisfy his need. *I don't believe it.*

When he looked toward Abel Veritt again, seeking to be told it was all some test that he had yet to find the answer to, the old man was no longer waiting patiently for Zeth's next question. He had tensed, leaning forward, his eyes ceasing to focus as he zlinned with Sime senses, which could perceive far beyond the range of vision.

Mr. Veritt rose, saying, "Someone is coming. One person. One Gen—alone?" He extended his sensitive laterals, the small, vulnerable, pinkish-gray tentacles lying smoothly against either side of the gnarled, weather-beaten hands.

"Two people," said Mr. Veritt. "No one else that I can zlin. Not a raiding party—one's a child. No . . . I think . . . Zeth, someone's bringing a changeover victim to the border! I've never heard of such a thing! That Gen is in danger—I can't tell how far the changeover has progressed." But as he mounted his horse he changed his mind. "I can't go down there. The Gen might turn and run—and be killed if the Sime reaches breakout. You go, Zeth. You're still a child. You won't frighten them."

Riding down the trail, Zeth soon saw a Gen woman driving a wagon, a blanket-covered form lying in the back. As he rode up, the woman halted the wagon. Her eyes swept over his untentacled arms. Then she said in uncertaim Simelan, "Fort Freedom. Is it still there?"

"Yes, ma'am," Zeth answered in English. "I live there."

"Oh, thank God!" She turned to the still form in the wagon. 'Marji! Marji, wake up! I'm going to have to leave you."

Zeth saw on the wagon bed a pretty young girl with

delicate features framed by curly light brown hair. She was either asleep or unconscious. The girl moaned, and tossed fitfully, exposing her forearms. The woman looked to Zeth. "She's always been such a good girl. Will you . . . will you take her for me? I can't come into Sime Territory again."

"Again?"

"I was born there. I grew up in Fort Freedom."

"Then you know we'll bring her through changeover just fine. What's your name?"

"Hope Carson."

"We've got a Tom Carson. A relative?"

"Tommy Carson? My husband's little brother! I wish—"

Zeth said, "You can come along. It's safe. Simes in Fort Freedom don't kill anymore."

"They don't kill real people. I know."

"No—they don't kill at all!" said Zeth, and then remembered what Mr. Veritt had just told him. "Your daughter will never kill," he amended. "One of the channels will give her transfer. If you grew up in Fort Freedom, you're not afraid to come back, are you?"

The woman studied him. "No," she said finally, "I'm not afraid. No one in Fort Freedom would hurt me."

"Then bring the wagon," said Zeth, and called, "Mr. Veritt! Mr. Veritt, this lady is from Fort Freedom!"

Mrs. Carson froze. "Veritt?" she murmured. "Is it Jord, or . . . ?"

Abel Veritt came slowly down the trail, getting off his horse a good distance from the wagon. "I won't hurt you, child!" he called. "Do you remember—?"

The woman jumped down from the wagon and stood in the trail. Veritt stopped, and the two just looked at one another, until finally he said, awestruck, "Hope!"

"Father!" Suddenly she was running toward him, only to stop a few paces away, hesitating.

"It's all right," he said. "I'm not in need."

She flung herself into his arms and they hugged each other, laughing and crying at once. Then Mr. Veritt held his daughter at arm's length, saying, "Oh, Hope, it's so good to see you again!"

"Mother?" she asked in a small voice.

'Your mother is fine. And Jord—well, he's had his problems since his wife died, but he's alive, too."

She nodded, fighting back tears as she led him toward the wagon. "I've tried to live a good life. I married Lon Carson."

"He was always a good boy," said Mr. Veritt.

"He's a good man, Father, but still—" She gestured toward the wagon. "Our daughter. Margid, but we call her Marji."

Veritt climbed up on the wagon, looking at the girl, then zlinning her. "My granddaughter," he said with a smile. "Lord, I thank you for allowing me to see this day."

"But, Father," Mrs. Carson said in anguish, "she's in changeover! In spite of all our efforts to do God's will—"

"Hope," said Mr. Veritt, "God gave you the courage to bring her here, that you might indeed see His will in action. Marji is not going to kill."

"Is she dying?" the Gen woman gasped.

"No! You will witness a miracle this day—a miracle we have seen so often it has become commonplace!"

She looked to Zeth as if just now absorbing what he had said.

"We've found the true answer," said Veritt. "Gens live safely with Simes in Fort Freedom now, freely giving of their life force without being hurt. We are putting an end to the kill forever." He tucked the blankets more securely around his granddaughter, then moved to the wagon seat and took the reins. "Zeth, take the horses back to the Fort. Tell Uel Whelan to meet us at my house. It's stage three. There's plenty of time."

Uel Whelan. For his own granddaughter, Zeth noticed, Mr. Veritt specified the only channel who had never killed.

At Fort Freedom, Zeth verified that Uel Whelan was still at the Farris Homestead. Then he galloped for home. Patches, tied to the porch earlier so he wouldn't follow Zeth, was now loose, jumping on the boy when he dismounted.

"Can't play now, Patches," he told the dog, and hurried inside. In the parlor were two Simes, obviously in need. Something was wrong. Normally Simes went directly to a transfer room for their appointments; occasionally someone might have to wait a few minutes in a shielded room, but if all the rooms were full, with a spillover into the parlor, something must be tying up all three channels.

Zeth headed toward the back of the house, but met Trina Morgan in the hall. She carried two cups of steaming tea. "Zeth! No, you can't go back there now. Everybody's busy." She set the tea glasses down on the edge of the staircase, and put her hands on Zeth's shoulders. "I know why Mr. Veritt took you out this morning, Zeth. You want to talk to your parents, but you're going to have to be strong until they finish their work."

"No," said Zeth. "It's a changeover! Mr. Veritt sent me for Uel Whelan."

"What stage?"

"Three."

"Then there's time." She nodded calmly.

"But the girl," Zeth began. "She's—"

Unhurried, Trina picked up the tea glasses and went toward the parlor. "Let me deliver this tea, Zeth, and then I'll go tell Uel for you."

Companions were supposed to remain unruffled in a crisis, but as Zeth fidgeted in the hall, itching to get back to the Fort, he thought that Trina was carrying things too far.

Finally Trina left the parlor. Zeth followed her to one of the insulated rooms, where she opened the door a crack and slid carefully inside, closing it behind her.

Zeth shifted back and forth from one foot to the other, until at last Uel Whelan came out. The young channel was clearly preoccupied. "Stage three, you said? Who told you?"

"Mr. Veritt. He—"

"How long ago?"

"Half hour, forty-five minutes. But—"

"Tell Abel I'll be there by stage five, maybe sooner." With that, Uel ducked back inside the room. Zeth wanted to shout after him that the victim was from out-Territory, Mr. Veritt's granddaughter—but he didn't dare interrupt.

So he rode back to the Old Fort, Patches loping along beside him. At the Veritt house, Marji had already been taken into the insulated room, where Mrs. Veritt made up the couch into a bed. Zeth noticed how Abel Veritt kept himself between his wife and his daughter like a channel or Companion. Mrs. Veritt was not in need, but she was past turnover. The wetness on her cheeks testified to her frustration that she dared not come near her daughter.

She took out her mothering instinct on her granddaughter, saying, "Hope, she's as beautiful as you were as a little girl."

Mr. Veritt turned when Zeth entered. "Did you find Uel?"

"Yes. He said he'd be here by stage five, maybe sooner."

"That's fine. I'll coach her till he gets here. Hope, you shouldn't stay. Marji will start responding to your field."

"Oh, Daddy, I can't leave her when she's in pain!"

Marji was struggling for every breath, the sound a strong counterpoint to their conversation.

"No," said Mr. Veritt, "she's not in pain, although she's uncomfortable because she has no training. She's not getting enough oxygen. If she knew controlled breathing, she'd be alert now, if weak."

Just then Marji cried out sharply, gasped, and fell silent. Mr. Veritt zlinned her, and smiled reassuringly. "There— stage four, and she's asleep, not unconscious. She'll gain strength for the last two stages. I'll stay with her. Zeth, please take care of my daughter.

So Zeth was to be chased away again. Well, maybe when Uel came he could sneak back in.

By this time, other Simes were on the porch. Mrs. Young came in to ask, "Who's in changeover, Margid?" Then she stared at Hope. "Is that—? Oh, it *can't* be!"

"My daughter," Mrs. Veritt said. "She brought us her daughter. Hope, do you remember Mrs. Young?"

"It's good to see you again," Mrs. Carson said, although even Zeth could see that only the formal good manners drilled into every child of Fort Freedom allowed her to speak politely to a roomful of Simes.

The Simes were equally polite. "You don't want a crowd, with your child in changeover," said Mrs. Young. "When it's over you'll feel like company. Margid, come help prepare the feast. You're our best cook, and it will keep your mind off—"

Quickly, Mrs. Young guided Mrs. Veritt out. The word would spread now, and no one would come near until the channel and his Companion were here to shield Mrs. Carson.

The Gen woman watched them go, muttering blankly, "What feast?"

"The changeover celebration for Marji," Zeth explained with the awkwardness of a child who knew more than an adult about a situation. "Every time a new Sime starts right off on channel's transfer, the family celebrates."

"I don't believe it," Mrs. Carson whispered. "I brought Marji here because at home she'd have been murdered or would have killed one of us. Here . . . can it have changed so much?" She looked around. "It all looks the same."

"Uh . . . you want some tea?" Zeth offered.

Mrs. Carson smiled through her tears. "Trin tea," she said. "The universal remedy. Now I know I've really come home again."

The Gen woman looked around the kitchen. "My mother's kitchen. But now she doesn't dare come near me."

"You'll learn to control your field," said Zeth. "Then you can be around Simes anytime." He put water on, and reached for the container marked "Tea," only to find it empty.

Mrs. Carson said, "Mother was always afraid we kids would break it. The tea is in the wooden box.

Not wanting to be the child who broke the delicate china tea container, Zeth set it carefully back on the shelf and finished making tea. Mrs. Carson sipped hers, studying him. "Zeth Farris. I don't remember any Farrises."

"My dad's a channel. He's the one who first discovered how to channel."

"What exactly is a channel?" she asked.

"A Sime who can take selyn from Gens without hurting them, and then give it to other Simes so they can live without killing. Your brother Jord is a channel." And Zeth found himself drawn into giving a detailed explanation of life at Fort Freedom, fumbling for definitions of new Simelan words like Companions, those special Gens capable of giving transfer to channels.

At length, Mrs. Carson put down her empty tea glass to go to the window. "It's all the same," she said, "and yet it's so *different*." She paced to the table and back to the window, plucking nervously at the curtain. "What's taking so long? Shouldn't that . . . channel . . . be here by now?"

"Changeover takes a long time," said Zeth. "When Marji went into stage four, that's about halfway."

She whirled from the window, wide-eyed. "But it's been—"

Just then the quiet was shattered by a piercing scream.

"Marji!" gasped Mrs. Carson, and ran for the insulated room.

Abel Veritt met them at the door, the terrified screams continuing behind him. "Hope—Marji doesn't know me," he said. "She came fully awake for the first time to find herself alone with a Sime."

"Let me—"

"You must not touch her. Stay by the door and talk to her."

Motherhood clearly had the best of fear in Mrs. Carson as she said impatiently, "All right—let me see her!"

Zeth followed them. Marji was sitting up, plastered against the wall as if to go through it. Her pretty face was distorted with panic—but the moment she saw her mother she stopped screaming.

"Marji, it's all right," said Mrs. Carson. "This is your grandfather. We're in Fort Freedom, Marji."

The girl began to sob. "Mama, I hurt! I'm so scared!"

"You'll be all right," said her mother, starting toward her. Mr. Veritt stopped her. "No, Hope. Stay behind me."

"Mama!" cried Marji again, reaching out. She caught sight of her own forearms, the tentacle sheaths showing as blistered lines from the wrists almost to the elbows. She shook her arms disgustedly, as if the sheaths could be cast off, then grasped her left arm with her right hand, scraping viciously. She screamed again in pain, and Veritt gasped, taking a step back before regaining control.

"No, Marji!" he said sharply. "You mustn't hurt yourself."

"No! No! No!" cried the girl, lost in her own panic.

Mr. Veritt grasped his daughter's hand and placed it in Zeth's. "Keep her here!" he told the boy, and strode across the room to sit on the edge of the bed, saying, "There's nothing to be afraid of."

"I'm cursed," Marji sobbed.

"No, you're not cursed, child. You are blessed with a mother who had the strength to bring you here."

"I don't want to be Sime. I won't kill!"

"No, Marji. You won't kill."

The girl stared wide-eyed from Veritt to her mother. "I—I'm scared, Mama. I don't want to die."

"You won't die, Marji," said Mrs. Carson, "but you won't kill, either. Have faith, and do what your grandfather tells you."

She looked at Mr. Veritt. "You're my grandfather? Mama always said—if I changed over—find you. But I don't want to change over!"

"It's not bad to be Sime, when you don't have to kill." Mr. Veritt sounded like one of the channels. "That's right—lie still now. Come, let us pray for the strength to accept God's will."

As Mr. Veritt's voice dropped to a murmur, Mrs. Carson

lowered her head, too. There was a short period of calm, and then suddenly the girl on the bed cried out in pain.

"It can't be!" gasped Mr. Veritt. "So soon! Zeth, go—" He turned, and saw Zeth holding Mrs. Carson back. "No. Stay with my daughter and keep her safe till this is over." He rose, saying to Marji, "I'll be right back."

Herding Zeth and Mrs. Carson out of the room, he said, "There's no time to wait for Uel. Where's Jord?"

"Out at our house, too," said Zeth.

The old man strode to the porch and called, "Ed! I've got an accelerated changeover, sixth stage. All the channels are at Farris. Get one here—fast!"

"Right you are!" Zeth heard, followed by the sound of galloping hoofs.

Mr. Veritt turned back toward the insulated room, saying, "Stay out here, Hope. I'll take care of Marji."

Mrs. Carson stared blankly at her father, her chin trembling. "What's happening? What's gone wrong?"

"Stage six is just starting," Zeth explained. "There's time for Mr. Whelan to get here."

The Gen woman began to pace. "Dear God, let her be all right!"

Zeth was more annoyed at being shut out than worried, although Mrs. Carson's pacing soon got on his nerves. *If I were a channel now, there'd be no problem.*

Suddenly a new sound came from the insulated room—not a child's scream of terror, but an animal cry of agony. Mrs. Carson went white, and dashed for the room.

"Don't!" Zeth cried, scrambling after her. "You can't go in there!"

She flung the door open before Zeth could catch her. Marji was straining to force her new tentacles from their sheaths. Zeth saw the membranes covering the wrist openings swell, then subside as Marji let her breath out in another feral grunt.

"My baby!" cried Mrs. Carson, as Zeth grabbed her arm.

"Hope, get out of here!" Veritt commanded, but she ignored him. "I'm not a channel! I can't shield you! Run!"

At that moment, with another intense effort, Marji's tentacles broke free. She collapsed on the bed as Mr. Veritt said, "Good . . . good. Lie still now; conserve your strength till the channel gets here—"

But the girl did not hear him. She sat up, eyes unfocused,

zlinning for selyn to satisfy her need—First Need, the most intense and terrible need most Simes ever knew.

Mrs. Carson's concern turned to terror as her daughter was transformed into nature's most perfect predator—stalking her. The Gen woman backed toward the door as the new Sime moved with astonishing speed. Mr. Veritt caught the girl's upper arms, but even though both were Sime, the strength of an old man was not equal to that of a youngster berserk with need. Marji flung him off, and went in pursuit of her prey.

Zeth could smell Mrs. Carson's fear—it prickled through his own body. There was nothing human about Marji now but her form. Like a stalking animal, her prey in easy reach, she approached Mrs. Carson, fixing her with empty eyes as she prepared to strike and kill. *I'll be like that!* thought Zeth.

Then Abel Veritt moved like a flash between his granddaughter and her prey, reaching for Marji's arms like a channel, laterals extended to twine with hers.

The moment lateral touched lateral, Marji jerked upright and in one fluid movement drew her grandfather into lip contact. *It's all right*, thought Zeth, weak with relief, but instantly he remembered, *No—he's not a channel!*

For a long moment the two figures remained thus intertwined and then Mr. Veritt collapsed. Marji let him fall.

He's dead, Zeth realized in horror, as Mrs. Carson screamed, "Father!"

But Marji was unsatisfied. Still in need, her restless laterals licking in and out of their sheaths, she began stalking her mother again. Mr. Veritt had entrusted the Gen to Zeth's care—*Keep her safe till this is over.* He had failed.

Marji took another deliberate step toward her mother. Zeth darted in front of Mrs. Carson. "Run! She can't hurt me."

He could hear Patches barking wildly. Time seemed suspended as he wished desperately that none of this was true, Abel Veritt dead, his granddaughter a berserker, his daughter a terrified Gen with only Zeth to protect her.

Then Mrs. Carson broke and ran. Marji moved to follow, but Zeth blocked the doorway.

Chapter 4

Facing the stalking Sime, trying desperately to believe that a Sime could not kill a child, Zeth reached for Marji's forearms. Suddenly, he was plucked up from behind and tossed roughly across the room.

Uel Whelan, Hank Steers on his heels, had thrown Zeth out of the way, then intercepted Marji as she came from the insulated room, intertwined tentacles, and touched lips. When they separated, Marji was a pretty girl again, completely bewlldered, but otherwise unharmed.

Hank Steers looked into the insulated room, and Uel Whelan started at his Companion's burst of emotion when the Gen cried, "Abel!" and dashed into the room.

Zeth was dumped unceremoniously to the floor, and realized that it was Jord Veritt who had caught him only when the channel stepped over him. As everyone converged on the other room, Zeth scrambled up to follow.

Marji Carson suddenly said, "Mama! Mama—what happened?"

Her mother retreated a step as Anni Steers said, "It's all right. She won't hurt you now."

"She killed my father!" Mrs. Carson cried.

"Abel's alive!" came Uel Whelan's voice.

Seth could see Abel Veritt lying still and white. Hank began to tremble with fear and hope at Uel's words. Jord, haggard, knelt beside the others. "What happened!"

"He couldn't let Marji kill her mother," Zeth explained. "He tried to be a channel for her."

"He would," said Uel, his voice choked. "Jord—?"

"I'm all right now."

"You and Hank give me a neutral field. God help me."
Lips moving in silent prayer, the young channel ran his hands

50

over Mr. Veritt's chest, laterals extended. "He's deep into attrition, but it hasn't been long. There's a bad nerve-burn. This is going to hurt like shen."

Zeth watched, fascinated, as Uel put pressure on Mr. Veritt's lateral extensor nodes to make the tentacles emerge. His handling tentacles remained sheathed, hands and arms flaccid in Uel Whelan's grip. Then the channel bent his head to touch lips.

Zeth saw color return to Mr. Veritt's hands and face. Twice there was a jerking motion, almost separating the two Simes, but Uel hung on. Finally he raised his head. Mr. Veritt lay completely still, but his lips were lip-colored again instead of blue, and Zeth could see his chest rise and fall with his breathing.

Uel Whelan leaned heavily on Hank Steers. "It was close. He almost shenned me, twice." His head fell to his Companion's shoulder, his eyes closing over some inner pain.

Jord shook his head wearily. "He's so old, and he's always been frail. You know he lives on faith as much as selyn. But his judgment has always been sound—until now. How—*how* could he have been so mistaken about the stage of changeover?"

"He wasn't mistaken," said Zeth. "It was just like we were taught, except the stages went so fast."

Uel raised his head, shaking off Hank's solicitude. "Because the girl's a channel!"

"She's his granddaughter," Zeth supplied.

"What?!" exclaimed Jord Veritt, his head snapping up. As his attention went beyond his father for the first time, he saw his sister. "Hope! It's your daughter—?"

"I didn't know what else to do," said Mrs. Carson.

"You did the right thing," said Jord, moving toward his sister. Margid Veritt took his place beside her husband. Marji Carson cowered against the wall, watching everything with round brown eyes—the same color as Jord's, but wide and bright, not sunken into permanent hollows as his were.

Jord made no attempt to touch Mrs. Carson, but said gently, "Welcome home, Hope. The child you have brought us is a greater blessing than you know."

He turned to the girl. "Marji," he said, holding out his hands to her. "Welcome to Fort Freedom. Thank God for your mother's courage to bring you here."

The girl raised her hands to push him away, caught sight of her tentacles, and moaned, "No! Oh, no! I killed him!"

"No you didn't!" Jord said quickly. "Come and look." With an arm about her shoulders, he led her to look at her grandfather, still on the floor. "Zlin him, Marji—like this—"

She glanced at Jord, then back at her grandfather. Her eyes went blank as she zlinned. Then Jord said, "You see? He's alive. You're never going to kill anyone, Marji. You're going to *save* lives."

Uel said, "Abel's improving. When he finds out you're a channel, Marji, he won't mind a little transfer burn."

Mr. Veritt stirred, and moaned softly. His wife bent over him, but Uel said, "It's all right, Margid. Don't zlin his pain—you'll just reflect it. Do you have any fosebine? Abel and I could both use some. It wouldn't hurt Marji, either."

By the time Mrs. Veritt returned with the medicine, her husband's breathing was quickening. Uel knelt beside the old man as he stirred slightly, winced, and opened his eyes.

Mrs. Veritt was right there with the fosebine. He drank the bitter stuff down without even a grimace, but remained very still as Uel zlinned him again.

Then the channel said, "Abel, don't try to talk. Save your strength, and listen. Your daughter and granddaughter are fine. You're the only one who got hurt, and you'll be over it soon."

Uel Whelan was entirely the channel now, his voice strangely unlike his usual speaking voice. Zeth listened carefully, thinking, *One day I may have such news to break to a patient.*

Weakness and pain prevented Mr. Veritt from more than a hint of a smile in response, but Uel went on in that same quiet way, "Your granddaughter is the new channel everyone's been praying for. You kept her from killing."

The impact of even those quiet words brought animation back into the old man's body. "Thank God," he said in a hoarse whisper, and struggled to focus on Marji. "Bless you, child."

Jord said, his voice not at all like a channel's, "Father, what made you do such a thing?" And then, with an impatient gesture, "No, don't try to answer. I know you thought you had no choice. I don't see how you survived!"

Mrs. Veritt answered for her husband. "God has more work for him. It was another miracle, Jord."

"We're all used to that," Uel added with a grin. "Abel,

we'll lift you onto the couch now, and then I want you to sleep."

"One thing," the old man whispered. "The bell."

"Don't worry—we'll let everyone know. Go to sleep, Abel. Fort Freedom will get along without you till tomorrow."

Mrs. Veritt helped install her husband on the couch, and left him asleep, Hank Steers in a big armchair beside the bed. "I'll get you something to eat, Hank."

"Thanks, Margid. Uel, I'll stay here tonight, unless you think a channel should stay by Abel."

"No—he's stable, Hank. Get some sleep yourself—this has been some day!"

Now Uel Whelan turned to Zeth. At the frown on the young channel's face, Zeth suddenly wished he had sneaked away earlier. "Now, young man, what were you doing when I arrived?"

"I was trying to keep Marji from killing her mother."

"By letting her kill you?"

"She couldn't. I'm still a child," Zeth pointed out.

At Zeth's words, Uel went white with fury. "You could have been killed! You would have been!"

"But I'm not a Gen—"

"Marji very nearly killed a Sime! She'd have stripped you and never known the difference! Zeth, you are the hope of this community. How could you be so foolish!"

Zeth gasped as Uel's fingers bit into his shoulders with Sime strength. The young channel flinched and suddenly his anger faded so that Zeth saw the fear beneath. "Where did we go wrong that you would think a child couldn't be killed?"

Meanwhile, with the ringing of the bell on the green, excitement stirred through Fort Freedom. Tragedy averted, rejoicing filled the air.

Mrs. Veritt and Jord put Marji to bed, and her mother managed to say good night to her. Jord told his sister, "Hope, you could stay at my house, but I'm afraid you're in no mood to let Uel or me take your field down."

"Zeth explained that you two are channels—but—"

"As you are now," said Jord, "you're a temptation and an irritant to every Sime past turnover. You can't stay here in that condition—"

"Stay?" she interrupted. "I can't stay at all! I've got to go home. My husband doesn't know where I am!"

"It's almost sunset," said Jord. "There's no moon tonight.

You can't find your way in the dark, but Simes can find you.
You have three choices. We can take you out to the Farris
place, where all our new, untrained Gens stay. Or you can let
us take your field down, and stay here or at my place next
door. Then you can leave in the morning, or stay for Marji's
feast. It would do her good to know you love her enough to
stay.''

"Lon will be so worried," said Mrs. Carson, "but Marji—"

"It's a once-in-a-lifetime experience. You've risked so
much to bring her. Won't you stay and help her through her
first day? I'm sure her father will understand."

She looked from Jord to Uel, then at her mother and the
door behind which her daughter slept. Zeth saw her throat
work. When she turned back to them, the worry lines between her brows were smoothed. "All right. But if I'm going
to stay, it's going to be here, with Marji. So tell me what to
do."

'Nothing. I do all the work—or Uel, if you prefer. You
should know he's a better channel than I am."

"But you're my brother."

Despite her brave front, Mrs. Carson's hands shook. Uel
moved to shield Mrs. Veritt as Jord said, "It's all right to be
afraid. Everyone is, the first time. Don't try to control your
fear, Hope—then you won't give me any surprises."

Zeth watched Jord's handling tentacles wrap about his
sister's forearms. She looked down, trembling, as the small,
moist laterals slid into place. "It's all right," Jord murmured.
Then his lips grazed hers, and he began dismantling his grip.

Mrs. Carson stared at him. "That's all?"

He smiled at her. "That's all there is to it, Sis. You're
low-field now."

Mrs. Carson was blushing as the blood returned to her skin
with the end of her fear. "Oh, Jord!" Suddenly she hugged
her brother, and the look of happiness on Jord Veritt's face
took years off his age.

Watching Jord hug his sister, Zeth found for the first time
that he believed what Abel Veritt had told him today. He was
flooded with compassion for Jord, for Abel, for all the people
struggling so desperately against what nature had done to
them.

Uel Whelan gave Zeth a strange look, and came to the
boy's side as Hope Carson turned from her brother to her
mother, holding out her arms. Zeth watched, knowing what

Mrs. Carson did not know—what he had been part of the conspiracy to keep her from knowing.

This morning I was so proud, wanting to be all grown up. And this is what it means, knowing things that hurt—

"Zeth," Uel Whelan said gently, "I'm sorry I scolded you—I forgot completely what day this was for you. I'll take you home now. Rimon would never forgive me if I didn't relieve him so he can come check on Abel and Marji for himself. I wonder if anyone rode over to Farris to tell them?"

Someone had, and Zeth's father was chafing at his own rule that there would always be at least one channel at Farris.

Thus Zeth received no more than a perfunctory examination from his father, and a hug from his mother, before they both galloped off into the twilight.

No light showed under the door of the room he now shared with Owen. It was too early to be sleeping, so Owen must not be there. But when he opened the door, he saw Owen at the window, sihouetted against the darkening sky. The older boy didn't move, and that in itself told Zeth there was something wrong.

Zeth came to his side, saying, "Owen—what's the matter? Haven't you heard the good news? There's another channel, Owen!"

Owen sniffed, and rubbed his hand against his eyes. In a voice thick with forced-back tears, he said, "Oh, fine! Another channel for me to hurt! They're gonna send me away, Zeth. They're gonna make me cross the border, and I didn't *do* anything!"

"What happened?"

"My donation. Jord was in need, and—Zeth, I didn't mean it!"

'You gave him transfer?" Zeth asked in an awed whisper.

"No! I didn't even try—but they'll never believe me!"

"Owen—Jord didn't attack you?!"

"Of course not. He's a channel. But he—he *wanted* me. How can I help feeling sympathy?" Owen stood and paced away. "I was holding back. Jord's not . . . flexible, like Uel. I was trying not to feel anything, but then he—"

"What?"

Even in the dim light Zeth could see the tears on Owen's cheeks. "For a moment I felt something—it was so great—and I thought, *maybe I'm the one who can help Jord*—and then he pushed me away and collapsed! Shenned himself.

Zeth, your dad thinks I tried to seduce Jord to transfer. But I didn't!''

"I know you didn't," said Zeth. "Anyway, you didn't hurt Jord. He was just fine this evening."

"Sure, once they got transfer into him. He had one of his attacks—voiding selyn. He almost died, Zeth."

"So *that's* what was going on here! But Jord's all right, Owen. You'd have sworn it was Dad, the way he handled Mrs. Carson."

"Mrs. Carson? What was the matter with her?"

Realizing Owen was thinking of Tom Carson's wife, Zeth said, 'No, Hope Carson—Abel Veritt's daughter!'' And he told Owen the whole story. "Didn't you hear?"

"I've been up here all day. I just didn't want to face your dad. He's going to send me away, Zeth."

"It wasn't your fault," Zeth repeated helplessly.

"Maybe it was. Maybe I can't help it any more than a Sime can. You don't know what it's like not to be able to help a Sime in need! The 'need to give,' your mother calls it. The Simes say that's gibberish, that Gens don't feel anything but sympathy, but they're wrong. You'll see—if you're Gen.''

"I'll be Sime," said Zeth, more positive than ever. The certainty was always strongest when he was around Owen, as if his friend's quintessential Gen-ness called to some opposing polarity in Zeth.

"Yes," said Owen glumly. "You'll be a channel, and you'll drive me crazy, too." He put his hand on Zeth's shoulder. "Zeth—promise me, when you're a channel—let me give you transfer!''

"I can't promise that, Owen. You know what my dad says—I might kill you!''

Zeth felt Owen's hand tighten, then very deliberately release him. Forcing calm, Owen said, "If not you, somebody. You found out today, didn't you? All the older Simes need direct Gen transfer every so often . . . so they can go longer between kills. Let me do that. Zeth! Promise me! I can stand to wait if I know I'm going to have a chance at—something real.''

A strange feeling stirred in the pit of Zeth's stomach at the idea of Owen giving transfer to someone who—He shoved the thought aside, and said, "Owen, we can't see what the channels see." As Owen pulled sullenly away, Zeth said, "Wait—this I will promise: when I'm a channel, I'll study you. If there's any way you can give transfer, safely, I'll find it.''

Owen sighed. "Thanks, Zeth. I know you would. . . but I'll be on the other side of the border before you change over.''

"No you won't! Nobody can force you to leave.''

"If I hurt people by staying here— Do you know what I've been thinking? Wild ideas. I could go into town and . . . and seduce someone into transfer. Prove I could do it!''

"Are you crazy? If you didn't panic and get killed, you'd end up with a dagger between your ribs.''

"Not from Slina, I wouldn't,'' Owen said thoughtfully.

"No, Owen!''

"Why not? She respects us. She sends her little girl to school here. Next time she's in need—''

"Do you want her to be like Mr. Veritt? Or Jord? Or your own pa? Do you deliberately want to hurt Slina?''

"Huh? What do you mean?''

"She raises Gens 'cause someone has to. I used to wonder how Slina could know us, and send Mona here, and still go on raising Gens for the kill. And kill every month herself. It has to be a choice she's made never to know, never to experience transfer without killing. Maybe you think that's a coward's choice, but maybe you just can't understand it. Maybe Gens can never—''

"Stop it!'' cried Owen, sinking onto his bunk. "Zeth— what's happened to you? You sound like your dad. Yes, I understand! I won't seduce Slina, or anyone else . . . not to have them go through what Pa does. But that means . . . if your dad tells me to leave, I've got to go.''

"He won't. What's it been—four months? It takes some Gens a year to learn everything a Companion can do. And you've been busy just getting well. Dad will understand.'' It was full dark by now. Zeth lit the lamp, saying, "I guess we better get to bed. But I'm hungry.''

"Me, too,'' said Owen. "I haven't eaten since breakfast.''

They went downstairs, past the room where Uel Whelan sat with his feet propped up, reading a book from the small collection kept at Farris. The community's real library, Abel Veritt's pride, was at the Fort. "What are you boys up to?'' Uel asked.

"We're just gonna get something to eat,'' said Zeth.

Uel looked up. "I'm sorry, Zeth. You missed supper at the

Veritts'. Hank puts his foot down when I forget he has to eat.''

"Did you eat today?" Owen asked suspiciously.

The young channel laughed. "Aye, sir, that I did. Hank and I had breakfast. And before you assert your Gen authority to remind me that Simes should eat twice a day, I'll let you bring me an apple, Owen.''

Zeth and Owen were eating sandwiches in the kitchen when Zeth's parents arrived home. Kadi Farris went straight to her son and put her arms around him. "They told us what you did today. Oh, Zeth, you could have been killed!''

"It's my fault, Kadi," said Zeth's father. "Shen and shid! How could I have let my own son think a child couldn't be killed? We're too casual, Simes and Gens together—the children think there's no danger . . . and then we have a day like today." He shook his head. "Sometimes I think Abel's right that God is personally looking out for us. We certainly put Him to the test today." He ran fingers and tentacles through his wiry black hair. "Owen. I meant to talk with you this afternoon, but we got behind, and then this thing with Abel's granddaughter—''

Owen had put down his half-eaten sandwich and was staring at Rimon as if waiting for a blow to fall. "I didn't mean to hurt Jord," he blurted out. "I was trying *not* to tempt him!''

"I know," said Rimon. "Jord told us. It wasn't your fault, but from now on I'll take your donations.''

The tension drained out of Owen. "You're not going to send me away?"

"No, of course not," said Kadi.

"But we must be more careful. I could throttle Jord," said Rimon. "After all that, daring to touch an out-Territory Gen—''

"His sister," Kadi reminded him. "Tonight, with his family home, he was closer to normal than I've seen him in years.''

"Dad, he did suggest that Uel Whelan take her donation," Zeth said, "but Mrs. Carson wanted her brother to do it.''

Kadi took her husband's hand. "You know what a difference love and trust make, Rimon.''

Zeth's father's sensitive lips curved in a reluctant smile. "I also know how dangerous it can be to rely on emotion rather than knowledge. But this time it worked. What a day!''

"How's Mr. Veritt?" asked Zeth.

"If I know Abel, he'll be up tomorrow, though my prescription would be a week in bed. Speaking of bed, why are you boys still up?"

"We were hungry," Zeth explained.

"Well, finish up and get to bed," said Rimon. He started to leave, turned back, and looked puzzledly at his son. "Zeth—before Mrs. Carson came, did Abel have a chance to tell you . . . ?"

"He told me."

"Rimon," said Kadi, "Zeth's tired. Don't make him think about that now. Zeth, you get some rest, and we'll talk when you're ready."

"I don't have to talk about it," said Zeth. "I understand."

"He really does," said Owen. "I said . . . some awfully dumb things a while ago. I don't think a channel could have made me see more clearly than Zeth did how wrong I was."

Kadi Farris' blue eyes swam with tears. "You mean on top of everything else, you had to counsel Owen, Zeth?"

"I'm sorry," said Owen. "I was so scared you were going to send me away that I didn't even think about Zeth's problems."

"Our son is growing up," Kadi said proudly.

Zeth felt himself blushing. "Maybe I am," he said, "but I'm not sure if I like it!"

The next day the one-channel-always-at-Farris rule was suspended, as the entire community of Fort Freedom poured into the Old Fort. There was a thanksgiving service, led by Jord Veritt, as Abel was still recuperating. Zeth heard more than one person speculate that Mrs. Veritt must have locked him in.

Mrs. Carson and Marji were the center of attention, as everyone had questions about friends and relatives across the border. As people found out who had married, who had children—and who had died or disappeared—Mrs. Carson's wagon piled up with presents, and messages.

Marji Carson, congratulated on every side for what she had always thought of as being cursed, answered politely but vaguely, one eye on her mother as if asking permission to speak to Simes. Mrs. Carson was surrounded by Companions, unobtrusively shielding her. Zeth wondered if she had any notion why his mother, or Anni Steers, or Trina Morgan, was constantly by her side.

Children Zeth's age and younger came to stare at the strangers, but soon ran off to play games. Like Zeth, they were too young to remember anyone who had crossed the border to Gen Territory. The younger Simes and Gens went to set up the tables for the feast. Jana, Owen's sister, went along to help, but neither Owen nor Zeth wanted to join them.

Owen hung around Mrs. Carson, listening. Zeth wondered if he was trying to act like a Companion, until there was a lull in the conversation. Then Owen asked hesitantly, "Mrs. Carson . . . do you know a Gen family named Lodge?"

"Lodge? Not in our village—but there's a big ranch run by a Glian Lodge."

Owen's blue eyes widened. "That's my uncle!"

"I've never met him," said Mrs. Carson, "though I've seen him at market day. He's a big blond, like you. And rich."

Owen laughed. "I'm rich, too—or my pa is. Del Erick. We raise the best horses in the Territory."

"Erick? But you said Lodge?"

"I can hardly remember my father," Owen explained, "but his name was Owen Lodge. That's my name, too—Owen Lodge Erick. Ma married Del Erick when I was just a little boy. He's been my father all my life, it seems."

"Perhaps Mr. Erick has relatives across the border, but I don't know anyone by that name."

"No—Pa came from in-Territory. And Ma always said she was the last of her family. Bresson. Carlana Bresson."

"Oh!" exclaimed Mrs. Carson. "That's why you look so familiar. Those eyes. Just like your mother's."

"That's what everyone says. Did you know her?"

"Not very well. She had just come to Fort Freedom when I left. But I remember how beautiful she was. Your father must have come here after I left."

Other people wanted to talk with Mrs. Carson, so Owen drifted away, Zeth following, Patches at his heels. Zeth wondered if Owen was remembering his real parents.

But Owen sat down on the steps of the Veritt house, saying, "There's something funny, Zeth. All those years, Fort Freedom sent Gens to that community across the border. And a lot of them got there, according to Mrs. Carson. But no Simes have come back."

"Well . . . Mrs. Carson was one of the first to be sent,

wasn't she? And her daughter's just old enough for change-over now. The others' children must still be too young.

"What about other people's children? There's a whole village of Gens—not just people from Fort Freedom. Why didn't they tell people about us?"

Patches butted his head against Zeth's knee for attention. He bent and hugged the dog as support against what he had to say. "Mrs. Carson said they'd have beaten Marji to death. They don't have channels or Companions, Owen. A new Sime always kills. Even Mrs. Carson thought Marji was possessed by a demon."

"But still she brought her here," said Owen. "If people over there know, how can they not tell their children?"

The door opened, and Hank Steers cane out onto the porch. Both boys immediately demanded, "How's Mr. Veritt?"

"Margid's helping him dress. He insists he's going to the feast."

"Dad said he would," Zeth commented.

"Yeah—that's Abel," Hank agreed, sitting down on the top step. "I heard you boys. You've never lived in Gen Territory. You don't know the fear the very idea of a Sime evokes—or the hatred. If your child turns Sime, he's not your child."

"In-Territory people think Gens are animals," said Zeth. "Still, folks show their kids the way to the border."

"Sure," said Hank. "If you're Sime, and your child is Gen, he's turned into something fragile and helpless."

Both boys laughed, for everyone knew Gens were tougher than Simes.

"No, no," said Hank, "not the Companions. Think of the new Gens at Farris, before they learn not to fear, in danger from people who love them. And outside Fort Freedom, Gens are fair game, so if parents feel anything but disappointment, it's that their child is in danger unless he can cross the border.

"But in Gen Territory—Zeth, you saw it yesterday. Marji would have killed her own mother. Few people who see a Sime in Gen Territory live to tell about it. The only Simes they ever see are berserkers or Freeband Raiders. Or hunting parties."

Hank did not elaborate, but Zeth knew that he had been brought in-Territory by a Sime hunting party. "I was taught," the young Companion continued, "that the only way to deal with a Sime was to murder him before he killed you. I don't think you kids born here have any idea of Mrs. Carson's courage in loading her child on that wagon and heading for the border.''

"No," said Owen, "I guess we can't imagine how they feel. But what will happen when they hear what's happened in Fort Freedom? Especially the ones who came from here?"

Zeth saw the faraway look in Owen's eyes. But before he could say anything, Abel Veritt came out onto the porch, leaning heavily on his wife. Hank jumped up and went to take his other arm. "Abel, you're really in no condition to go out."

Mr. Veritt gave him a weak smile. "Nonsense. I've just had another dose of fosebine. The worst I can do is fall asleep in the middle of the festivities." He looked toward the two boys now standing on the steps. "Zeth . . . son, I have you to thank that my daughter is alive, and my granddaughter did not kill. May God bless you for your courage . . . and protect you from ever being so foolhardy again."

"Thank you," Zeth said uncertainly, but was rescued from further embarrassment by other people surrounding the Veritts.

The two boys hung back to let the crowd pass. Then Owen said, "I've got to find Pa."

"Why?" asked Zeth.

"Look at that wagon. Did you see the stack of messages? I want to go with Mrs. Carson. Living proof, Zeth! I want to see Gen Territory—and then I'll bring back messages. And I'll tell all the young people there how to get here if they have to." And he hurried off to find his father.

As Zeth watched him go, a strange, numb feeling spread through his body. *It's just one trip*, he told himself. *He doesn't want to go over there to live.*

But the sense of celebration had gone out of the day.

Chapter 5

If only he wouldn't be so blameblasted independent!

Zeth often found himself thinking that, angrily, in the days that followed. Ever since that day of the raid, he had given all his strength to making Owen fend for himself.

But as the days passed after Owen left Fort Freedom, Zeth began to realize what that meant. His friend, an adult Gen, had to leave him behind just as a Sime left his childhood friends behind. Zeth finally let the unthinkable thought surface. *Will he stay in Gen Territory?*

One day when Owen had been gone for two weeks, Zeth encountered Marji after lunch, sitting on the back porch. She was depressed, caught up again in the teachings of her former spiritual leader, Mr. Bron, who held that Simes were possessed by demons.

"Marji, it's turnover depressing you," Zeth told her. "I've seen Simes possessed by evil—those two who cut off Owen's arm. If you'd seen *that*, and compared them to people like your grandfather—"

A stern voice interrupted from the top of the steps. "What's going on out here?"

It was Kadi Farris. She came swiftly down the steps and sat on Marji's other side. "What's wrong, Marji? Turnover?"

Marji jerked her head in a reluctant assent, then began visibly relaxing as the field of a skilled Companion did its work. She asked in wonder, "How can you tell?"

"Gen secret, as Hank likes to say." She smiled the radiant smile Zeth loved. "Actually, Marji, I haven't the least idea *how* I do it—I just let it happen. Now, what has my insensitive son been doing to upset you so?"

Marji shook her head. "It's not Zeth. I expected to hear from home by now. I guess I'm afraid of bad news."

Zeth's mother said positively, "If Owen had been thrown out, he'd be home by now."

"If no one got him along the way," said Zeth gloomily.

His mother frowned at him. "I'd stake Owen against the Border Patrol any day!"

As his mother took Marji into the house, Zeth decided to take his new horse out for some exercise. He whistled for Patches and went out to the barn to saddle up.

The bay filly had been a birthday present from the Ericks, although it was Jana who had presented her, saying, "She's from Owen, too, you know." But Owen had missed Zeth's eleventh birthday party, and the surprise party for Abel Veritt, too.

Zeth had named the horse Star, thinking, *Now I can keep up with Owen wherever he goes!* And then he remembered Owen was an adult, and he was just a kid. It would be that way *forever!*

Zeth remembered how he had felt just before Owen left— the irrational, total conviction of his imminent changeover. That conviction, more than anything, had sustained him as Owen struck for independence. Now that certainty of impending changeover had deserted him, and he felt lost.

He walked Star out of the barn, then turned onto the road and gave her an easy warmup until they were cantering breezily along the road. Patches ran ahead or behind, darting off to chase rabbits, barking joyfully.

Zeth was deep in his own thoughts. *This is why Dad always says it's bad to get too dependent on a certain person.* Of course, Rimon Farris was referring to the dependence of a Sime on a certain Gen, or vice versa. *But this is how it must feel. I'm afraid of losing Owen.* In changeover class, they'd taught him that that was the way a Sime in need felt about a Gen he'd fixed on. It was what made a Sime attack, strip selyn by force from the Gen—and kill.

The specter rose before his eyes—Owen dead, white and drained falling from Zeth's own hands.

No! I won't.

The walls of Fort Freedom loomed before him, the gate lookout hailing him with a friendly wave. Unable to think of anything else, he said, "I came to talk to Mr. Veritt."

"He's at his house!" called the lookout, and Zeth walked Star on into the circle of clean, white houses. Mrs. Veritt was on her front porch, hemming a dress.

"Hello, Mrs. Veritt," said Zeth, getting down from his horse. "Is Mr. Veritt home?"

"Yes, but he's about to go into town," she replied, just as her husband came out.

"Hello, Zeth, can I help you with something?" Abel Veritt appeared completely recovered.

"I . . . just wanted to talk."

"If it's something we can talk about on the road, how about riding into town with me?"

Zeth accepted eagerly—children were not allowed to go into the town across the creek except with an adult.

Slina, Mr. Veritt explained, had a Gen she didn't want killed. "It's getting harder on her every year," he said sadly. "Someone has to run the local pen, and Slina does it as humanely as possible. I suppose she can manage as long as there are those who have need of it." He abruptly changed the subject. "Well, Zeth, what did you want to talk about?"

If it's Marji's turnover, thought Zeth with sudden insight— "It's your turnover day! I'm sorry, Mr. Veritt!"

The old man smiled. "You're very sensitive, son. Usually no one notices but the channels. Let's talk about you, not me."

"But that's just it. Turnover. Need. I . . . I don't think I want to be Sime!" It was out before he thought. If any Sime hated being in thrall to his selyn system, it was Abel Veritt.

As if reading his mind, the old man said, "Your father will see to it that you don't kill, Zeth. Then you'll learn control. Look at Uel—not even your father notices Uel's turnover. Hank always knows, but I'm certain he just keeps count, as part of his job."

Hank and Uel. All his life Zeth had heard the two spoken of in one breath, like bread-and-honey. "But what if Hank died or something?"

"Merciful God!" said Veritt, pulling his horse up short, whitelipped with shock.

"I'm sorry," Zeth said hastily. He didn't know where his manners had gone. Things just came blurting out. "It's just that I don't see how anyone can be sure of anything in life." That wasn't what he meant to say, either. He bit his tongue, afraid to make it worse.

With studied calm, the old man urged his horse up beside Star. The hot summer sun glared down from a cloudless sky. A lark took flight and Patches ran off, barking merrily.

"I understand how you feel, Zeth," said Veritt quietly. "It's a feeling no Sime can escape save for a few blessed moments after—a transfer."

"It doesn't mean I'm going to be Sime, though."

"No," agreed Veritt, more readily than Zeth wanted him to. "There's no way to know that until the first sign of changeover, or establishment." He sighed. "You tempt me to my worst fault, son—presuming to know God's will. Yet He has allowed me to know it at times. He allowed me to recognize your father. Our community must have other such channels, and you may be one. My granddaughter is also a channel, though. She will require—and need—a Companion."

"She's getting along fine with Trina."

"For now. But if you should establish, Zeth, you'll inherit your mother's abilities. She brought your father to his current capacity. There is a direct relationship between capacity and sensitivity—ask Rimon to explain it."

"You think maybe I was meant to be Marji's Companion?"

"Perhaps. Or perhaps you'll both be channels. God does not act without purpose—even if it's sometimes difficult to discern that purpose. He does not offer us certainty, Zeth, but observing His moves, we can find confidence and security in the goodness of His purpose. Whatever happens, it is for the best—when you've placed your trust in God."

But have I? Zeth always felt uncomfortable when Mr. Veritt spoke of his God. His parents respected the strange beliefs of Fort Freedom, but taught that the Creator of the world required nothing of man but to know Him through His works, and gave nothing to man but the capacity to gain such knowledge.

"I think I placed my trust in God when I prayed for Owen to be Gen. But I don't see what good it's done him—or me. I know you've placed your trust in God—I tried to tell Marji that when she was going on about you being a demon. But—I don't see what good it's done you. You still—oh, shen!" *He's in need. Why can't I remember that!*

Veritt didn't even admonish him for his language, though. "What's this about Marji?"

Zeth recounted his brief conversation with her after lunch. "You're not possessed by any evil spirit!"

"Yes, you are right. The need to kill comes from within me—not from any outside entity. I alone am responsible for the fact that despite years of effort I remain joined to the kill."

"Joined—?"

"While I've been recovering these last two weeks, I found it hard to zlin. The nerve-burn made me hypersensitive and it was like coming out of a dark cave into bright sunlight every time I went hyperconscious. But when I did zlin other Simes, I found a . . . thread . . . a characteristic binding all of us who have been unable to turn wholly to channel's transfer."

"How come my dad never noticed?" asked Zeth.

Veritt shook his head. "He took it for granted. He's zlinned it all along; when I pointed it out to him, his reaction was, so what? Perceiving a common characteristic in the nager of all Simes who kill is no help in teaching them not to kill."

"I don't understand."

"Other Simes say we are unnatural. Surely the purity of the nager of Simes who have never killed is the natural state. The mark of the killer is the mark of corruption—it unites all those who bear it, from the most vicious of Freeband Raiders to those who struggle to kill only once or twice a year.

"To be a killer is to be joined to the kill. *Junct.* Each of us must break free of this bond, Zeth. We must become *disjuncted!* Yes, that's the right word for it."

"But why make up a new word?"

"The word is the symbol for the thing. Most Simes can't perceive the thing itself. I could not until my injury left me oversensitive for a while. I—" He glanced over at Zeth and seemed to come back from a far distance. "Zeth, what I want you to understand is that our faith doesn't claim to make life easy. But by putting our trust in God, we find the effort of living becomes tremendously worthwhile. Owen is a treasure in our community. Thanks to your efforts, he has found a purpose in life. You did this for him, and for our whole community, when you put your trust in God."

They were crossing the wooden bridge to the road through the small town, riding toward Slina's pen with the crisp green flag flying above its buildings.

The town had changed, even in Zeth's lifetime. There was still a saloon, but it was no longer part of a ramshackle row of buildings. Now there were neat shops, a bank, and the magistrate's office at Slina's pen. Three years ago they had succeeded in getting this end of the Territory declared a county, so there was now at least nominal law and order. The transients who used to gamble and carouse here, and raid across the border, had been driven to find a new stamping ground.

Nonetheless, it was a community of killer Simes. Feelings toward Fort Freedom ranged from sympathy to grudging respect. Either community would rally to support the other, but the feeling here, even to a child, was entirely different from the easy give-and-take of life at home.

For these Simes had no Gens living with them in day-to-day camaraderie. Slina's Gens were all drugged into complacency, their nagers neither irritating nor soothing.

Slina was irritated anyway, nervous and edgy even though Zeth could not see any symptoms of actual need in her. "Well, I'm glad you finally got here!" she greeted them.

"Zlin me, Slina," said Veritt. "I'm now technically in need and can legally claim the boy. Yesterday—"

"Shen, I'd've fixed the papers! I wish you'd've took him yesterday. I don't want that sort of thing here!"

"What sort of thing?" Veritt asked.

"Come on—I'll show you."

Slina led them to a holding room where one boy sat alone on the bench. He jumped up with a smile when Slina entered.

The boy was twelve or thirteen, a head taller than Zeth and as sturdily built as Owen. He had curly dark brown hair and bright brown eyes—obviously undrugged and alert. He looked them all over curiously, but his engaging smile was for Slina. It was easy to see why she could not let him be killed.

"He seems completely recovered," Veritt observed, and Zeth realized this must be the boy the channels had cured of an intestinal infection.

"Yeah—he was tearing up the infirmary, so I put him in here till you came. This morning I thought I'd give him one last dose of fosebine. Watch." Slina filled a wooden bowl with cloudy fluid and approached the boy. He backed off, then tried to push the bowl away, screwing up his face.

"Come on, drink it," said Slina. "It's good for you." She grasped the boy's hands, twining tentacles about them.

"No!" exclaimed the boy, shaking his head. "No, no!"

Slina dropped his hands and backed away, trembling. "That's what he did this morning. Shen and shid! Ain't never seen one come to life right here! And I never want to see it again—take him out of here, all right?"

"God be praised!" said Mr. Veritt. "He's been undrugged only—how long?"

"Nigh three weeks now, but he was so sick the first week he was unconscious most of the time."

Zeth wasn't surprised. He'd seen a number of pen-grown Gens learn to talk once released from drugs. " 'No' is always their first word,'' he said.

"So it seems, Zeth,'' said Mr. Veritt, "but it's usually months before they speak. Has this boy had special treatment?''

"Not till he took sick," Slina replied. "Just get him out of here, will you, Abel?''

But the boy wanted to stay. "You've been kind to him,'' said Veritt as he pried the boy away from the Gendealer.

"Ain't kindness—just protectin' my property. Your property now, and your problem.''

Zeth held the chain attached to the boy's collar while Slina made over his papers to Mr. Veritt. *If I establish, I'll have to come here for papers that say I'm someone's property. That say I'm not a person.* Owen had such papers, sealed with Slina's dagger-shaped mark.

Such legalities meant nothing to the people of Fort Freedom—but they did to the Territory Government. *So if I'm Sime, I'll be dependent on Gens. And if I'm Gen, I'll be someone's property unless I want to cross the border.*

As they took the new boy out to the horses, Zeth remained buried in his own thoughts. But the words "Freeband Raiders'' caught his attention.

". . . over in the west part of the Territory,'' Slina was saying. "Militia chased 'em over the border—they come back across beyond Ardo Pass, but the Wild Gens, they don't know Freeband Raiders from any other Simes. They come swarmin' across 'long about where the Raiders first crossed. Word is, Farris was hit real hard.''

"Rimon's father—?''

"Oh, he's all right. We'd've heard if anything'd happened to Syrus Farris.''

As they tried to get the Gen boy up onto a horse, he began to fight them. Slina and Mr. Veritt had to overpower him with sheer Sime strength.

"You don't know when you're well off, kid,'' Slina said, turning to go back inside. Suddenly, she froze, and Zeth saw Mr. Veritt stiffen at the same time.

Both Simes looked off beyond the western edge of town. Veritt's face crinkled into a delighted smile. "Owen!''

Sure enough, a large well-laden farm wagon came down the trail as fast as the big draft horses could pull it. Flash was tied behind the wagon. Zeth let out a whoop of pure joy, kicked his horse, and galloped to meet his friend.

Owen hit the wagon brake with one foot, and hauled back on the reins. Zeth dived from his horse onto the wagon seat, hugging Owen and demanding, "Where've you been? I thought you weren't ever coming back!"

Owen wrapped the reins around the brake and hugged Zeth. "It took longer than I expected. At first nobody would listen to me, and then everyone wanted to send presents, and I went to see my uncle—" He broke off as Mr. Veritt rode up. "Abel! What're you all doing in town? Am I glad to see you! I've got to tell someone! You won't believe what those people think!"

Then he took in the Gen boy with Veritt, still wearing the plain gray pen smock, and the collar and chain. "I'm sorry. I didn't think you'd—but why'd you bring Zeth?"

Veritt smiled. "This is a new adoptee, Owen. Now come along home. Everyone is anxious to hear your adventures."

Owen was as full of news as the wagon was of presents. Stacks of letters answered the ones e had carried across the border. The Old Fort was full of tears that evening—many of joy, but some of sorrow to learn of deaths or disappearances. Some who had been sent from Fort Freedom in Farewell Ceremonies had never reached the Gen community on the other side of the border.

Later that evening, Zeth's family gathered with Owen's and the Veritts around the Veritt kitchen table. Owen sat beside Zeth, his fingers wrapped lovingly around a glass of trin tea. The talk swirled over Zeth's head while he reveled in his friend's return—the relief leaving him sleepy.

Owen had brought a book for Mr. Veritt from Mountain Chapel's spiritual leader, Mr. Bron. Abel held it between his hands, idly gazing at his tentacles gracing the cover. "Owen, I understand this Mr. Bron's problems very well. It took great courage for him to allow you to speak of Simes as human beings with souls capable of salvation."

"Well, he did ask me not to talk about souls and salvation, but when I insisted I'd donated selyn, and Mrs. Carson told him she had, too, he said it was better to speak freely than to have it pass in whispers."

Mr. Veritt nodded. "A wise man."

Owen's eyes fixed on Veritt's tentacles. Zeth, too, was

fascinated by the old Sime's display. In Fort Freedom, it was impolite to unsheath tentacles except for work.

"Abel," said Owen shakily, "you're not going to teach from this book the way Mr. Bron does? I read some of it along the road—what it says about Simes— That's where they get all their sick ideas! It's all twisted!"

Mr. Veritt shook his head. "There is great wisdom in this book, Owen—along with much unintentional error. It belongs in our library. I'm pleased to have a copy again, after all these years. I wish I could thank Mr. Bron."

Zeth knew how precious books were to Mr. Veritt. Everyone who traveled away from Fort Freedom kept an eye out for volumes to add to the growing library—but how could Mr. Veritt be grateful for one such as Owen described?

Owen took a deep breath, and Zeth thought he would voice the protest. Instead, he said firmly, "I'll tell him—or you can write to him and I'll take the letter. Next time I go."

So bloodyshen independent! Owen's casual announcement sent chills up Zeth's spine, dispelling his contentment.

In the months that followed, Zeth experienced that same shock each time Owen left again for Gen Territory. He was the only boy anywhere near Zeth's age, so when he was gone there was just nobody to talk to. Life slid down into a slump; it wasn't worth getting out of bed in the morning.

Zeth's lackluster attitude did not escape notice for long. One day he was called to his father's office. Rimon was alone. "Sit down, Zeth. We've got to have a talk."

"Yes, sir," said Zeth, heart racing. He didn't have to hitch himself up onto the chair seat anymore, and for the first time he noticed his heels touched the floor.

"Your mother is upset—partly because you've been doing only a halfhearted job with your chores lately."

"I promise I'll do better."

"I rather expect so. But that's not what worries me. Your behavior has been erratic lately. I want to know why." The note of challenge faded from his father's manner as he added, "Might it have something to do with Owen?"

Zeth gasped. Was he that transparent? "I don't know."

"Look, Zeth, we're all proud of the job you did, helping Owen get back on his feet. Even if he can't work as a Companion, he's found himself a job only he could do for us. We couldn't spare a working Companion; we couldn't send a Sime, or a child. Only someone like Owen can do the courier's job—and Abel and I agree it has to be done if our way of life is to have any meaning. We owe that to you, in a way."

"Yeah—I guess—"

"Zeth, you're on the verge of growing up. You may not have realized it, but you're the heir not only to my position here but perhaps to all of Farris. We can only hope you'll be full-grown before you have to step into my shoes."

He reached to take both of Zeth's hands into his own. "I don't mean to frighten you, son, but you've surely heard the talk of the Gen raid on Farris in response to a huge swarm of Freeband Raiders that's moved into the Territory."

"Yeah, I heard about it."

"There's no telling where they'll strike next—or what the out-Territory Gens are going to do. If Owen can bring Mountain Chapel to understand the difference between Freeband Raiders and law-abiding citizens—that will be only your first contribution to the dream we're living here. Sometimes I'm so proud of you, I don't know how to express it!"

"I didn't do it to make you proud of me. I did it to make it up to Owen."

"Yes—and you have done so. But that is in the past. Recently, there are moments when I can't believe what I learn about Zeth Farris could concern any son of mine. Like yesterday, when you 'helped' feed the chickens at Fort Freedom, and left the gate open so they spent the rest of the afternoon chasing birds all over the common! Or last night, when I found Star hadn't been unsaddled. Or this morning, when—"

"Yes, sir, I know," said Zeth in his quietest voice.

"Zeth, one day lives will depend on you. If you're irresponsible in one thing, it will undermine your sense of responsibility in others. That's not the way Farrises behave."

"Yes, sir."

"I understand that you miss Owen. But that must not interfere with your responsibilities. If you're going to be a channel, Zeth, you've got to learn to put aside personal desires. Now is a good time to learn that lesson."

"Yes, sir. I'll try."

"Actually, it could turn out to be good that Owen is gone so much of the time. If he's not here when you go into changeover, it will be a lot easier on him. Since he's your friend, that should matter to you."

Stunned, Zeth said, "I'd never thought of that!"

"Well, think about it. Today ends this nonsense. Saddle Star and take a ride, think it through. Next time I see you, I don't want three people following you with complaints!"

The joy of a whole day free to ride was tarnished by the admonition. Zeth went to Fort Freedom, but Abel Veritt was busy in a meeting with most of the other men, making battle plans against the Raiders. All the children were in school, and everyone else was working.

He found Mrs. Veritt canning tomatoes. She gave him a new hat she'd knitted, saying, "It's getting chilly already. I'll warrant there'll be an early snow this year!"

He was on his horse and riding before he remembered he'd meant to apologize for the chickens.

Zeth took the back trail out of Fort Freedom, up around the hills and over by the Old Farris Homestead. They still grew mushrooms in the tunnels his parents had built, but there was nobody there today. Before long he found himself on the border overlook. The last time he'd been here, Abel Veritt had told him the adults' secret—and Marji had come.

Star grazed happily and Patches chased rabbits while Zeth climbed onto a rock and stared morosely out into Gen Territory. Somewhere out there Owen was adventuring, and here Zeth sat, tied to within an hour's ride of home in case he should go into changeover. *Shen!*

"Shen!" He said it aloud. He'd been such a silly child to think he was really that near changeover. He'd probably be Gen after all, and the Companion Owen could never be. Then how would Owen feel about him? Whether he became Sime or Gen, he was losing his only friend.

He let himself cry, until he felt Star's nose nudging his wet cheek. Reaching up, he buried his face in her warmth, apologizing over and over for leaving her saddled and uncombed. Patches came back from his rabbit chase and added his licking to Star's attentions. "I'm all right," Zeth assured them. "I won't forget my responsibilities again. Honest."

A few days later, news reached them that two of the largest bands of Raiders had joined forces with a band from some other Territory. The three bands had picked one section of the Territory clean, and were now heading this way.

Furious activity sprouted up—last-minute attempts to get in the late crops, hammers reinforcing the stockade at Fort Freedom, windows being boarded up, troops practicing battle formation on the green.

Zeth overheard his mother and father coming home late that night. "We'll just have to stand them off alone," said Rimon Farris grimly.

"I just don't see how they could refuse our request for troops," said his mother. "We're a county and we pay our taxes—it's got to be illegal, what they're doing to us."

"Probably, but that doesn't change anything. Tomorrow we move valuables and crucial supplies out to the Old Homestead, and prepare shelter for the children there. Everyone else is to meet at the Old Fort at the first sign of Raiders."

So Zeth found himself ignominiously herded with all the little kids into the tunnels that honeycombed the hill under the house in which he'd been born. Jana, Owen's sister, was the oldest child in the group, but ever since Zeth had thrown her out of Owen's room, he'd felt more grown up than she was. And he was finally as tall as Jana.

Mrs. Veritt was lookout for the children—someone had to do it, and her love of children made it acceptable to her to be away from the fighting. Zeth knew she feared for her husband. So did he. His own parents, and the other channels and Companions, wouldn't be fighting—they'd be healing the wounded. Abel Veritt, though, would be right out in front, wielding his whip with that astonishing skill he'd learned in his days as a Freeband Raider. Old as he was, he'd never let younger men fight without him.

As Mrs. Veritt's tension communicated itself to Zeth, he thought for the first time of a future without Mr. Veritt. When Marji had almost killed her grandfather, Zeth had felt sheer terror, and then intense relief when Uel was able to revive him. The possibility of Fort Freedom without Abel Veritt had not been forced on him then, as it was now.

It wasn't that he had not known death, even among people close to him. The first time Zeth could remember was when Willa Veritt, Jord's wife, died. Then later, Owen and Jana's mother, Carlana Erick.

But some people seemed . . . immortal. His father would always be there, and his mother, and Abel Veritt. Without them, how could there be a Fort Freedom?

As tension mounted with waiting, Zeth felt more and more restless. Mrs. Veritt spent most of her time atop the hill above the old sod house, scanning the trails. In direct charge of the children was Wik, the Gen boy Mr. Veritt had taken from the pens the day Owen returned from his first trip out-Territory. Wik was an astonishment to everyone. Only four months free of the drugs that inhibited the mental development of pen-grown Gens, he had already learned to talk and to ride, and just before being assigned this task he had given transfer for the first time. Therefore he had to stay inside the heavily insulated house, lest his strengthening field attract scouting Raiders.

Wik took his first leadership assignment seriously, scolding the children if they climbed the hill or wandered into the tunnels. He couldn't seem to understand childish energy and curiosity—*well, he never had a childhood,* Zeth told himself as he tried to be patient with Wik.

When the bell from Fort Freedom sounded through the cold air one bright morning, Zeth's heart gave a painful leap. If only he could zlin! If only he were grown up, and could be down there fighting!

He avoided Wik and Jana and followed Mrs. Veritt to where they could see the Old Fort. It was so far away that only the fact that people were riding in from both the New Homestead and the town could be discerned. In the rising clouds of dust, it was impossible to make out individuals.

Watching the gathering, Zeth didn't notice the yellowish cloud on the southeast horizon until Mrs. Veritt whispered, "God help us!" Then he realized storms never came from that direction. The cloud was the dust of the largest alliance of Freeband Raiders the Territory had ever seen.

The Fort had been preparing for weeks. The walls were strong and well defended . . . but Freeband Raiders berserk with killust would swarm over them, not caring if they died . . . and some would get through. As the cloud grew, Zeth's heart sank.

So many—ranks upon ranks of killer Simes, headed for the border—for Gen Territory—destroying anything that aroused their lust for pain and fear. When they finished with Fort Freedom, they'd plunge across the border—and find Mountain Chapel . . . and Owen.

As the dust settled around the Old Fort, Zeth saw the futility of their preparations. They had to wait for the Raiders to come to them. If only they had Gen guns, to cut them down at a distance—

"Zeth, go inside with the other children," said Mrs. Veritt

distractedly. The worry in her voice cut through Zeth like a knife.

And in that instant, his plan came to him, full-blown. "Yes, ma'am," he said meekly, and started back toward the Old Homestead, not daring to look back to see if Mrs. Veritt followed him until he approached the open door to the old house. From inside, he heard Wik call, "Zeth?" For a moment, he thought he was trapped, but when the Gen didn't come out after him, he realized he was searching the tunnels for him.

He had to hurry, before Wik got Mrs. Veritt to zlin for him. He ran down the hill and across the trail, then along the creek to the old threshing floor. There, out of sight of the trail, was an old barn housing the horses and wagons that had brought the children out here.

Zeth saddled Star, and led her through the creek, angling through the brush to meet the trail. Then he swung into the saddle and urged Star up the hill to the border.

All Fort Freedom's children knew the way to Mountain Chapel—but Zeth's heart pounded with trepidation as he kicked his heels into Star's sides. As he passed irrevocably beyond the point where Simes could safely follow him, doubts rose. He had never felt so alone in his life. Although he was dressed warmly, his woolen cap pulled down over his ears, he shivered in the crisp air.

I'm going to Mountain Chapel, he instructed himself firmly. Then out loud to Star he said, "We're going to get the Gens with their guns to come and drive the Raiders from Fort Freedom." If not for their relatives, he figured, they'd do it to keep the Raiders from reaching their own homes.

It was so simple, so obvious. Why hadn't the adults thought of it?

When he reached Mountain Chapel, Zeth quickly found out why. He'd crossed rugged uninhabited terrain, and begun wondering if perhaps he'd lost his way, when suddenly he came around a rocky hill to look down into a small valley, still green from the summer, as if the frosts had missed that pleasant and protected land. Nestled in the bend of a winding river was a town, the homes surrounding a large stone structure exactly like the chapel in Fort Freedom. Zeth knew he had found Mountain Chapel at last.

He wanted to gallop down there and shout out his news, but the mountainside was steep, the trail hardly more than a track. He rode into shadow, shivering. Night fell before he reached the town.

As Star's hoofbeats clattered on the bridge across the river, people came out with lanterns—and guns.

Zeth found himself facing a semicircle of men studying him suspiciously. "Who are you, boy?" one of them asked.

"Zeth Farris—from Fort Freedom."

The tension relaxed a little. "All right, son, get down from your horse, and let's have a look at you."

Zeth dismounted, saying, "I'm looking for Owen Lodge Erick. It's important. I mean—" as it dawned on him that although he personally longed for Owen, his message had to be delivered at once to the town's leader, "I've got to talk to Mr. Bron."

One of the men handed his gun to another and approached Zeth. "You're safe here, Zeth. I'm Lon Carson. I have a great deal to thank you for. You come on home with me—"

"No, you don't understand!" Zeth protested. "I came for help—"

"You'll find it here," said Mr. Carson, putting his arm around Zeth's shoulders. Then he whispered, in Simelan, "Come in the house with me before you say anymore!"

The other men parted to let them pass. Zeth let himself be led into one of the houses. When Mrs. Carson saw him, she cried, "Zeth!" and enveloped him in a warm hug. "But what are you doing here? Have you established? Surely you're not old enough—"

It was happening again. No one would take him seriously because he looked so young. "No," he said impatiently, "but Marji and everyone at Fort Freedom are in terrible danger!"

Mr. and Mrs. Carson looked at one another in shock. Then Mr. Carson said, "What's wrong?"

"Freeband Raiders!" Zeth spilled out his story, ending breathlessly, "And if you won't bring your guns and help, the Raiders will destroy Fort Freedom and then come right across the border and attack you here!"

Mr. Carson nodded. "You've done a good job, Zeth. I'll get the other men with family at Fort Freedom. Hope—"

"I'll take care of Zeth," she said. "You must be hungry."

He hadn't eaten since breakfast. He wasn't hungry, but he had been brought up on a strict regimen. "Yes, I should eat something. But where's Owen?"

"He was supposed to be back in town this evening. Mr. Bron always insists that Owen stay with him. Zeth, you must understand how difficult it is for people who did not come from Fort Freedom to believe there are Simes who don't kill. Mr. Bron is . . . much like my father. He sincerely wants to do God's will, but until I returned from Fort Freedom with Owen, he was positive it was God's will that all Simes be destroyed on sight."

"But there are lots of people here from Fort Freedom—"

"Not even a third of the town," she replied. "And what could we say before last summer? Our own parents killed someone every month. Now we say they don't anymore . . . but how can I persuade anyone that it's real? If it weren't for Owen, I might think I dreamed it myself."

Mrs. Carson took Zeth into the kitchen, where she fed him while they talked of Fort Freedom. "So the real drive of the Raiders in our direction started after Owen left," he concluded, dabbling with his soup. It tasted funny, although he recognized the recipe as one of his favorites that Mrs. Veritt often made.

When Mr. Carson returned with a dozen other men, Mrs. Carson tried to herd Zeth off to bed. "But I have to explain what's happening!" he insisted.

"We all know about Freeband Raiders," said Mr. Carson grimly. "We're all going. What we have to decide right now is, who we dare ask to go with us."

"But it has to be the whole town!" Zeth exclaimed.

"You don't understand, son," said a swarthy man with thick black hair. "We have to think of our wives and children—especially our children. Right now that means heading off the Raiders. But when we get back—"

"We'll worry about that when we *get* back, Joe," said a man in a plaid shirt. "I think I can talk Cord Ashley into helping. He's allowing his son to court my Nancy."

"Webb Simmins lost his boy to changeover two months ago," said a grizzled, bent-over man so thin he might have been Sime. He coughed, then went on, "He said to me next day he wished he could've sent him to—'that Fort Freedom place,' he called it. If he won't come along . . . at least I don't think he'll try to stop us."

At an imperious knocking on the back door, silence fell. The men glanced anxiously at one another, and Mrs. Carson pulled Zeth against her protectively. Lon Carson opened the door.

For one incredulous moment Zeth had the impression that it was Abel Veritt at the door. Then the man moved, Zeth's eyes focused on him, and he didn't know why he should have thought it. This man was much younger, a tall, slender Gen with dark hair untouched by gray and grave brown eyes that swept over the men in the Carson kitchen with a sad bewilderment that did nothing to undermine his authority. In another reversal of impression, Zeth realized that that was what reminded him of Mr. Veritt: the ability to acknowledge his feelings without losing his dignity.

"So," he said in a tone of disappointment without accusation, "the children of Simes counsel together in the night."

Zeth's hackles rose. "They're here because of me," he said. As the man's eyes evaluated him, he added, "And I'm *not* a child of Simes. I'm the child of a Sime and a Gen, and if you want the only place in the world where that can happen to survive, you'll get your gun and join us in driving the Freeband Raiders from Fort Freedom."

Out of breath, his charge of adrenaline abating, Zeth plunged into acute embarrassment as the man stared at him in silence before he said, "You must be Zeth Farris. Mountain Chapel welcomes you, and thanks you for preserving the life of Mrs. Carson."

At the man's completely reasonable tone, Zeth wished he could sink through the floor. Then he remembered why he was here, and forced himself to say politely, "You must be Mr. Bron. I'm honored to meet you—but Fort Freedom needs your help." He stumbled over the English word "needs," but knew it was the right word to convey his meaning.

Mr. Bron's level gaze swept the assembled men. "Is that what you were counseling about? Whether you dared ask my help? Are you afraid to confide in me?"

The thin, bent-over man rose. "No, we're not afraid. We are going to help our friends and families on the other side of the border. We'd welcome your help."

"To go to the aid of . . . Simes?"

"Simes who don't kill," said Lon Carson, "under attack from Simes who do. Freeband Raiders, Mr. Bron. It's not a moral issue from what Zeth tells us. It's a plain practical one: either we join forces with Fort Freedom and stop the Raiders there, or we risk their destroying the Fort and then descending on us."

Mr. Bron nodded slowly. "I see. On the 'plain practical'

side, if we ride in force across the border, can we hope to avoid detection? Or will we be branded Sime sympathizers, and have the militia down on us?" At the murmur of protest, he raised a hand. "I understand fully that that question is academic if we are attacked by such a huge band of Raiders. I've seen those monsters of depravity—and I share your desire to fend them off."

At the common sigh of relief, however, Mr. Bron shook his head. "Can you not see that this is not a secular issue, but a high moral one? God is testing us. Listen to me!" he urged as the men began to mutter again. "Each time young Owen has come here, he has brought an invitation to me to visit Fort Freedom, to see for myself Simes who have overcome the kill. Has God become impatient? Is this a test? Are we being asked to show charity to those we wrongly thought of as inhuman?"

A chorus of yeses echoed around the room.

"You may be right," said Mr. Bron, "or this may be the Devil's work drawing us into sympathy with demons, to lead us to our deaths in that sin. Tell me, Zeth Farris, why would Fort Freedom send a child for help? To play upon our sympathies?"

"I wasn't sent," said Zeth. "I came by myself. Now I see why my dad or Mr. Veritt didn't send someone: they knew you'd refuse. Mr. Veritt knows all about the Church of the Purity. He must've known it'd be no use asking *you* for help!" Frustrated tears stung Zeth's eyelids. He felt hollow. "D'you think *they'd* refuse to help *you?*"

"Son," replied Mr. Bron, "surely you know I have no way to answer your question." He turned to the assembled men. "I must pray for guidance. Tomorrow I will gather the elders—"

"You do that," said Mr. Carson. "We're going on ahead. I got a brother and a daughter over there. Last summer I didn't have the courage to help Marji—she's alive only because my wife dared risk her own life. You want miracles? Take a look at Hope. I'm going to go help my daughter, and afterward, I'm going to beg her forgiveness."

"Mr. Carson—Lon. Give me time to consider."

"But the Raiders are attacking *now!*" said Zeth, his head spinning as he tried to make these men see him as more than a hysterical child.

Mr. Bron ignored him. "Don't be impetuous, Lon. A few

more people for the Raiders to kill will not help Fort Freedom. I will pray for a sign from God this night. If He indicates that we should help Fort Freedom, we will attack as a concerted force. If He reveals a trick of the Devil . . . then I fear if you go, you cannot return to Mountain Chapel.''

Only then did he turn to Zeth. "You look tired, son. You are welcome to stay at my house. Your friend Owen may have arrived by now. I thought he was the one I would find here, not you.''

Zeth wanted to see Owen the moment he arrived. "All right. Thank you, sir."

Despite Mr. Bron's lantern and the smooth, well-tended path, Zeth stumbled like a small child clumsy with sleepiness. Although he was dreadfully tired from the long, hard trip and the letdown after pleading his case, he didn't feel sleepy, but his stumbling gait felt like one of his nightmares.

When he actually fell heavily to his knees, Mr. Bron helped him up, saying, "You're out on your feet, child." Zeth wanted to escape, to crawl away into a hole somewhere, he was so ashamed.

As Mr. Bron helped him up his own porch steps, the front door opened and a woman stood silhouetted against the light. "Maddok? What did they want you for? Oh—a child escaped from the Simes?'' The woman closed the door as Mr. Bron led Zeth to the couch, then joined them, saying, "But surely he's too young—''

"I think he's ill, Sessly,'' said Mr. Bron, and the woman placed a cool hand on Zeth's forehead.

"He's feverish. Poor little boy. Don't worry—we'll take care of you.''

"Zeth,'' said Mr. Bron, "this is my sister. Sessly, this is Zeth Farris.'' Zeth wouldn't have had to be told the two Gens were brother and sister—it was the same face, as if he were seeing double, but while the high forehead, deep-set eyes, and determined mouth and chin spelled strength in the man, in the woman they formed a face that at best would be called "plain" or "homely."

The woman was almost as tall as the man. Zeth felt small and frightened. He knew they meant to help him, but their proximity grated on his nerves. If they'd just go away—

The woman held out her hand to Zeth in a Gen gesture of friendship. Some people said it went back to the Ancients, but Mr. Veritt said it was more probable that it had developed as a way of displaying the forearm to show the absence of tentacles. Whatever the motive, Zeth knew he had to touch her—and he had no idea why he desperately wanted to refuse.

When he lifted his hand, a dull pain, like sore muscles, spread from wrist to elbow. He'd been hauling on Star's reins all day, guiding her through the rough terrain. There were spots of soreness on his hand, too, which might have been blisters if he hadn't had calluses.

Telling himself to be grateful for being treated like an adult, Zeth shook hands, ignoring the faint twinges of pain and the illogical sense of revulsion.

"I think I can find pajamas to fit you. A good night's sleep and you'll be fine. Zeth Farris," she added thoughtfully. "You're Owen's friend. He should have been here by now."

"Perhaps he decided to stay over with the Nortons," Bron suggested. "I think he's seriously interested in Eph Norton's daughter."

Zeth fought down panic. Was Owen planning to *stay* this side of the border? "Can't you send for him? His pa's at Fort Freedom, and his sister's hiding with the kids. Owen has the right to know what's going on."

"Of course," said Bron. "In the morning I'll send someone. If he were coming tonight he'd be here by now. Sessly, you take care of Zeth. I must go to the chapel and pray for guidance."

"Guidance? Maddok, what is happening?"

He explained briefly. Sessly looked back to Zeth. "Oh, you poor, brave child! No wonder you're exhausted. Come along and get ready for bed now, and I'll bring you some hot milk."

She showed Zeth the bathroom and the guest room, and gave him some pajamas. It seemed to take every ounce of his strength to change in the cold bathroom. Chills shook him, followed by a sudden sweat. Nausea hit so fast that he barely managed not to vomit on the floor.

Trembling, gripping the cold stone appliance for support, Zeth felt the ache in his forearms again. He could no longer deny the facts, the unconscious knowledge that must have been with him for hours.

Fever. Exhaustion. Pain in his forearms. Nausea.

This time you've really done it, he told himself, fighting tears of weakness. *Disobedience has finally brought you into Gen Territory, into the house of the Spiritual Leader of the Church of the Purity . . . to go into changeover!*

Chapter 6

Think!

Zeth knelt in the bathroom, panic clutching at his vitals. He had to get to Owen—

No. He thrust the absurd thought aside. He had to get home, to his father. *Think*, he told himself more calmly, reminding himself that fear was the greatest enemy of the changeover victim.

I'm still hours away from breakout and First Need. Mrs. Carson got Marji to Fort Freedom in a wagon. I can go much faster on a horse.

With that thought firmly in mind, he found the strength to open the window, airing the sour smell out of the little room and clearing his head. If he went out that window now, Sessly Bron would discover in a few minutes that he was gone, and raise the alarm.

He had to pretend nothing was wrong, and go to bed. Then, as soon as he was sure she was asleep, he would sneak out, find Star, and ride for home.

And what if you can't get to your father? the voice of fear demanded.

I'll get there somehow! Get out of Gen Territory first, then worry about reaching Dad.

In the Bron guest room, he was laying his clothes carefully over a chair, ready to get into quickly in the dark, when Sessly Bron came in. Although he knew he could have no sensitivity to fields yet, her presence made him uneasy.

She's not going to guess, he insisted to himself as she set a steaming cup on the table between the two beds, and turned back the covers on one of them.

"Hop in now," she said cheerfully, reminding Zeth of Mrs. Veritt. "Sleep, Zeth. You're a brave boy to have come all this way. Say your prayers and trust in God to help you. Here—drink your milk," she added, handing him the cup.

Obediently, Zeth pretended to drink the milk, actually taking only a tiny sip. "Thank you," he said. "Good night, Miss Bron." He yawned, and half closed his eyes. To his intense relief, the Gen woman left.

Zeth set down the milk, and pulled the blankets up to his chin for warmth. He could hear Sessly Bron moving about. He hoped she would not stay up to wait for her brother. Then he heard her coming down the hall . . . opening his door. He closed his eyes and tried to breathe deeply and evenly. She came in, turned out the lamp, and took away the cup of milk.

Zeth waited. If she had gone to bed, how long would it take her to fall asleep? He couldn't hear anything. Perhaps if he got up and listened at the door—

Zeth woke with a start, feeling hollow. He was panting, his skin pricking, and he barely had strength to turn over. He realized he had passed out.

His heart pounded and he struggled for breath until the disciplines the channels had taught him took hold. This was stage two. He began the rhythmic breathing exercises, and soon his gasping eased. He didn't know how much time had passed, except that it was too much. He'd have to ride like the wind.

Forcing himself out of bed, Zeth pulled on his clothes, counting breaths hypnotically. His body was leaden. His boots almost defeated him, searing pain shooting through his arms as he hauled on their tops. He had to sit on the edge of the bed to steady his breathing again before he dared try his escape.

He was sure the sound of opening the window rang through all of Mountain Chapel. When no one stirred, he climbed out, stumbled to his knees, and forced himself to stand. Where was Star? Mountain Chapel was much like Fort Freedom— there had to be a stable. He looked around, grateful for the illumination of the waxing moon, even though it might reveal his presence.

The narrow chapel windows glowed with dim light. Maddok Bron, praying for his sign from God. *In the morning, when they find I'm gone, will they ride to help Fort Freedom?* Zeth wondered sadly. But he had no choice. *If I stay, I'll kill.*

In the moonlight he spotted a large, barnlike building just beyond the neat rows of houses. Even though he tried to stay in the shadows, it should have been a brisk three-minute walk. Instead, it became an endless and familiar nightmare, his legs too heavy to lift. He struggled and plodded, trying to get to Owen, who lay dying—

Gasping again, Zeth pulled himself together. This was not a dream, and Owen had nothing to do with it. *But why isn't he here? He'd help me get home. Owen*—

Forcing one foot in front of the other, Zeth made his way toward the stable, fending off fear. "Don't panic," he remembered Abel Veritt telling the changeover classes. "There is nothing to fear in changeover now. God has given us channels. Changeover is no more than any other natural process in growing up."

And I'm supposed to be one of those channels, Zeth thought. *I will be. I'll get home in time.*

His father had explained how fear killed many Sime children of Gens. Even if such children escaped being discovered and murdered, their terror at becoming Sime used up their last reserves of selyn. If that happened before breakout, they died of attrition.

That won't happen to me, Zeth told himself firmly. He was creeping up to the door of the stable, smelling the good clean smell of horses, hoping Star had had enough rest to carry him—

He slid the heavy stable door open just enough to slip in, and a sudden fury erupted out of the darkness—a barking, snarling, growling dog snapping at his legs. Zeth danced back in startlement, the rhythm of his breathing broken, a stab of fear shooting straight down through his middle.

The dog kept up a steady racket, horses snorted and stomped, and a voice called, "Who's there?"

Zeth backed against the door, trying to slide it open again, but the dog growled and snapped at him, pinning him effectively until the light of a lantern made him blink and wince. "Who are you?" the voice demanded.

"Zeth Farris. I've come—for my—horse." He could hardly get the words out. "Call off—your—"

His strength gave out, and he collapsed to his knees, the dog moving in with a threatening growl. The man—hardly more than a boy—moved closer to play the lantern over him. Instinctively, Zeth clutched his forearms across his middle, giving himself away.

"Hold him, Brownie!" The note of fear drove the boy's

voice up. "Get away from that door—now, or I'll sic him on you!"

Zeth eyed the dog, which seemed ready to go for his throat. If he tried to protect himself . . . now, of all times, he could not afford to be bitten on the arm.

So he crawled away from the door, pleading, "Just let me—have—a horse!"

"No, you'll steal no horses here. C'mon, Brownie!"

Keeping the dog between him and Zeth, the boy edged out the door, stationing the dog outside. The click of the bolt locking him in was the loudest sound Zeth had ever heard. The stable boy ran out into the night, shouting, "Sime! Sime! I've locked a Sime in the stable!"

Pure terror prickled through Zeth. He was panting and gasping, weak and helpless, on the verge of fainting except that panic kept him alert. The alarm bell, so much like Fort Freedom's, rang into the night.

Soon the stable would be surrounded—he had to get out! But he couldn't even get to his feet. As his eyes adjusted to the darkness, he made out dim moonlight filtering through a crack high above him. It took shape as he stared at it— outlining a door up in the hay loft.

For all the good it was to Zeth, that door might as well be on the moon! He could hardly crawl along the floor, let alone drag himself up a ladder . . . and the ladder lay beside the stack of hay thrown down from the loft.

Zeth had to set up the ladder, climb to the loft, jump to the ground, and run! Run? He couldn't even walk. He tried to lift the ladder, but the best he could do was slide it a hand's span across the floor—and even that left him sick and trembling as he heard voices outside.

"Get around back—he could break out the back door."

Back door? Oh, no—he might have gotten out by now— with Star!

"Cord—Trent—train your guns on that loft door. They can jump on you like some mountain cat!"

They think I'm a full-grown Sime, Zeth realized. *If I were, I'd be out of town by now.* Then he heard Lon Carson's voice. "What is it? A Sime? Hey, in there! You from Fort Freedom?"

Angry questions from the gathering men, and Mr. Carson's protest, "*One* Sime doesn't attack a town! Someone's come after the boy!"

"No," came the stable boy's voice, "it *is* a kid. Change-over."

"Who is it?" another voice demanded on a note of anxiety.

"I don't know him. Never saw him before."

Then Sessly Bron's voice. "It's Zeth! He's gone from—"

"Dear God!" exclaimed Mr. Carson. "Zeth, is that you?"

"Yes!" he managed to choke out. "Mr. Carson—let me go—please! Got to—get home—"

"You hear that?" Mr. Carson said to the others. "That boy was perfectly all right a couple of hours ago—there's plenty of time for him to get to Fort Freedom, to one of their . . . channels."

"No Sime is all right, and no damn Sime sympathizer!" came another voice.

Someone else responded, "Turn him loose so's we can shoot him! Damn demon monster!"

"My daughter is neither demon nor monster!" Lon Carson said angrily. "She could help this boy. Give him a horse—or I'll take him in my wagon. He came to us for help—are we going to murder him?"

"Lon." Maddok Bron's voice, calm and reasonable. "We must do what is right, Lon. You know that."

"Are you so damn sure you know what's right? You'd have murdered Marji—"

"Stop! Before you say something you may regret forever. I know you feel shamed that your wife took your daughter across the border without your help—but how can you be certain Hope is not being used?"

"She saw—"

"She saw what they chose to show her."

Heart vibrating madly, darkness closing in on him, Zeth lost track of the argument as the transition to stage three struck him. The stable dwindled to a black box, a coffin, the walls closing in. He choked, fighting spasms in his chest, and fainted.

He woke to a dull ache spreading through all the nerves of his body. That he could breathe again was little relief in the presence of indefinable ugliness. But it came from outside himself—he could get away from it if he could move.

Sitting up, he found his head clear again. He saw the dim inside of the stable, smelled the horses, heard the voices outside. The ugly sensation dimmed before the senses he was familiar with—and then as he focused on the angry voices, it returned in a most peculiar way.

Through the walls came a glow of darkness—his mind twisted, trying to find words to describe it, but he didn't have them, even in Simelan. "Darkness visible," Mr. Veritt had once said, was the way an Ancient poet had described hell. It seemed to fit the sensation he was getting from several people . . . yes, those were people surrounding the stable, hating him, fearing him.

". . . get him out of there," someone was saying, "*whatever* we do with him then!"

"Shoot him!"

"Let's smoke him out!" someone suggested.

"You fool! Burn down the stable with all our horses? Just keep him in there. If he survives, he'll come out looking for someone to kill, and we'll shoot him. If he doesn't come out by tomorrow night, we'll know he's dead."

It wasn't even cruelty, Zeth somehow realized. He was not human to the men talking so casually of his death.

He was going to die. He should have some strength at this stage, but he could not even crawl to the water trough to assuage his thirst. Fear had consumed his selyn reserves.

If by chance he survived breakout, he knew he would not be able to think rationally in First Need. He would be driven to seek selyn, find his way out of the stable—and be shot on sight.

At least I won't kill. He considered that, then thought, *I haven't asked God for anything since I prayed for Owen to live. Now I have one last request, because I won't be able to control it myself. If I don't die in changeover . . . don't let me kill anyone before they shoot me.*

Abel Veritt called it "putting one's trust in God." Somehow, Zeth felt better, even though he was terrified of what was yet to come.

He was a channel, all right—his changeover was progressing even more rapidly than Marji's had. If they let him go right now, and he galloped for the border, breakout would come long before he got home. A berserker, he would attack the first Gen he found. *Or the first Sime. My father killed a Sime in First Need.*

With sudden clarity, he knew why he was here: to die without killing, the shock that would rouse the community of Mountain Chapel to go to Fort Freedom's rescue.

It was all part of God's plan that Abel Veritt spoke of, that Rimon Farris said it was man's only duty to seek to perceive. If Zeth had obediently stayed with the other children, he'd have gone into changeover just the same. With Freeband Raiders surrounding the fort, there'd have been no way for Mrs. Veritt to get him to his father.

Wik would have tried to give him First Transfer—Wik, who could easily serve any other changeover victim, would have thus ended his brief life, so full of potential. And Zeth would be junct—joined to the kill. With the voracious need of a Farris, he might have gone on to kill Mrs. Veritt or one of the children.

Instead, he would be a martyr. His death would unite Fort Freedom and Mountain Chapel. His name would be carved on the Monument, and his grandchildren would tell his story to their grandchildren.

It did not occur to Zeth just then that if he died in change-over he would have no grandchildren. He lay on the stable floor, shivering as the night cold crept into his bones, while the men outside futilely argued his fate.

What roused Zeth from his torpor was a new sensation . . . no, a change in the same sensation of feeling the people outside. Beyond the muddy, unpleasant miasma, he sensed a brightness like sunrise. But it wasn't the sun, wasn't light at all, although it gave promise of warmth to ease his chill.

Galloping hoofbeats, the bright presence swamping all the others, suffusing him with hope. Outside, a familiar voice asked, "What's going on?" Owen.

"Changeover," someone replied. "We got 'im trapped."

"Thank God I decided to ride on over here. Whose child is it?"

Another presence, nothing to Owen's, but without the ugliness of the men who waited to murder Zeth, joined those gathered at the door. Owen identified it. "Mr. Bron! I can save that child from killing. Tell your men to let me through."

"Are you a witch, then, Owen? A sorcerer who can consort with demons and emerge unscathed?"

The annoyance in Owen's field penetrated Zeth's numbness. "Let me save a life tonight, and we'll argue theology in the morning. Where are the child's parents? Surely they will want their child to live . . . and not to kill."

"None of ourn," said the man who wanted to shoot Zeth. "Some kid from across the border."

"But who would—?" Then Owen was at the door, the bolt creaking as he withdrew it. "Zeth! Zeth, is that you?"

The numb chill had taken Zeth over completely. Though his lips moved in an attempt to answer, no sound came.

Meanwhile, he heard a scuffle outside the door, Owen demanding, "Let me go! He needs me! He's a channel, and he could die, you lorshes!" He was apparently dragged away from the door, and Zeth's spirits sank. Then he remembered that Owen, despite the magic of his field, could not be a Companion. They were right to keep him from Zeth.

The ugly fields were at the door again, Owen's somewhere beyond them, maybe with Bron's. The cold within Zeth's body was no longer unpleasant. Perhaps all feeling would disappear, and he would just quietly die.

Then Owen and Bron were back at the door, Bron saying, "Open it—but keep your guns ready." Bron, too, was armed with a shotgun.

Owen dashed to Zeth's side without a false step, and dropped to his knees, taking Zeth's right hand in his. Zeth felt his presence, but could not feel their hands touching.

"He's freezing!" Owen exclaimed.

Bron peered down at them. "Is he dead?"

"No, he's not dead, no thanks to you!" Owen snapped. "Can't you feel his need?" He pinned Zeth's hand under one knee so he could roll up the boy's sleeve. A stab of fear and pity went through his field. "Look what you've done to him!"

Bron frowned. "I don't see anything."

"His tentacles aren't developing to match his state of need." Owen's fingers gently probed Zeth's forearm. "They're there, but stunted. You terrified him, locking him in here, and now the temperature's dropped. I *wish* we had a channel!"

As he spoke, Owen was rolling Zeth's sleeve down again, and pulling his unresponsive body against his own warmth. "You'll be fine now, Zeth," he said reassuringly. "I'm going to take care of you."

Within the aura of Owen's field, Zeth could not help but believe it. The moment he accepted that he would live, it seemed, his body began to tremble with the cold again, the hollow weakness returned, and an indefinable sensation sprang from his chest out to his shoulders and down his arms. Even when it passed, his shivering continued convulsively.

Owen looked up at Bron. "That was stage four transition.

I've got to get him someplace warm, or he'll use up his last selyn reserve just trying to raise his body temperature. You wanted a sign? Zeth is that sign, and you were too blind to see it. If you'll give us a warm place, lock us in together, in the morning you will witness a miracle. We'll both be alive and well. Could you ask better proof of what Mrs. Carson and I have told you?"

"And what if you're *not* both alive?"

Still shivering uncontrollably, Zeth looked at the gun Mr. Bron had pointed at him, and somehow found his voice. "If I killed Owen," he got out through chattering teeth, "then I'd *want* you to shoot me."

"Maddok—please!" Sessly Bron appeared from behind the armed men. "If they're right—Maddok, don't you want to believe?"

"This town is my responsibility. If I were wrong—"

"What if we've been wrong all along, shooting down helpless children? Since Mrs. Carson took Marji across the border, two children have been shot down like mad dogs. You paced the floor for nights afterward. If you don't give these boys a chance . . . will you ever sleep again?"

The man looked from his sister to the two boys. "I place it in God's hands. What do you need?"

The word sent a shudder up Zeth's spine, but Owen replied, "A warm place. Blankets. Hot bricks."

Sessly Bron took a horse blanket from one of the stalls, and wrapped it around Zeth. He hadn't even thought to look for one!

The scratchy wool didn't bother him, nor did Miss Bron's proximity, with Owen's field shielding him. "Let's get you home and back to bed," she said. "You men get out of the way! You can come surround our house, or you can go home and get warm."

Owen managed to get to his feet, supporting Zeth. "Can you walk if you lean on me? The only way I can carry you is over my shoulder."

"I'll take him," said Maddok Bron, handing his gun to his sister.

Terrified of being handled by an untrained Gen, Zeth clung to Owen—but he couldn't walk. He couldn't even feel his feet. "Owen—please!"

"I'm here, right beside you, Zeth. Let Mr. Bron carry you." Owen held Zeth's hand, the only thing that kept him from becoming hysterical as he was carried back to the Bron house, into the room he had escaped from a few hours ago, and deposited back in the same bed.

Owen pulled off Zeth's boots and his jacket, but left the rest of his clothing on, piling the blankets from both beds over him. But there was too little warmth in Zeth's own body for it to do him much good, even with towel-wrapped hot bricks at his feet. Finally Owen closed the door against all the other fields, saying, "Don't come in again, and keep those men away from the house. Zeth will be zlinning right through the walls soon, if he's not already. When it's all over, we'll come out."

Zeth's shivering shook the bed, and a sudden wave of dizziness made him clutch at the pillows in irrational fear of falling off. The numbness was gone; he was aware of every twinge of penetrating cold. Despite the blankets, he felt as if icy blasts of air were blowing across him. "C-cold!" was all he could force out.

Owen studied him for a moment, then gently probed at the back of Zeth's neck. Zeth groaned as he touched the tender swelling there. "Stage five," said Owen. "Just relax now. You're going to be fine." But Zeth could sense his worry at the rapid transitions without proper tentacle development.

"Can't get warm!" Zeth was too miserable to be embarrassed at the whimper in his voice.

There were no more blankets, so Owen climbed under the covers beside Zeth. As Owen's warmth gradually transfused from the Gen's body to his, Zeth stopped shivering and fell into exhausted sleep, no longer caring that he would probably die despite Owen's best efforts.

He woke at dawn, feeling too warm, and stretched out full length, shoving at the heap of blankets over him. Owen sat up and helped him turn them back neatly. His arm had been under the covers, yet when he felt Zeth's forehead now, Zeth perceived his hand as cool. He reached to take Owen's hand in his, puzzled at the difference in sensation.

Owen smiled reassuringly. "When you touch me, you feel like a Sime now, Zeth. Let's get your shirt off, all right? You're going to make a grand mess at breakout."

Even with Owen's help, the sliding of the flannel shirt irritated Zeth's arms. "Look!" said Owen when they had completed the task. There they were: tentacles, small but definite, lying quietly in their sheaths.

"Beautiful," whispered Owen, relief suffusing his field. "Now don't get overanxious. You're safe now; I'm here. We have all the time in the world."

"How did you talk Mr. Bron into letting you help me?"

"He's not an unreasonable man . . . and his sister has a kind heart. It seems their younger brother, Frid, changed over a few years back . . . and Mr. Bron had to shoot his own brother to save Sessly." He shuddered. "That's what it's like out here, Zeth. People harden to it, the way junct Simes harden to killing. But there are those who can't help knowing that there ought to be a better way. Your dad, my pa, Abel Veritt. Everyone at Fort Freedom now, but you're too young to remember when your folks first came."

"What if I kill you, Owen?"

"You won't. I won't let you."

"Suppose I hurt you? I'm a Farris. I have a need like my father's."

"And I have a field to match. It's over a month since I donated—I can feel how high-field I am, and still climbing."

Zeth, too, could feel the warm glow of promise, increasing as cold emptiness sucked him down and down into a bottomless chasm—need. Despite Owen's hypnotic nager, fear remained. "Dad says—"

"Your dad says—and I've heard him—'Poor Owen. What a great Companion he'd make, if only he had both arms.'"

The bitterness in his friend's tone and nager was agony to Zeth. "Owen—"

Instantly, the bitterness was gone. "It's all right. You made me realize I can still do anything I really want—and what I really want is to give transfer. That's why I stayed away from Fort Freedom. To be around Simes in need, wanting to help and not being allowed to—"

Zeth squirmed under that painful frustration. It was more than knowing how Owen felt—it was feeling it.

Owen fixed Zeth with a piercing stare, all tension resolved. "They say Gens can't feel what Simes do. Well, Simes can't feel what Gens do, either, or your father would never have forbidden me transfer. This is what I was born for. I've found myself. This is what I need, Zeth."

Zeth, giving himself up to Owen's certainty, realized that his friend's awkwardness was gone. He was Gen-graceful now, precise slowness in his every move, evoking in Zeth a

trust he had never known before. For the first time, he really
believed Owen could serve any need, even Zeth's.

"Rest now," said Owen. "Sleep some more if you can.
Save your strength for breakout."

"I'm too excited to sleep. Did anyone tell you why I
came?"

"Mr. Bron told me. You were very brave to come for help,
Zeth . . . and when they see us after our transfer, you'll get
it. I wish I'd been here when you arrived! You really gave me
a scare, going into stage four without the slightest visible sign
of tentacles—but you've come back to a normal pattern now."

Normal for another Sime, maybe, Zeth thought, *but normal
for me?* His need was deepening, but his tentacles showed no
sign of being ready to emerge.

"Where were you so late?" he asked to change the subject.

"I left the Nortons in plenty of time to get here by dark,
but I ran into some soldiers from the garrison. Bunch of
fools!"

"Why would Gen soldiers stop you? You're Gen."

"They knew that, and they knew I wasn't running guns or
Gens. They just thought they'd have some fun tormenting a
one-armed kid—and I had to put up with their questions
'cause if they'd searched me and found my tags I'd be in real
trouble."

"But what did they want? Do they know you go back and
forth across the border? Owen, what if they'd arrested you?"

"Will you relax?" Owen's field soothed Zeth. "They
didn't arrest me. They were drunk. When I told them I'd been
visiting a girl, they wanted to know all about Sue."

Zeth remembered Mr. Bron mentioning a girl Owen was
interested in. "Are . . . are you gonna marry her?"

"Not unless I can persuade her to move to Fort Freedom,"
Owen replied. "Especially now that I'm going to be your
Companion! But my Uncle Glian and Ed Norton would like
us to get married. Ed lost his son to changeover, and Uncle
Glian has no kids, so I'm his closest kin. Their ranches
border on each other, and they've got it all planned that Sue
and I should get married and unite the two ranches!"

"But . . . do you really want to get married?"

"I'm not ready. It's not even a year since I established . . .
but . . . I really like Sue. Zeth, an awful lot of girls pity me,
because of my arm. Sue's different. Reminds me of Jana, the

way she speaks her mind. We're comfortable together. Friends.''

"How did you get away from the soldiers?" Zeth asked.

"Oh, they let me go after they'd had their laugh. It was late by then—I thought about going back to the ranch, or I might have camped out if it hadn't gotten so cold. Something told me to come on to Mountain Chapel." He turned to Zeth. "I'm the one feeling cold now. There's a warm robe hanging on the door—see? I'm not leaving you, Zeth. I'm just going to take off my shirt and put that robe on. Otherwise I'll have to put on a sweater, and we'll have a real tangle when it's time for your transfer."

As his need deepened, Zeth was terrified to have his Companion move the slightest distance from him, but Owen's field was so reassuring that he gave a grim nod to the common-sense suggestion. Besides, Owen's shivers were renewing his own.

Despite his handicap, Owen quickly skinned out of shirt and undershirt, and shrugged into the robe, wrapping it properly and tying the sash with the aid of his teeth. It was not in Owen to be sloppy—even when they were kids, Zeth and Jana might have run around with their shirttails out, but never Owen.

Owen sat on the edge of the bed, facing Zeth, glowing. Zeth blinked, but it was still there, not just the morning sunlight glinting off his friend's blond hair, but a golden glow suffusing his whole body. He realized it was the same sensation he had been—zlinning?—all along, but this was the first time Owen had sat still, completely in his field of vision. In his dreams, Zeth had seen his mother glow like that.

Owen examined Zeth's forearms again, and the newly formed tentacles squirmed slightly, sending new sensations through Zeth's nerves. "Good," said Owen, "they're forming nicely now that we've got you warm. Here—take my arm between both of yours. See if my field can encourage faster development."

Zeth did as he was told, pushing back the sleeve of Owen's robe, and felt conflicting sensations: the proximity of his developing laterals to the source of life-promise was keenly sweet, while the touch of Owen's skin was somehow rough against his swollen, oversensitive forearms. The swelling increased, and soon it felt as if the fluids in which the tentacles writhed were boiling, burning him alive.

He sucked in his breath through gritted teeth, and convulsively pulled his arms against his chest, clenching his fists in helpless spasms.

"No, Zeth!" Owen said warningly. "Not yet!" He pried one hand open, but the moment he let go to reach for the other, Zeth's fist clenched uncontrollably. "Shen!" muttered Owen. "I thought I was over wishing for two hands!"

Somehow, that struck Zeth as immensely funny. He broke into giggles, watching Owen try to capture both his hands in his one. "What's so shenned funny?" Owen demanded.

"If you had two hands, we wouldn't be here. You'd be a Companion, but my father'd be giving me First Transfer, if I'd stayed in Fort Freedom."

Owen s anger evaporated. "Yeah. And I have the feeling . . . it's almost going to be worth it!"

Yesterday, that idea would have been incomprehensible. Today, hovering on the brink of Simehood, experiencing the growing void of need as unbearable pleasure because Owen was there to fill it, Zeth understood. The experience was all—and it had to be with Owen. If his father walked through that door right now, he would fight him off, tooth and nail.

His spasms had relaxed. He placed both hands on Owen's forearm and looked into his friend's eyes. "When this is over," he promised, "you won't say 'almost.' "

With Owen coaching him, Zeth saved his strength until the actual breakout contractions began. Then he worked with the spasms, feeling his newly formed tentacles writhe and press against the wrist openings, where the membranes swelled but did not break. That pain was good pain, negligible beside the agony/bliss of his growing need.

For seconds at a time, the world blotted out before his emptiness and Owen's undefined but potent presence.

Owen shoved a corner of the blanket into Zeth's hands. The rough texture of the wool triggered even stronger contractions. The membranes covering the wrist orifices bulged, and Zeth grunted and strained to break them, ran out of breath, and fell back panting.

"Zeth!" said Owen. "Come on now! I can't do it for you!"

A Sime could have wrapped tentacles about Zeth's arms to force the fluids against the membranes. A Gen could have done almost as well with fingers—but it had to be done to both arms at once.

"Here—hang on to me," said Owen, thrusting his arm against Zeth's palms. Zeth's fingers dug into the hard Gen muscle for the final contraction. It had to be the last one, or he'd surely die of attrition before breakout.

"Owen—" he cried, helpless before the pain, but the cry cut off as he strained once more, tentacles burning in the searing fluids, pressure too much to bear.

Owen bent over him, reaching for the fifth transfer contact point. As the Gen lips touched his, Zeth was seized with yet another spasm, peaking before the last one abated. Unable to breathe, blackness closing in, Zeth strained toward the promise of life.

In the moment when he had given up, the tension burst, membranes parting before eager tentacles, spraying both him and Owen with hot blood and fluids. In the shock of cold air, his new tentacles locked themselves around Owen's arm, and Zeth fell forward against his friend in blessed relief.

As Zeth relaxed, Owen gently untangled himself and pushed Zeth back onto the pillow, grinning at him as he said, "Congratulations, Zeth."

Need surged back over Zeth, washing out hearing, smell, touch, and vision. Despite his training, he panicked, clutching at the single bright warmth in his darkening universe. It was there, real and solid before him, stable, dependable. He perceived the long-denied, chronic yearning in his friend easily matching his own sudden, acute need. Owen's selyn— his life force—etched out the Gen nervous system in magnificent patterns.

He was held in that beauty, wavering on the brink of death yet braced by infinite strength. He reached out, his laterals in startling negative contrast to Owen's brimming nerves. His left hand seated itself, but his right hand groped, perceiving through the ultra-sensitive lateral tentacles the field pattern of Owen's left arm—yet there was nothing there for him to close upon.

Owen moved the arm that Zeth held, and in panic Zeth gripped tighter, the flash of pain through Owen's nager jolting him into savage need. A strong flood of reassurance overtook him, and his head cleared. *Owen's arm is gone— can't use this grip.* Even with that knowledge, though, he couldn't release Owen's arm. But he let himself move with Owen—and then Zeth's hand rested on Owen's left shoulder, near the bright pattern of selyn flow at the back of Owen's neck. His left hand released Owen's right arm and sought a symmetrical grip, laterals seating themselves automatically. Owen's arm came up against his back, enclosing him in the vibrant circle of Genness . . . and then, without volition, he felt Owen's lips make the last, vital contact, opening the flow of selyn.

All his life Zeth had imagined transfer—but nothing had prepared him for the combination of relief, release, and joy. His sensations and Owen's were so bound up together that he seemed to be giving and receiving at once—*sharing. This is what I was born for!* There was no surprise, only the fulfillment of highest expectation, rising to a thrilling crescendo, peaking—and abruptly starting all over again at a lesser intensity. *Two selyn systems. I am a channel!*

When it was over, Zeth and Owen clung to one another, Zeth tumbling back to normal perceptions as he felt his hands against Owen's cool skin, smelled the salty odor of his flesh. Then he sat back, seeing that Owen had pushed his robe down off his shoulders so Zeth could find his transfer grip unhampered.

He fumbled for Owen's wrist, and saw the red marks of his fingers and tentacles. They would be nasty bruises soon. But when he looked at Owen's face, all thought of apology disappeared. Never before had he seen such satisfaction—a perfect reflection of his own feelings—wiping away the deadening ordeal Owen had undergone since the loss of his arm.

A grin spread across Owen's face. "You were right, Zeth: there was no 'almost' about it!"

They hugged each other, laughing, then drew apart in distaste at the sticky mess Zeth's breakout had made. "Come on," said Owen. "Get dressed. They're waiting for us." He stood, reaching for their shirts. Then he turned and looked back at Zeth with a grin, stretching like a lazy cat. "I feel so *good!* As if I'm completely healthy for the first time in my life, only I never knew I was sick."

Gingerly, Zeth climbed out of bed. He felt normal—like Owen, the best he'd ever felt. A new Sime had to be able to flee if necessary—he should have no problems.

Except for his total contentment, Zeth felt so ordinary that he had to look at the tentacles now neatly sheathed along his forearms to believe he was truly Sime. He had returned completely to the senses he'd been born with—hypoconsciousness, Simes called it. The normal state after transfer. He'd have to make an effort to zlin.

"What are you making such faces about?" Owen asked.

"I was zlinning. Now I can't."

"Sure you can," Owen said confidently. "Focus on me. My field will be low, but it's there, 'cause I'm alive."

And sure enough, when Zeth concentrated, he suddenly saw his friend surrounded by a hazy luminescence that pulsed brighter with each passing second. He was both seeing and zlinning: duoconsciousness. "I *can* zlin!"

"Of course you can," Owen said casually. "Shen—half the time I think I can do it myself!"

Shivering, the boys washed with cold water from the pitcher on the washstand, then dressed and straightened the room. Owen glanced at Zeth, and Zeth gave him a nod, ready now to face anything.

Owen opened the door, calling, "It's me, Owen. It's all over. We're both fine."

In the hall, Mr. Bron was waiting with his shotgun. Zeth stared uncomfortably at the gun, zlinning the tension in the man holding it. At this distance, a Sime ought to be able to sense the decision to shoot, and wrest the gun from a Gen's hands before he could fire. But Zeth was so newly Sime that he had little control of his reflexes, and only a vague idea of what he zlinned. Furthermore, if he made the wrong move he was too far outnumbered to get out of Mountain Chapel alive. He couldn't even protect Owen.

Mr. Bron backed away into the main room. "Come out here where we can see you." Mr. and Mrs. Carson and Sessly Bron were there, the women seated on the couch, Lon Carson also with his gun ready—but Zeth was unsure exactly where he might aim it.

When Zeth stepped out into full daylight, Mr. Bron studied him with a puzzled frown. "You don't look at all like a Sime. What happened?"

Zeth was wearing the long-sleeved flannel shirt he'd had under his heavy jacket. Slowly, trying not to frighten anyone, he rolled up one sleeve to show the neatly sheathed tentacles.

The start that went through Mr. Bron caused Zeth to tense, but he was replete with selyn, and Owen was at his side. "You have nothing to fear from me," he said honestly.

"You asked for a sign," said Owen.

Zeth recalled, "Mr. Veritt always says to think carefully about what you pray for—because it's what you'll get."

Mr. Bron stared at him for a moment, as if trying to decide whether to take offense—and then his face lifted into a smile. Zeth had the feeling that the expression was new to those grave features.

"I am convinced," said Mr. Bron. "Seeing you together—" He shook his head in wonder.

Mrs. Carson came over to them. "Zeth . . . congratulations." She held out her arms, letting him make the decision—just as he had been taught always to let a Sime decide to accept or reject contact even with a child. He didn't hesitate, but hugged her. She kissed his cheek, then Owen's.

Lon Carson offered Zeth his hand, stumbling over the idea, but managing to say, "Congratulations, Zeth." When they touched, Zeth felt the urge of his tentacles to seal the grip, but quelled it. He dared not frighten or offend.

"Lon—call the men together," said Mr. Bron. He and his sister were both watching avidly, tense but unafraid. Zeth remained duoconscious without effort now.

Sessly Bron approached Zeth, wonder in her nager, but no fear. "It is your custom . . . to congratulate—?"

"Yes, ma'am," said Owen. "Zeth's grown up now."

She looked into Zeth's face, and he perceived in her field a mingled joy and sorrow. Her eyes were misted as she said, "Congratulations, Zeth." Then she turned to Owen. "You must teach me to do what you did for him."

"Sessly!" gasped her brother.

She turned fiercely. "I shall learn it! We will shoot no more children down in the streets of Mountain Chapel!"

"We can take them to Fort Freedom," said Mrs. Carson.

"If there still is a Fort Freedom," Zeth said, suddenly terribly aware that a whole day had passed since the attack of the Raiders had begun.

"There will be," said Maddok Bron. "Zeth—Owen—you must show my people. We will drive off the Raiders, to preserve a place where—God be praised—it is no curse to be Sime!"

They went out onto the porch of the Bron house. Pale morning sunlight was melting the light frost across the grass, but although Zeth wanted to savor the crisp morning air, his attention focused on the gathering crowd of armed men. To one side were Lon Carson and the others Bron had called "children of Simes," but far outnumbering them were other men, shotguns and rifles held ready. There was the same ugly sensation he had felt outside last night—a mingling of hate and fear.

Behind the men stood women, some holding babes in arms, others with older children by their sides. Zeth was sure the whole town had turned out to judge him.

Mr. Bron stepped forward, his voice carrying clearly in the morning air. "My people—since last summer, when Hope Carson took her Sime daughter across the border, to return with tales of Simes who do not kill—since that day, we have lived in doubt and dissension. If before we were concerned about the children of Simes living among us, now suspicion divided us, dread fear lest we misinterpret God's will. The Holy Book said Simes are demons. Killers. Yet if what Mrs. Carson told us was true, it was possible that any child of ours who turned Sime . . . might . . . not . . . kill."

He waited for the ensuing murmur to die down before he continued, "We prayed for a sign. Last night a child came to us from Fort Freedom, claiming not to be the child of Simes"—he glanced sidelong at Zeth with a faint smile—"but of a Sime father and a human—normal—mother."

Now there were open exclamations. Bron nodded. "You have heard of this boy, Zeth Farris, from Mrs. Carson. We have wondered at the stories she and Owen Lodge have told us and, if they are true, what we are being asked to do.

"Last night Zeth came for help against killer Simes attacking his home. No adult of Fort Freedom dared—but the faith of a child led him here, to beg aid of strangers."

"Why should we help Simes fight Simes?" shouted a portly man in the back row, whose nager was a sullen umber. "Let 'em kill each other, and good riddance!"

"As you would have killed last night, as we have killed our own children for generations!" Bron replied. "You all heard the alarm last night. Those of you on schedule came with your guns. The rest . . . you looked into your children's rooms, did you not? And before you went back to sleep, you thanked God it was not your child . . . this time."

At the whisper of assent, Bron continued. "When Zeth told me about the Raiders, I went to pray. God forgive me—He had sent the sign we sought, and I would not see it. I went off to pray without recognizing that the child who had come to beg our help . . . was in changeover!"

Starts of fear ran through the crowd, followed by puzzlement as Zeth stood quietly on the porch. Owen edged nearer
as the questions rose. "How could he be?" "Look at him—
that's no Sime!" "But I saw him in the stable last night.'
"But look—he's just a little boy!"

When the crowd had settled, Mr. Bron said "Zeth? Show
them?"

Zeth stepped forward, Owen at his side. "There's nothing
to be scared of," he said. "Owen's Gen, like you, but he
knew what to do for me. I'm Sime—but I'll never kill."

With his right hand, he once again unbuttoned his left cuff
and rolled the sleeve up to expose his sheathed tentacles.
Owen, standing to his left, took Zeth's hand, lifted it—and at
last Zeth allowed his handling tentacles their way, sliding
over Sime and Gen flesh, binding their hands for all to see.

There were gasps from the crowd, and instinctive move-
ments of guns. At once Maddok Bron stepped in front of
Zeth. "There is nothing to fear. Rather rejoice in God's sign
to us. Think of your own children, brothers, sisters. Will you
chance their becoming demonic killer Simes? Or would you
have them like this boy—lucid, controlled . . . harmless?"
He moved to Zeth's right side and added, "Innocent."

Firmly, Bron held out his hand to Zeth. Sensing that the
man knew, as Abel Veritt always did, the gestures that would
convince people only partially swayed by words, he took his
hand, letting his tentacles wrap about it. There was a collective sigh from the watching crowd.

Then Lon Carson raised his gun over his head, shouting,
"For your brothers, your sisters, your children—ride with us
to save Fort Freedom!"

With a shout of assent, people scattered to their homes.
Zeth was left standing between the two Gens, retracting his
tentacles. Mr. Bron examined his hand, front and back.
"They're not—"

"No, they're not slimy!" Owen supplied with a laugh. "I
don't think I've convinced Uncle Glian of that. Oh!" he
added. "I've got to ride to Uncle Glian's ranch! He'll bring
his men to help."

"I've got to get across the border," said Zeth. "I'll be safe
enough. You go for your uncle, and I'll ride with Mr. Bron."

"You're not going anywhere but back to bed!" Owen said
firmly. "Zeth, you're a brand-new Sime and a channel at
that. If you don't rest, in a few hours you'll collapse."

"And so will you, Owen," said Sessly Bron from just inside the door. "You had no rest last night, either. Maddok, send riders to the ranches. And you boys come inside and have breakfast. I'll heat some water so you can have a bath, and then—"

There was no use protesting that both Zeth and Owen were grown men by Fort Freedom's standards. Besides, as his tension relaxed, Zeth found his mind refusing to obey his will, fixing with utter fascination on trivial things such as the rippling pattern through the walls of a house as men rode by behind it. "Well, maybe you're right," he conceded, glad to have Owen beside him to shield him from the chaotic nager.

Still, he fidgeted nervously as they watched the men of Mountain Chapel ride out to defend Fort Freedom. Would there be anything there to defend? Was he the last channel left—untrained and nearly helpless?

Owen put his hand over Zeth's restless tentacles and said, "We'll ride home tomorrow."

Chapter 7

The sun was low when Zeth and Owen topped the hill that gave them their first view of home. The air was very cold. A pall of smoke hung over the valley. Only large landmarks could be distinguished. The Old Fort stood amid columns of black smoke. Where the town had been, there was nothing—even the wooden bridge across the creek was gone, along with Slina's pens.

They had found the Old Homestead deserted but unharmed. Mrs. Veritt and the children must have gone home. That was the only hopeful sign. Well beyond the Fort Zeth could see other columns of dense smoke, and concluded that his own home was also a casualty.

He urged Star forward, insisting to himself, *if the children are home, Fort Freedom drove the Raiders off.* Immediately, though, he wondered: *At what price?*

Zeth reached forward, his laterals extending themselves to zlin, and was bombarded with excruciating pain, anguish, fear, grief.

It was not until Owen stopped both their horses and reached out to shake Zeth that he was able to stop zlinning. "Zeth—what's wrong? What happened?"

Forcing calm, Zeth said, "Down there. It's awful!"

Owen looked from Zeth to the scene below, and back again. "You can't zlin that far!"

"Are you going to tell me what I can and can't zlin?" Zeth snapped, rubbing his hands over his aching lateral sheaths.

"No, of course not," said Owen. "Here—stop that! You want to injure yourself?"

"I'm all right," Zeth said. "Come on—let's get home."

"What did you zlin?" Owen asked as they started down.

"Pain. Probably a lot of people hurt. I'm scared, Owen."

104

The path to the Fort led through heaps of dead bodies. Zeth saw Simes going through piles of corpses, separating the dead from the living. Scarecrow forms of Freeband Raiders were flung limply on the blood-churned stubble. Among the piles of enemy dead were other bodies, Simes and Gens, some he knew and some he recognized as out-Territory Gens: they had died defending people they had always considered enemies.

And I'm responsible, Zeth thought, as he turned his eyes from an upturned face bearing the hideous rictus of fear that marked death by the kill. But the Fort stood. One wall was partly burned and partly smashed in; several houses had been burned; but the chapel stood unharmed, and the people he saw were not Freeband Raiders. *I'm responsible for that, too,* he consoled himself. The bullet-ridden Raider corpses made it plain that the out-Territory Gens had saved the day.

Zeth and Owen headed toward a large group of active people—and naturally, they found Rimon Farris and Abel Veritt at its center. There was a whip slash across Abel's forehead, blood congealed in his white hair. He limped heavily, but he was the same unstoppable Abel.

Rimon, though, was almost unrecognizable. His clothing was in ashy tatters, his hair singed, his eyebrows gone. From his thighs to his boots, his trousers had been burned away, his legs a mass of burns and blisters. He was too busy healing others to think of himself. Rimon looked up with a start. "Who's—? Zeth!"

Until the past few minutes, Zeth had never before zlinned any Sime, but zlinning his father, he felt that he'd have known that field anywhere. He could feel worry and annoyance vying with the pride of winning, and the easy meshing of their fields as his father zlinned him in return. Zeth slid down off his horse, but dared not embrace Rimon because he zlinned another painful burn across his back. Rimon held out his hands, and they entwined handling tentacles in the gesture of deep friendship Zeth had so often seen his father exchange with Del Erick.

Some overlying anxiety rang incomprehensibly through Rimon's field. Then he was called to help by Hank and Uel, working nearby. Zeth flicked back to duoconsciousness as Abel moved in to hug him, tears in his eyes, saying, "Fools and children! Somehow God takes special care of them. Bless you, Zeth Farris. For all I could turn you over my knee like a child too young to be reasoned with, what you did saved Fort Freedom.''

In the background, Owen called, "Pa!" and ran off toward Del Erick, who was carrying a limp form. Del did not seem harmed at all, though his clothes were dirty and smeared with other people's blood.

He carried a boy no bigger than Zeth, Sime, emaciated, dressed in the rags of the Freeband Raiders.

"I left this one for dead a few hours ago," said Del as he joined them. "I suppose I should have just broken his neck and had done with it."

"No, Del," Abel said gently. "You're a fine fighter, but you don't murder the helpless. What's wrong with him?"

Zeth zlinned the boy, finding pain, swelling, and pressure on his lateral sheaths. His eyes told him the cause. "Whip burns," he said, fighting off nausea as his own laterals buzzed in sympathy. "A hard blow to his right outer lateral. The swelling is keeping him unconscious." When Abel and Del stared at him, he added, "I'm sorry—that's all I can tell. I don't know what to do for it."

Del gave a grim laugh. "What are you—two days old?"

"Less," Owen contributed with proprietary pride.

"And already you can zlin that accurately? You'll be a better channel than your dad, Zeth. Congratulations."

"You shouldn't have moved this boy, Del," said Abel.

"I know—but I couldn't bring him around. Better disorientation than freezing to death."

Abel said to the Simes waiting to help, "Take that boy inside and have fosebine ready if he comes to. He'll send every Sime in the Fort into screaming fits, and we can't have that with all these untrained Gens around."

Rimon, hearing the last part, said, "Put him in the back room of the chapel, away from the Gens." The stone chapel, the best-insulated building in the Fort, would be used as an infirmary for Gens. Zeth walked over to his father and Uel. They had a Gen male face down on a blanket, blood pouring from the lower left side of his back. Blood stained all down his left trouser leg, indicating that he had remained on his feet or his horse despite the wound.

Uel was saying, "I don't know how you can heal him, Rimon. His field is melting away. While you're working with him, others may die who might have recovered."

Again Zeth automatically zlinned—and instantly recognized the man's field, weak as it was. "Mr. Bron!"

Abel said, "Their leader. Rimon, can't you save him?"

"Dad," Zeth pleaded, "he took me in in changeover. He persuaded the Gens to come help us. Uel—can't I do something? So Dad can—?"

"Your father ought to be in bed himself!" Uel snapped. Hank put a hand on his arm, and he calmed. "I'm sorry. We've been through so much here, I forget what you've been through." His expression brightened. "Hey—you *are* a channel, aren't you? Congratulations." The smile faded. "Oh-oh. Trouble."

Several Gens from Mountain Chapel were approaching, guns ready, suspicion in their collective nager. Both Hank and Owen immediately moved between them and the Simes.

"Let us through!" one of the men demanded. "We can take care of our own."

"No," said Hank. "Our channels are his only chance."

Hank, having come from Gen Territory, spoke the Gen language without even the faint trace of accent of the bilingual children of Fort Freedom. Zeth observed the consternation in the Gen fields as they tried to place him. Owen spoke up. "I've told you about Fort Freedom. Now see for yourselves. The Simes here don't kill—they save lives. Please—if Mr. Bron is to have any chance at all, don't interfere."

"What're they gonna do to him?" another man asked.

Zeth began to zlin what his father was doing. He was, to all appearances, simply standing beside the fallen Gen, but nagerically he was projecting need. The cells of Bron's body responded by producing selyn, and, Zeth discovered with absolute fascination, producing more blood. He zlinned his father avidly, wanting to know how a channel—

A gently impinging field brought him duoconscious. Owen was circling Zeth's left wrist with his hand, not touching, but interfering with Zeth's perception. When his eyes focused, Owen said, "Wake up, Zeth. We're going inside."

Hank Steers was standing beside Owen. "There, you see, Owen? It worked. But keep an eye on Zeth. A new channel can drift off for hours, and you'll find out he was zlinning the bumblebees working in a field of clover!" Hank added, "Hey, Zeth, congratulations. And, Owen—you certainly showed 'em! The Companions have been on your side all along, you know, but we couldn't argue the channels down. Any problems—just ask!'' And he hurried after Uel.

In the chapel, rows of beds and pallets held the wounded Gens, many already treated and resting. Whip cuts, knife wounds, broken bones—all would respond to simple treatment. Fort Freedom's Gens moved among them, lest Simes inspire fear. Zeth followed the party carrying Maddok Bron toward the far end, where heavy hangings shielded the part of the chapel where the channels were treating the most seriously wounded.

Owen's sister Jana was plumping pillows and carrying water. She dropped everything, though, when she saw her brother. "Owen! Oh, you're back!" She took his hand, oblivious to Zeth, and pulled him toward one of the beds. "Look who's here!"

The man in the bed was big and blond, like Owen—Zeth knew even before Owen exclaimed, "Uncle Glian!" that they had to be related. Only the eyes were different—this man's were hazel, not the startling blue of Owen's and Jana's.

Glian Lodge pushed himself up on the pillows, wincing at the pain from broken ribs. "Well, hi there, son. You're a hero, I'm told!"

"Not really," said Owen, and Zeth could zlin that the thought surprised him. "Zeth saved Fort Freedom—and you, and all the others who came to help."

"Hell, a chance to shoot them slimy sons of—" He broke off. "Yeah—I know. All Simes aren't alike." He called to the man in the next bed. "Hey—Eph! Wake up and see who's here!"

"Hello, Mr. Norton," Owen said politely when the other man opened his eyes. His head was swathed in bandages, covering an array of painful cuts. Owen pulled Zeth forward to be introduced.

They had already exchanged the normal pleasantries when Lodge said suddenly, "Hey, wait!" His field jarred with startlement, and Zeth clenched his teeth and backed a step toward Owen. "You're the kid went into changeover—?"

"Yes, sir," he replied. "Don't worry—I won't hurt you. No Sime here would."

The Gen shook his head. "I'll be damned. You seem like any normal, healthy kid."

"I am," said Zeth, although he wasn't really a kid anymore. Eph Norton stared at him. "Dear God," he whispered, and turned his head away. Zeth felt the tears stinging the Gen's eyelids as he pretended to fall back to sleep. He remembered that the man had lost his son to changeover.

When Zeth and Owen continued toward the insulated hangings' Owen said, "Let me go first, and *don't zlin* until you look first. This is one shidoni-be-flayed experience to throw a new channel into. Let me shield you. No heroics.

Zeth nodded and followed Owen through the curtain. Each of the severely injured Gens was surrounded by heavy hangings cutting the fields to a shattered haze so the channels could work without interference. One of the compartments, though, throbbed with a ruddy glow that drew him helplessly, and when he pushed the hangings aside, he saw what he already knew: his mother, lying in the bed unconscious. Her field was so strong that he was surprised to see three other people there: Marji Carson in the channel's position beside the bed, Trina Morgan assisting her, and Marji's father, Lon Carson, watching his daughter work.

Owen started to pull Zeth back, but when he saw Kadi Farris he followed Zeth, his field marbled with concern and sympathy.

Marji looked up. "Your father said you were home, Zeth. He was just in—Kadi came conscious for him."

"How bad—?"

"They were caught in the fire. Both of them have bad burns on their legs. Rimon threw himself over Kadi when the roof fell in—he has even worse burns. Kadi has lung damage from smoke—and your father says there are scars from another time."

"Gen raiders burned their first house down around them when they started to homestead here. Marji," said Zeth, "will she live?"

"Oh, yes! I'm sure. Rimon will be back later—she responds best to his field, but I can maintain her."

Zeth began to zlin his mother. She could hardly breathe. The burns on her legs were painful, but the dark anomaly of failing cells was in her lungs. Marji was projecting need, encouraging Kadi's cells to produce selyn—to live and work and sustain her—but his mother's field resisted full cooperation with the young channel's. As Zeth pored over what he zlinned, the fields became abstract designs, fascinating in their complexity. He allowed his own field to impinge on the linked fields before him. Kadi's field responded—and then she became aware of her pain, crying out, "Rimon!"

"No, Mama, it's me—Zeth."

She turned to look at him. Her eyes were normally deep blue, but now pain had drained the color from them until they seemed almost gray. Her hair was dull with smoke and soot—she was faded, not the flaming-haired angel he remembered. Then she smiled, and was his mother again.

"Zeth. My baby. They told me—"

"Don't try to talk, Mama. Yes, I'm all right, and I'm a channel, like Dad."

"You feel like your father," she murmured. Zeth didn't know what to make of that, but didn't ask because he could see how it hurt her to talk. ". . . so proud of you," she whispered, and then could not stay awake any longer.

"She must be getting stronger," said Marji. "She could hardly talk to Rimon." Zeth let himself become duoconscious again, but could comprehend nothing more from Kadi's field. As he turned to go, he passed Lon Carson, who was projecting a savage pride as he watched Marji. His nager didn't interfere with her work. Probably Rimon had decided making Lon go would create a greater disturbance.

Owen held the hangings aside. "Zeth, can you hear me?"

"Sure."

"Well, *listen!* Stay with me and let me shield you—you can't go drifting off in a hospital!"

"All right, Owen," said Zeth with absolute intent as he followed along in Owen's wake . . . until the flow-pattern of the ambient nager became an irresistible lure. He turned around, caught in the intensity of ebbing and flowing energy.

This time Owen shook him impatiently. "Come on, Zeth, the channels will throw us out of here!" He led Zeth on to where, heavily shielded with many layers of drapery, the channels were treating the critically wounded patients. Zeth jolted back to hypoconsciousness when he zlinned that the body being carried out by Dan Whelan and Del Erick was dead. The bodies out in the field had not bothered him—but this one meant the channels had failed to save someone. Bron?

No, Maddok Bron had been laid on a table, still unconscious. Duoconscious again, Zeth perceived the fighting strength that denied Bron's state of depletion.

Two Mountain Chapel Gens with guns had accompanied

the party into the chapel. Their fields thrummed with suspicion as Rimon bent over the still form of their leader. "You gotta take the bullet out," one of the Gens insisted.

Zeth's surprise and revulsion were reflected in his father's field, and Rimon fought irritation, fatigue, and pain before he answered calmly, "Then he would surely die. Prying about inside the wound would start the bleeding again, just when I've managed to stop it."

"Whad'ya mean, you stopped it? You didn't do nothin'. We watched you the whole time."

Again Rimon gathered patience before replying, "I'm sure you're aware that Simes can sense a Gen's life force. Those of us who are channels can sense such things as the bullet inside Mr. Bron—and just as a Gen's field affects a Sime, a channel's field can affect a Gen. I'm afraid I can't explain further in terms you can understand." He paused. "How did this man get shot? There were no Simes with guns."

One of the men explained, "When most of the ranchers went down, we were ready to retreat. Mr. Bron wouldn't let us. He rode through the ranks to lead us—I think he must have gotten in the way of someone's shot. I don't think he knew he was hurt till the battle was over."

Rimon nodded. "A brave man. Now will you allow me—?"

Maddok Bron suddenly surfaced to semi-consciousness, flaring pain. Both Rimon and Zeth turned at once, and the Gens raised their guns by reflex. Owen moved to shield Zeth, who suddenly realized Rimon was working without a Gen. "Go help Dad," he urged.

Rimon motioned Owen back, saying, "No—he's so weak I shouldn't have any field interfering. I worked alone when I healed you, Owen. Stay with Zeth—he has no experience."

Bron was lying on his side. Rimon carefully placed his hands over his back and abdomen, the wound between them. One of the Gens gasped, "What are you doing?"

"If he moves, he could start bleeding again," Rimon replied. "He could go into shock. How can I make you understand that the best thing is to leave him here?"

Astonishingly, Bron fought his way up to full awareness. His eyes opened. "Don't move!" Rimon said sharply.

Bron's dizziness and nausea came sharply to Zeth, even through Owen's field. How did his father stand it? Fear, pain, anxiousness—"Who are you?" Bron whispered. Rimon, still bearing the effects of the fire, looked like an apparition straight from the hell preached about in the Church of the Purity.

"You're in Fort Freedom," Zeth said quickly. "My father is treating your wound."

Confused, Bron struggled to peer at Zeth. It was several moments before he whispered his name.

"That's right," Zeth said, trying to project encouragement. "You're safe. Because you came to help, the Raiders are gone."

Bron had no strength, and was both chilled and sweating. Shock. They could lose him right now. Bron knew it. "I'm dying," he murmured. "Tell my sister—"

The two men with guns immediately started toward him. "No!" said Rimon. "Mr. Bron, you won't die if you can tell these men to stop interfering with your treatment."

Bron was shivering steadily now. Owen tried, "Please, Mr. Bron. Rimon can't work with Gen fields interfering. I know you can't understand, but—"

"Not understanding," Bron whispered with a beatific smile. "Faith. You said it, Owen. I asked for a sign." He drew a long, shuddering breath. "Go, Cord, Vern. I don't need your protection here—I have God's." He managed to remain conscious until the two men left the room. The instant relief in the ambient made Zeth's senses reel.

Forcing himself back to duoconsciousness, he heard his father saying, ". . . blankets and a warming pan. Wik should be out there somewhere. Send him."

Owen said, "I'll be right back, Zeth. Rimon, should I take him—?"

"No—just hurry back." When Owen had gone, Rimon said, "Zeth, I can't take Hank and Uel or Jord and Anni away from the wounded Simes. Marji—"

"I know. I saw Mama. She talked to me."

Rimon breathed a sigh of relief. "She's getting stronger, then. I hate to leave her with Marji, but she can hold Kadi's field and she can't do what I'm doing. When Owen gets back, we'll see if you two can help me."

Owen returned with blankets. "They're warming bricks on the chapel stove to warm the beds. I sent Wik—Rimon, the way that kid has changed while I've been away!"

"You forget he came out of the pens," Rimon agreed. "He'll be a fine Companion when we have time to train him—but meanwhile we've got to make do with what we have. Owen, support Zeth—if you don't let his attention wander, we can put his condition to good use.''

Zeth was about to protest their talking about him as if he weren't there, but then he realized that his father was according Owen the status of Companion, and felt a warm glow of pride for his friend.

"All right, Zeth," said Rimon. "First healing mode. Zlin me, and then try to mesh your field with mine.''

Zeth zlinned how his father's field shifted, and found he could shift to match. He felt his father's surprise and pride, followed by a tug which drew him back to duoconsciousness.

"Very good, Zeth. Now, maintaining healing mode, put your field and Owen's, and all the leakage through the drapes, into balance, so it's as if Mr. Bron and I were alone together. Here—zlin me doing it.''

Suddenly Zeth stood in a bubble of clarity centered on his father. Duoconscious, he could hear the steady hushed din from the chapel, but his whole body felt *silence*.

"Now, you try it," said Rimon, slipping back into healing mode, his attention going wholly to Bron.

Owen moved automatically to where his field balanced the most intense external fields. But when Zeth tried to compensate for the fields flowing through the hangings, the patterns distracted him again. Twice Owen pulled him back, once with a tug of his hand, then with a flick of his field.

Zeth bit back frustration at his inability to concentrate, and flung himself into the task again. The bubble of quietude formed around them all, and Rimon looked around with a smile. Then Zeth was holding the incredibly beautiful and complex pattern of shifting energy fields.

A Gen approached. At first Zeth felt annoyance at the distortion, but he found he could weave the approaching field into the bubble, a bright tang of curiosity almost as ravenous as his own, contriving as naturally as Owen did not to interfere.

Zeth tried duoconsciousness, and found that he could still hold the fields. It was Wik who had entered, to place the towel-wrapped hot brick at Bron's feet. Rimon dared not move, but he smiled at his son and said, "Good work, Zeth."

Zeth envied his father's ability to divide his attention—but the instant his mind wandered, the field pattern collapsed. As he groped for it again, both Gens stepped automatically to positions which negated the worst effects. *How do they* do *that?* Zeth wondered, but was too busy to think about it further.

He rebuilt the bubble of silence. As soon as he had it again, Wik left. Zeth caught up the pattern, proud of his control. He spared a portion of his attention to watch what his father was doing, lost the pattern, gained it, and again peeked at his father. He couldn't count how many such cycles he went through, but by the time the people outside the curtains were falling asleep, leaving for the night, or settling into vigils, Zeth was able to watch his father and still hold the bubble steady.

Once, he sought to pick his mother's field out, but Owen brought him back to attention. Another time, a Sime poked his head through the hangings, radiating anxiety—and left, disappointed. Some time after that, another Sime approached. This time Zeth recognized Abel Veritt, also rife with anxiety— but as the old man hesitated at the entrance, Rimon's field suddenly flared relief, and Zeth was brought all the way down to hypoconsciousness, seeing his father leaning heavily on the table where Bron lay, looking unutterably tired, but also satisfied.

On that note, Abel entered. "Rimon—"

Rimon smiled at him. "He's all right, Abel. He's out of shock and sleeping."

"Yes, I'm very glad, but . . . Rimon, you must—"

Zeth sought duoconsciousness to ferret out the terrible worry he had sensed in Abel Veritt. His overstrained, unpracticed system rebelled. He started to black out. The two Simes turned, but Owen was at his side, easing him to the floor. He was as exhausted as when fear had drained him in the last stages of changeover.

If Owen hadn't been there to lean on, he would have fallen right off the world. At least that was his impression. Both Abel and Rimon bent over him. Rimon said, "I'm sorry, Zeth—you weren't ready for that. Relax. You'll be all right in a few minutes. Abel, I put him straight to work doing field balances and he held steady until just now!" Rimon's pride warmed Zeth despite the exhaustion.

"Owen," Rimon added, "let Zeth take a transfer grip. Zeth, relax against Owen's field. Let anything happen that happens—you won't hurt him. You're high-field."

Owen knelt in front of Zeth, who found it nearly impossible to lift his leaden hands to Owen's shoulders. But then his tentacles spread naturally, and he rose to duoconsciousness, at rest once more in the safety of Owen's nager.

They were in that state, Owen's back to the sudden flare of nageric horror, Zeth shielded, Owen unaffected except that his field somehow strengthened for a moment as— Abel gasped, staggering, turning toward the agonized tumult in the ambient as Rimon emitted a harsh, hideous sound like nothing human and dropped with a lifeless thud. But his body moved, muscles contracting unnaturally, his field a torment of uncontrolled spasms, driving his body into convulsions as Zeth struggled helplessly to focus—

Abel pulled himself together, dropping to his knees beside Rimon's thrashing body, yanking off his belt to thrust the leather between Rimon's clenched teeth as footsteps pounded up outside the enclosure and Trina Morgan flung open the hangings, crying, "Rimon—come quickly! I think Kadi's dead!"

Chapter 8

Zeth woke at dawn. Something new had happened to him while he slept. He knew that the sun was just below the horizon. He knew exactly where he was—not just that he was in Abel Veritt's house, but *where* the house was, in a strange new perspective.

Beside him, Owen slept soundly. He lay still so he wouldn't disturb his friend. He could zlin the whole house without moving—or right out through the walls. The ambient nager was no longer a mere blur of interesting patterns. He could sort out the fields of Simes and Gens, noting them as individuals, even though he could not yet put names to many of them. The fields no longer ran together in foreshortened layers; he knew exactly where each person was.

He zlinned the room next door. Empty. Across the hall . . . Margid Veritt, asleep. Out in the main room, some Gens slept in exhaustion. One field he knew: Lon Carson. Yes, he remembered vaguely, they had given sleeping room to several uninjured men from Mountain Chapel.

Other memories of yesterday—and very early this morning— suddenly returned. *Mama's dead!* He sat up in shock, and Owen stirred and muttered in his sleep. Kadi was dead, and Rimon very ill. Abel had seen Rimon go into convulsions like that before; he had known just what to do. Then Uel Whelan had come. The rest was a blur.

Had Rimon survived? Abel would know. He located Abel in the kitchen, his field still and controlled. Zeth slid out of bed, trying not to wake Owen. For the first time in his life, he tiptoed silently through the house without tripping or knocking something over. Not one of the men in the main room stirred as he passed.

Abel Veritt was seated at the kitchen table, his chin resting on his folded hands in an attitude of prayer. But the old man's field did not suggest peace. Something dark and tense dominated Abel's nager—something not there last night.

When Zeth entered the kitchen, the dark nageric cloud retreated, but didn't dissipate as he looked up and answered before Zeth could ask, "Rimon is alive, Zeth. He went through worse than this before you were born, when he was learning . . . not to kill." The darkness flared and retreated at the words. He added, gravely, "It will be very hard for him without your mother. It will be hard for all of us—but I don't have to tell you that you and your father are like family here. No—you *are* family."

Abel prepared two glasses of tea. As he put Mrs. Veritt's wooden tea box back on the shelf, he took down the delicate china container, and placed it in the center of the table.

Duoconscious, Zeth studied the container. It had a single white glaze on the inside, but the outside had been glazed with two other colors, and had a tiny delicate tracing of gold. Incredible luxury for Fort Freedom. But what caught Zeth's attention was the way Abel's field was distorted through the various layers of glaze. Zeth moved his hands, his laterals perceiving from various angles—

He pulled himself back to duoconsciousness, annoyed at drifting off again, and shook his head. "I can't seem to keep my mind on anything!"

"That's normal," said Abel. "You're rediscovering the world. Thank God there's no guilt to interfere with your development, Zeth. Ask Uel—I suppose he'll take over your training until Rimon's on his feet again. I'm afraid you'll be put right to work."

"I don't mind. I feel fine this morning."

"You recover quickly—just like your father."

Margid Veritt came in, tying a crisp white apron around her waist. Zeth recalled that he'd run away from her just before the attack, and babbled an apology.

"You did what you had to do, Zeth. I've lived with Abel long enough to understand that sometimes a man has to follow the inclination God sends him."

She picked up the china container. Abel reached out and covered her hand with his. "Leave it."

"But it's empty, Abel."

"Use it. Put tea in it, Margid. That's why I got it for you.

All these years you've said the children might break it—but there are no children in our house any longer."

Margid stared at him, and he added, "For me. Don't you think it's time I got to see you use it?" She nodded silently, poured the tea into the china container, and placed it once more in the middle of the table.

Owen was soon up, Margid busy putting food before him. "You must eat too, Zeth," she fussed contentedly. "You're still growing."

Owen's hunger inspired Zeth's, but after a few mouthfuls he didn't want anymore—and he still had half a slice of Margid's delicious bread. He reached for the jam. Owen dropped his cereal spoon and grasped Zeth's arm. "Hey—I didn't bring you through changeover so you could poison yourself!"

Strawberry jam. For the first time, Zeth realized there were some things he had lost by becoming Sime. Not just some of his favorite foods, but any real pleasure in eating. There were new pleasures to savor . . . but he wondered if many Simes felt nostalgic for the old.

Lon Carson joined them, asking, "Marji still asleep?"

"Oh, no, Lon," answered Abel. "She slept about two hours, and then went back to work. You were wonderful with her—I think you did her as much good as her Companion."

"She's my daughter and I deserted her when—"

"You were there last night. The first time a patient died under her care—" He shook his head. "Having her father there, accepting her, was as important as anything Trina could do."

The other men from Mountain Chapel did not join them in the kitchen, but accepted the food Margid took in to them. They would leave this morning, along with most of the other uninjured men from Mountain Chapel. Many of the ranchers had been killed or injured, leading the charge against the Raiders. Glian Lodge, though, turned up in the Veritt kitchen, a bit leery of the Simes gathered there. He was seated between Owen and Lon Carson.

When Del Erick, Slina, and Uel Whelan arrived together, carrying extra chairs, Zeth realized that this was a planned meeting—but no one suggested he and Owen should leave. The conversation was conducted in English—in which, if possible, Slina's grammar was even worse than in Simelan. She wasn't embarrassed; she spoke fluently, if inventively.

Uel's report, from the channels, came first, so he could get back to Rimon's side. Zeth's father, he reported, was stable, but still unconscious. "And that puts me out of commission until I dare leave Rimon for more than a few minutes at a time." His mouth set grimly. "We lost three Gens during the night, and five Simes. At least a dozen more people ought to have a channel in attendance, and we can't *spare* one! Marji's trying to handle the Gen ward with just Trina and Wik. Nobody's attending the Simes at all right now, till I get back and relieve Jord with Rimon. He and Anni are working together better than usual, but we all know Jord's pattern."

"I'll come and bring him home as soon as we're finished here," said Abel. "How many people are left to care for?"

"A few are up and about," said Uel. "Mr. Lodge, here, insisted on getting up this morning."

"I'm fine," the rancher said, although Zeth could zlin the throb of his injury.

"Your friend Mr. Norton can be moved out of the infirmary later today, but neither of you is in shape to ride for home yet. Three other Gens won't require channel's supervision anymore, leaving twenty-one in the chapel. The Simes are recovering rapidly—fifteen left the infirmary this morning. That leaves forty-three patients." He shook his head. "And we're out of fosebine."

Slina put in, "Ain't none at my place—ain't no *place* no more. Filthy lorshes burnt it down. Winter settin' in—"

"I know," said Abel. "We'll get to your report, Slina, but let Uel finish so he can go back to Rimon."

"That's it, except for the three Raiders we captured. Two died in the night, but the kid's still alive, screaming with disorientation. Without fosebine or a Companion to spare, there's nothing to do for him but confine him in that back room. Oh, yeah—we'll have a problem in the Gen ward with Hapen Young's transfer burn. His last dose of fosebine will wear off about noon, and he'll have that sick headache for *days*."

"But, thank God, he survived," said Abel, adding for the benefit of Glian Lodge and Lon Carson, "Hapen established as a Gen only six weeks ago. He hadn't even donated to a channel yet, but he somehow managed to keep from resisting when one of the Raiders got to him."

"Resisting?" asked Lodge.

"That's how Gens get killed," Uel explained. "They resist

letting a Sime take their selyn, and the forceful drain burns out their nervous systems. Maybe we can move some insulating curtains from around Maddok Bron to insulate poor Hapen.''

"How *is* Mr. Bron?'' asked Zeth.

"Your father brought him through the immediate crisis. If we can keep him from dying of secondary infection, he'll recover. Abel, work with him, all right?''

"What can *I* do? I'm no channel.''

"You can pray with him. You speak his language. Oh, yes, someone ought to be keeping a close eye on Bekka Trent. She'll be approaching crisis soon.''

"I'll remind people,'' said Abel.

The grim statistics soaked through Zeth's numbness. Fort Freedom might not survive. There just weren't enough channels.

When Uel had gone, Del Erick reported that both the New Farris Homestead and his own home had been set afire. The stone walls of the New Homestead were still standing, but the outbuildings were gone. "My horses, and Fort Freedom's sheep and cattle, are scattered all over the range. I set some of my men to milking the cows that had come back to the New Homestead—they didn't much care for the job, but we've got Gens and children to feed.''

"Good work, Del,'' said Abel. "Shelter is a problem. We've lost the town, your place, and Rimon's. We have what's left of Fort Freedom, and the Old Homestead. It seems best to rebuild right here before the winter really sets in—and try to keep the mixture of people stable by shuttling some out to the Old Homestead.''

Zeth noted the careful wording. Obviously, no one had informed their rescuers from out-Territory that mingled with the Simes who didn't kill were those who had to kill occasionally, and those from town who killed every month.

Lon Carson said something similar to what Zeth had been thinking when he resurfaced into awareness. "We can spare some supplies, maybe even a milk cow.''

"We can contribute,'' said Glian Lodge for the ranchers. "Owen, the next time you—''

Zeth managed not to squirm, and Owen quickly answered, "I won't be crossing the border anymore, Uncle Glian. But we'll find other couriers, and you're always welcome here.''

Zeth's blur of relief ended only when the ambient nager shifted with the departure of Lodge and Carson. Then the group around the table could tackle the most serious problem: the lack of Gens for those who had to kill.

Slina's Gens had been brought to Fort Freedom before the attack and sheltered in three houses near the wall. Their nager had attracted the Raiders; they had smashed the wall and killed more than half the Gens by setting fire to the houses to drive them out. Others had died in the fires. "We got a two-week supply left," said Slina. "That's a two-week *normal* supply. Sick Simes, they need extra kills. Abel, we'll be out in ten days, easy."

"How long—?"

"I sent Risko over to Ardo Pass this morning. Ol' Mack owes me a favor, but no way is it gonna stretch to a month's supply, 'specially this time of year."

"Then," said Abel very quietly, "until you have replenished your supply, we cannot allow any Gens to be killed."

"Hey, now," Slina began, "there's no way—!" Then she stopped. "You mean everybody should—? The channels—?"

"Slina, that is the *only* way—unless you want to see Simes mad with need cross the border to kill the very people who just saved our lives?"

"Shen," she murmured, staring at her tight-clasped hands, handling tentacles wrapped protectively around them. "I don't think I could stand—" Her field ached with revulsion.

'No one is asking you to disjunct," said Abel. "This is a severe emergency. Everyone must accept channel's transfer once, twice at the most. But we must have your permission to have the channels draw selyn from your Gens today—that way, they'll produce a new supply. And we must have your cooperation in persuading the townspeople."

"You gonna try to convince 'em to take up your ways?"

"Slina," Abel said gently, "have we ever tried to persuade you?"

"Naw," she admitted. "That's why I trust you with my kid." She sighed. "It gives me the creeps to think it. But if anybody knows how hard it is to be sure everyone who needs a Gen can get one, it's a Gendealer. Shen and shid! This coulda happened at least five times since Rimon come here, 'cept you people come and healed my sick Gens and stretched the use of healthy ones. I owe you. The townspeople owe you. I'll convince 'em. Go ahead and have the channels take all the selyn they can from my Gens." But Zeth could feel her horrified shudders as she made the commitment.

When the meeting was over, Zeth and Owen went to the chapel, where Rimon was shielded in one of the back rooms. In the other room was the young Freeband Raider. Being moved while unconscious had distorted his Sime sense of precisely where he was in the world—the new sense Zeth had awakened to that very morning. Owen put his arm about Zeth's shoulders as they passed, to be sure Zeth did not get caught up in the boy's nager.

Owen remained precisely at Zeth's left shoulder as they entered Rimon's room. Channel and Companion, they could thus refrain from disturbing the nageric balance of the sickroom.

Rimon Farris lay unconscious, Uel Whelan beside him, while Hank Steers lay sound asleep on a pallet on the floor. Yet even in sleep Hank's field was a steady support for Uel.

With the dirt and soot washed off his face, Rimon appeared dead, pale, his breathing so shallow as almost not to disturb the covers that were heaped across his middle. His blistered legs were smeared with shiny salve. Pain penetrated even Rimon's unconscious state.

Last night Rimon had been vigorous, animated. Now Zeth could find almost no trace of his father in what he saw or what he zlinned. Zeth had been relieved to find Fort Freedom still standing and all the channels alive and working, but he realized as he watched the still form of his father, *The battle isn't over; it's just begun.*

Wishing he could help, but glad Uel was there to take the responsibility, Zeth moved closer, automatically sliding into healing mode. Uel said, "Zeth—where did you learn that?"

"From Dad, last night."

"Of course. Someone said they put you right to work, poor kid. And we'll have to work you some more. We're out of almost all our medicines—Mr. Lansing brought his last aloe plant for Rimon's burns. He and Len Deevan are going out to the Old Homestead to harvest mushrooms today. Then they'll head down south to sell them for medicines and herbs. In the meantime, all we've got are channels."

"What do you want us to do, Uel?" asked Owen.

"Relieve Jord. He's going to try to give a couple of transfers this morning—after that, do as much as you can with the Simes. Owen, you keep Zeth doing what he's assigned, and *not* trying anything else."

"We'll manage," said Zeth, trying to hide his apprehension. Just as they came out of Rimon's room, Glian Lodge emerged from the main room of the chapel, half leading Eph Norton. "Owen," said the rancher, "can you show me the Deevan house? They told us we could stay there."

"Yeah—probably in Len's room, while he's away. It's the house with the big apple tree—about five houses down the street."

They had to raise their voices over the moans coming from the room where the young Raider was. Suddenly the incoherent shouts turned to words: "Papa! No, Papa, no!" A thud, as the boy hurled himself against the barred door.

Simultaneously, Zeth realized that the boy was shouting in English and that Eph Norton's field had suddenly gone wild. "No!" he groaned. "Jimmy! Oh, my God. Oh, my God!"

Owen was trying to step in front of the door to stop the flaring Gen fields from irritating the boy inside, and at the same time maneuver Zeth to where he was shielded, too.

Eph Norton took the move as if the boys were trying to bar *him* from the room, demanding hoarsely, "Who's in there?"

"One of the Raiders," said Zeth. "A young boy—can't be many months past changeover."

"A young boy? Jimmy?"

As if in answer, the boy inside the room cried, "Papa! Please, Papa! Don't lock me in the barn! Let me out!"

Norton was white with shock. "That's my son! Dear God, why?"

Glian Lodge was staring at Zeth and Owen. "A Raider? What can you do with him? He's a raving monster."

Zeth said, "I don't *know* what we're going to do with him, but we can't just murder him, can we?" *The way I was almost murdered.* He forced the thought aside.

"I meant to," said Norton. "I locked him in the barn, went for my gun—he broke out! I never saw him again. It wasn't three weeks later I met Owen, and he told me about— I could have sent him—" He broke into sobs.

"Eph, you can't be sure that's Jimmy," said Lodge.

"It's Jimmy. I want to see him."

"No," Zeth and Owen chorused, Zeth's sympathy for the boy's situation putting him a beat behind. Then Owen continued, "He can't help himself, Mr. Norton. He's been living like a Freeband Raider for months. Now he has an injured lateral and he's hallucinating. It could make him do *anything.*"

Glian Lodge said, "You don't have to guard the door,

boys. I'll see that Eph doesn't do anything stupid. Come on now—if it is Jimmy, you can't help him now." He looked to Zeth. "Do I understand right that his upset will upset the boy?"

"That's right."

"So the best thing you can do is let me put you back to bed. You were only supposed to walk down the street." As he led the man out, he added, "We'll talk to this Abel Veritt. He seems a good sort—you even forget he's a Sime, y'know?"

The Raider boy—Jimmy Norton, apparently—continued to sob. Grimly, Zeth led the way out through the chapel. There were only a few Gens left now, none seeming critical to Zeth. Despite heavy curtains hung about one bed, Zeth felt the aching and sick headache which identified Hapen Young's transfer burn. Without fosebine, the boy would suffer, but he'd survive.

The insulated hangings around Maddok Bron's bed were turned back so that Marji Carson could sit beside him and still keep an eye on the other patients. Trina Morgan looked tired, but was awake. Bron was sleeping.

A good smell permeated the air, and Zeth looked up to see some women wheeling in a cart with a huge pot. As they began handing out bowls of soup, Maddok Bron came awake. "Good morning, Mr. Bron," Zeth said, though it was almost noon.

Bron forced an unconvincing smile. When he tried to lift his head, a spasm of pain shot through his lower back. Marji said, "Don't move. Let us help you, Mr. Bron."

"Marji? They told me—I didn't believe it. God bless you, child, and forgive me for thinking you a demon."

"You couldn't know," she replied. "Even Mama didn't know. But everything's all right now." She blinked back tears. "You're hungry. That's a sign you're getting better."

Cautiously, Bron asked, "You can read my thoughts?"

"No, only feelings."

"A gift. And you're a healer, too." Zeth felt the man's awe, akin to his own—but while Zeth was perceiving his familiar world in a new way, Bron was encountering a world he had never dreamed possible. "So much to think about—"

"Not today," said Zeth. "You're much better, but you're not well. Eat, and then go back to sleep."

Bron looked from Marji to Zeth and back again. "Children

tending the injured? Are things that bad, then?'' He tried to peer out into the main room.

"We're not children; we're channels,'' Marji said firmly. "Don't worry—Mountain Chapel will manage till you're well. Daddy and some other men are going home today. They'll take care of everything. You concentrate on healing.''

As Bron had used up his strength, he allowed Marji and Trina to prop him up with pillows. He didn't flinch when Marji extended handling tentacles to steady the bowl of soup, but ran a hesitant finger over one of her dorsals, saying in a bemused tone, ''I don't understand. I must pray and meditate, for there is too much I do not understand.''

Zeth had not meant to stay so long in the chapel. As he and Owen hurried out the front, they met a gruesome sight: rows of dead bodies laid out on the cold ground, not even blankets to cover them. Four Simes were digging a trench in the unused portion of the cemetery, while the ranchers and the men of Mountain Chapel loaded onto wagons the bodies of their own dead.

Zeth flinched, and backed against Owen, who could hardly soothe Zeth because he was shivering in horror himself. Zeth did not see his mother's body. Someone had taken it to prepare it, as he saw people taking other bodies off now . . . and one being brought back, wrapped in fine linen cloth. There was no time to make coffins.

Abel Veritt, crossing from his house toward the Sime infirmary, met them. "I didn't think,'' he said. "I should have warned you.''

"Mama?'' Zeth asked hesitantly.

"She is in heaven, Zeth. Her earthly remains are being prepared . . . but that is not your job, son. We all have other duties, even before we can hold the memorial service.''

Abel's field was comforting. Zeth felt Owen choke back tears as he squared his shoulders and followed the two Simes along the path lined with corpses.

Abel took Zeth and Owen into the Brandon house, now turned into an infirmary for the most seriously wounded Simes.

Jord Veritt looked as bad as Zeth had ever seen him, older than his father, eyes sunk so far into their perpetual dark circles that his face appeared a skull. His field felt very different from those of Rimon, Uel, or Marji—a peculiar sense of precarious balance, as if his systems held only a tenuous grasp on their selyn, and his control might at any moment dissolve into explosive release.

But he was working, Wik at his side, Anni Steers sleeping in the armchair in the corner.

"Jord," said Abel, "you've done enough now. You may be needed elsewhere later, so you must save your strength."

Jord gave a bitter smile. "You mean I'd better not get sick myself. It's all right, Father—I know my limits." He looked at Zeth and Owen. "You're supposed to relieve me?"

"I learned to balance fields last night," said Zeth. "I can do healing mode. Let's hope nothing else is required."

"Show me," said Jord, and Zeth went into healing mode as Rimon had taught him. "Good," said Jord, "but you're projecting for Gens, as if you were in need. For Simes, you have to pretend to be Gen. Like this."

Zeth strove to mesh fields, but the anguished fear that underlay Jord's projection of repletion repelled him. Forcing himself, he managed to imitate the repletion only. Jord said, "That's it, Zeth—keep that up, and you'll have everyone comfortable." Zeth realized that Jord couldn't tell the difference between their fields—night and day to Zeth. If another channel couldn't tell, he decided, then the Simes who were to benefit probably couldn't either.

Soon Zeth's mind was occupied with the new experience of balancing Sime fields as opposed to Gen fields, Owen drawing him back every so often to be sure he didn't miss a crisis. There were other Simes caring physically for the patients; fortunately, nothing happened that Zeth and Owen together couldn't handle. It would be weeks before he knew enough to realize how badly an untrained channel might have mishandled an emergency; on that day he felt proud and grown up, totally in control.

Late in the afternoon, Uel Whelan came in, checked out the ambient, and said, "Zeth, you've been a tremendous help—I think we dare leave this ward without a channel now." They left the house in charge of one of the Sime women.

Zeth was tired again, but by leaning on Owen's field he was able to walk back to the Veritt house, where another conference was in progress. He sat with a glass of tea in his hands while Owen, who hadn't eaten since breakfast, consumed a huge bowl of vegetable stew, but he came out of his weariness when Wik came in. "Marji wants you to come," he said. "Rimon's awake."

Zeth hurried eagerly to the sickroom, but when he entered his elation vanished. Although Rimon's pain was the first thing to shock Zeth, even worse was the fact that Rimon didn't mind it. Then came an even greater horror: Rimon was in need—and he didn't feel it!

Rimon looked at Zeth casually, without interest. Zeth wasn't even sure he recognized him. "Dad?"

"Zeth. How are you?" It was a polite formality.

"I'm fine," Zeth answered. "Mr. Bron's better—you saved his life. The people from Mountain Chapel—" Rimon wasn't listening. His eyes drifted away from Zeth's, but he wasn't zlinning. "Abel will be here soon," Zeth tried. No response.

Uel put an arm about Zeth's shoulders and led him out. "Your father is still in shock, Zeth. Jord was like that after Willa died. It will take a long time. He can't even grieve—he's too close to need."

"Who's going to—?" Zeth began in panic, hating himself for being glad that Owen was too low-field to provide the transfer Rimon would soon need.

"We'll manage," Uel said firmly. "Zeth, your father's been a fighter all his life. He's the first Sime ever to stop killing. He's not going to give up now . . . and do you really think that if he tried, Abel would let him?"

But Zeth could not shake off the feeling that even Abel Veritt could not make his father want to go on. Abel spent hours with Rimon, talking, praying. Each time Zeth walked in on them, however, he would zlin the dark cloud upon Abel's nager. Did Abel fear that Rimon might be reduced to Jord's state, living for his duties, a life without hope or joy?

The morning of the funeral service, Jord and Uel together got a transfer into Rimon. "He'll be all right for a couple of weeks," Uel told Zeth. "We forced him, the way we have to force Jord sometimes. But maybe now he'll fight that infection. What he really needs is a good transfer from a Gen."

Owen!

As if reading Zeth's mind, Uel said, "No, not Owen. Zeth, your father actually expressed interest this morning, the first sign of recovery. He said he won't touch Owen—you're not to attempt to do with a substitute until you're fully trained. Even if I didn't agree, which I do, I'd take Rimon's advice about what's best for you, Zeth."

His own fears relieved, Zeth asked, "Then who?"

"Hank, probably. I manage when he gives transfer to Abel. Marji and I are pretty close in our cycles, and she volunteered Trina for me without batting an eye." He shook his head. "She doesn't seem nearly as dependent on her Companion as the rest of us, maybe because she had First Transfer from a channel? There's so much we don't know!"

And I thought Dad had found out everything about channels!

Both Rimon and Maddok Bron developed infections. Bron's kidney infection, though, responded to the herbalist's concoctions combined with fosebine. Slina's man, Risko, brought back only ten Gens from Ardo Pass, but at least he picked up a good supply of fosebine. After that, the chapel cleared quickly . . . and it was time for the memorial service.

The bodies had been buried days before, before the ground froze. The cold spell that had come in with the raid had now lasted almost a week; people shivered in their warm coats, and started talking about early snow.

What they got was freezing rain, coating the half-unleaved trees with ice and making both walking and riding treacherous. Zeth's dog Patches came in from herding sheep, his feet bleeding from sharp ice trapped in the fur between his toes. Although he was given a rug to lie on by the fire, when Zeth and Owen left for the memorial service, Patches insisted on going along. He left them as they approached the chapel . . . to lie on Kadi's grave.

Zeth stared after his dog. "How could he know? He wasn't even here."

The benches were back in the chapel except for a space left for the pallets of those too weak to sit up through the service. Lamps shone on the memorial to the martyrs to the cause of Sime/Gen unity. The last name was still Teri Layton, killed in the raid in which Owen lost his arm. Although the stone slab was large, Zeth wondered if it would be possible to get all the new names onto it . . . and if they did, how long it would be before they'd require another monument, and then another, and another—

He pulled his mind away from the thought, zlinning the people in the chapel. The Simes from town were off in one corner toward the back, insulated from the rest of the congregation by high-field Simes interspersed with Gens who could handle them if necessary. Otherwise, the people of Fort Freedom took their usual positions.

Their usual positions. Although Zeth knew why people never took the same place twice in the chapel, this was the first time he could perceive the fields that dictated the arrangements.

Today, those fields were somber. With all the work to provide shelter for survivors, to care for the injured, to prevent an accidental kill, there had been no time for grieving.

Rimon Farris was still in the insulated room at the back of the chapel. His burns had developed such an infection the channels had decided not to move him, but if two doors were left open, he could hear everything. *If he cares,* thought Zeth.

The severely wounded were the last to be brought in. Maddok Bron was among them—he was laid on the floor, near where Zeth and Owen were sitting. Only Gens were now left recuperating; the Simes had either died or recovered. Slina, well past turnover, jarred the ambient as she sat down behind Zeth and Owen. She had taken over care of the sick Gens as soon as they could forgo a channel's supervision. Certainly their local Gendealer knew how to care for Gens, but Zeth wondered what the people from Mountain Chapel would have thought had they known the occupation of their rough-spoken nurse.

Del Erick slid onto the bench beside Slina, reaching out to squeeze Owen's shoulder to tell him he was there.

Change was the subject of Abel Veritt's eulogy. He skipped over the details of the long struggle against the kill lest questions be raised in the minds of their out-Territory guests, and spoke of the breaking up of families when Gen children had to be sent across the border.

"We prayed for their safety," he said. "We never dared hope to meet them again in this world—but God has more than answered our prayers. Our children have come home— and brought us new friends, who risked their lives to save ours. Since the day He sent Rimon and Kadi Farris to Fort Freedom, God has given us cause after cause to rejoice."

He paused, looking out over the assembly. "Today we gather in mourning for those who died defending our way of life. It is right to grieve—and to question. Only by questioning can we receive answers. Why should we lose so many we love? We must be willing to die for what we believe in. Of those willing—some will die.

"All of us have lost a friend or relative—and everyone, even those who never knew her, has lost Kadi Farris. Kadi

taught Rimon how to live without killing. She was the first
. . . because she was willing to lay down her life to save
Rimon's. God did not claim her sacrifice at that time.

"And Rimon—how often has he risked his life for you? To
save my life he gave up his own selyn—and did not die.
And—for the first time—I did not kill. Surely no one who
remembers that day can doubt that God is guiding us. Why
He brought the Raiders here—"

Zeth, who had so often heard Abel Veritt turn terrible
events into occasions for rejoicing, noticed the reaction of the
out-Territory Gens. Their sorrow was tinged with curiosity,
perhaps a bit of resentment. Except for Maddok Bron. Bron
listened intently, his field falling into synchronization with
those Simes closest to him, the way a Companion's did. He
didn't resist emotionally, like most of the other Gens.

A painful, harsh sorrow swept through the ambient nager,
and Zeth surfaced long enough to hear Abel calling those who
had died martyrs, encouraging the cleansing grief that would
allow people to accept and go on. Beside Zeth, Owen dissolved into wracking sobs. Del leaned forward and put his
arms around his son. Zeth saw Jana, sitting on the raised
benches of the children's choir, trying to keep composure.
But soon tears were coursing down her cheeks.

Zeth let himself become hyperconscious again, lost in a
world of nageric patterns. The Gens joined in the outpouring
of emotion. Slina, need preventing her from full response, sat
gloomily awash in other people's grief. Her little girl broke
away from the family she'd been left with and climbed onto
Slina's lap. Her mother held her tightly, as if someone might
try to take her away. Abel Veritt's orchestration of the service
was long-practiced, but far from cynical. When the grief had
been vented, he went back to the subject of change. "Change
for the better," he insisted. "There is never progress without
loss in this world—but we have not lost those we love. Surely
they wait for us, even now. Their task in this life is finished;
God has further progress to ask of us."

Zeth lost track of Abel's speech again as he read the
astonishing change in the ambient. By the time the choir sang
out again, an emotional healing had taken place in that chapel
as effective as the physical healing done by the channels.
What would Fort Freedom ever do without Abel Veritt?

When they stood to leave, Owen whispered, "Zeth—are
you all right?"

"Of course I'm all right. Why wouldn't I be?"

Del also studied him with an air of concern. "Zeth—don't deny your grief over your mother's death. It's not a time to put on a brave front, son."

"I'm not," said Zeth, quite astonished. Then they were moving out of the chapel, conversation becoming difficult as they worked their way through the crowd.

At the back, off to one side, stood the Raider boy, Jimmy Norton, his face streaked with tears. On either side of him stood tough Simes from town, but the boy didn't look in any shape to make trouble. Even a few months of the harsh Raider's existence had taken their toll. He was emaciated, his hair stringy, although he was well scrubbed and dressed in clean clothes. Zeth had overheard the women discussing how to rid him of lice.

As Zeth passed, Owen moved automatically to Zeth's left, as if to protect him—and the boy saw the stump of Owen's missing arm. A scream of utter terror broke from him.

"The one-armed Gen! The wer-Gen! Don't let him kill me!"

Chapter 9

It was a wonder that the Raider boy's panic didn't cause a riot. Still radiating terror, he was hustled away from the vulnerable Simes. Wik broke out of the crowd, using his field to calm the boy.

Owen stood frozen until Zeth started after the boy in avid curiosity—then he ran after Zeth. Eph Norton headed toward his son, cut off by Abel Veritt and Del Erick.

The explanations came in the Veritt kitchen. Jimmy Norton was seated, Wik on one side and Hank Steers on the other keeping him steady enough to face Owen and explain, over half an hour's patient coaxing, why he was so terrified. Eph Norton listened, grim-faced, as his son told what he'd learned in his three months as a Freeband Raider.

"Everybody knows—even in the cities—that in Fort Freedom they live on Sime-kills instead of Gens," Jimmy blurted at last.

"How could they 'know' such a thing?" asked Abel.

"The town here used to be a good raiding stopover. Now everyone who comes to raid disappears!"

Under Abel's gentle prodding, Jimmy described the burgeoning reputation of Fort Freedom. "Yeah, we heard the way you give selyn to Simes—it ruins the"—he eyed his father—"*appetite for the kill*," he finished in Simelan, his nager sick with conflict.

Owen said, "It wasn't a channel who frightened you."

"Fort Freedom's Gens can't be killed. Everybody knows the Giant Killer Gen came from here. Your Gens can kill! Just a flick of their monstrous fields and—" He broke off, choking.

"Is that why," asked Abel, "the New Farris Homestead

132

was attacked last spring? Because people are afraid our Gens can kill—supernaturally?''

"Well—it certainly isn't natural!" Jimmy's eyes fastened on Owen's missing arm.

The silent tension stretched until suddenly Abel lunged with the swiftness of a killstrike, tentacles out, grabbing at Owen's bare neck. With a faint flicker of adjustment, Owen turned to Abel, holding the same warm compassion he gave Zeth.

Zeth came to his feet, every fiber resonating to Owen's betrayal. Before the feeling could take hold, Abel relinquished. He had never tried for lateral contact.

Only then did Zeth become aware of Jimmy Norton. The boy was also on his feet, the two Gens beside him still seated, holding him by their focused attention. Zeth understood. It was one of Abel's demonstrations, much more eloquent than words. *Our Gens do not kill—nor do we.*

Just then Marji Carson and Jord Veritt appeared, supporting Maddok Bron between them. Bron said, "Will one of you get me a chair, please? Eph—even though you and your son never joined our church, I want to help."

"Jord," said Abel, "bring in the big armchair for Mr. Bron. His counsel will be welcome."

Bron was settled and brought up to date. While they talked, Zeth watched Jimmy scanning the room. He looked from Abel to Jord, Wik, Hank, Uel, Eph, and then Zeth and Owen. His eyes skittered over Owen, but hungrily devoured everyone else with a sharp edge of hope.

Finally, Owen leaned forward and said, "Jimmy, we've never met before. Why are you afraid of *me?*''

"You can never be Sime again, can you? They turned you Gen so you could live without your arm—but—can they do that to anyone? Can they do it to me?"

Wik broke into giggles. "That's just silly!"

Zeth let his shock recede amid the laughter. Jimmy's awe reminded him so of how he'd felt when his father had announced Owen's establishment that Zeth said, "It does seem like magic, Jimmy, when the channels save people's lives. But it's not. Nobody can turn a Sime into a Gen—or vice versa."

"But he was in changeover when they cut his arm off!"

"No," said Uel and Jord almost in unison. Then Uel

added, "I was there, Jimmy. The tale has been exaggerated out of fear."

"I think I know how," said Owen. "The people who did it kept saying they *wanted* us to die in changeover. Someone overheard and misunderstood."

Wik nodded. "Uel's a channel," he said reassuringly. "He'd know a changeover."

"What's a channel?" asked Jimmy, his nager calming.

As everyone gave his own definition, Zeth pondered a new thought. He had led Owen and Jana into the battle where Owen had lost his arm. So in a way he was responsible for the reputation that had brought the Freeband Raiders down on them.

Maddok Bron was saying, "Jimmy, you must understand. I am here only because these Simes do not kill. Ever."

All this time, Eph Norton had been sitting silently, on the brink of tears. Now he said, "Jimmy—oh, son, please listen to these people!" He turned to Uel. "Can you teach him to be like you? Can you . . . make him my son again?"

Uel looked to Abel, who said cautiously, "We can try. But, Mr. Norton, we cannot *do* it to him. Only if he *wants* to stop killing can we help. It's a long, difficult process."

Jimmy was staring at his father. "Papa—you *want* me as your son?"

"Of course I do! If I'd known this place existed, I'd have brought you here myself."

Zeth understood the rarity of Norton's attitude from Jimmy's tremulous hope, a hope the boy didn't quite dare feel.

"Jimmy—" Norton looked around. "I can't be alone with him?"

"It's not safe," said Uel.

"No, Papa, it's not," said Jimmy. "I can't—trust myself. That's the worst part—you go crazy, and then you wake up and you've killed someone—"

In answer to Eph Norton's flare of horror, Abel said, "The Freeband Raider pattern. He's never been through a normal need cycle. Mr. Norton, we're doing our best to protect all the Gens from out-Territory. You will go home safely if you'll observe one precaution: *always* take a Sime's word if he tells you *not* to trust him."

But as father and son wanted badly to talk, Jord and Wik accompanied them out. As the others rose to leave, Abel said,

"Stay for a moment, please. Maddok, there is something you urgently have to know. Do you feel up to it now?"

"Tell me, Abel," said Bron, settling back into his chair. Zlinning, Zeth decided he could take perhaps ten minutes of sitting up.

Abel steepled his fingers, tentacles retracted. "Maddok, we have not lied to you. However, you do not know the whole truth.

"I gathered as much, from what you said to Mr. Norton." His eyes were fixed on Abel's hands. "God will not hold you responsible for what you did before you knew there was another way. The important thing is that you have stopped killing."

Pain swirled through Abel's nager, but he looked straight into Bron's eyes. "No," he said quietly, "I have not stopped."

The only emotion in Bron's field was disbelief.

Abel went on softly. "I have been trying for nine years to live entirely on channel's transfer . . . but at least once each year—"

"It's a physical problem," Uel interjected. "Mr. Bron, no one who had been Sime for over a year when Rimon discovered how to channel has been able to disjunct—to stop killing."

"Rimon had been killing for four years," Abel said dully. "It should be possible for anyone who really wants to."

"And we'll find out how," said Uel. "Zeth will be as good a channel as his father. Working together—"

Abel managed a weary smile. "You don't understand, Uel—and Zeth never will, either, thank God. Maddok," he continued, shaking off his depression, "you see here a community in transition. All our young Simes—those who changed over after Uel—have never killed. A few, who came to us from across the border, have killed once, and never again. In another generation, Fort Freedom will be in truth a community in which no Sime kills, ever."

Zeth watched Bron's nager with interest. His adjustment hardly seemed as radical as Zeth's when he'd first learned the dire secret. Bron began to ask searching, technical questions that Abel, the channels, and the Companions stretched their English to answer, for many of the words had just been invented in the last nine years, and they were all in Simelan.

Bron ran out of strength and shook his head wearily. "One thing is clear. Mountain Chapel must have people who can prevent a child from killing at changeover."

"I'm sure we'll find volunteers among our Gens," said Abel. "I wish we could send a channel, but a Sime on your side of the border—"

"Would bring down on us the same sort of raids you have been suffering," Bron agreed. "I must learn—and teach all my people—to give transfer."

"No!" It was a chorus from everyone else in the room.

Astonishment rang in Bron's field. He appealed to the Companions, "Hank—Owen—do you think yourselves better men than I am?"

"That's not it," said Uel. "It's not something you can do just because you *want* to!"

"Don't be dumb, Uel," said Hank. "That's exactly why I was able to do it for you—or are you getting so old you can't remember your changeover?"

"There's wanting, and then there's wanting," Uel muttered.

Bron smiled. "I know the difference. Owen—when Zeth was in changeover, didn't you say that you would not let him kill you? I have much to learn before I can be so confident. So I must start now. Abel—" Bron's eager smile turned him into a different man from the dour minister Zeth had first met. "Abel, if you refuse to kill—surely you will allow me the right to refuse to die?"

Fort Freedom also refused to die. Slina's emergency Gen shipment—technically top government priority after a raid—was delayed first by bureaucratic fumbling, and then by the weather, as the first snow filled the mountain passes. On the heels of the storm, however, the tax collector made her rounds—nothing ever seemed to stop her. Slina sneered, indicating the empty spot where the pens had stood—but managed to get Fort Freedom into a fine fix, as the inspector insisted on a house-by-house search. And Fort Freedom was full of out-Territory—untagged—Gens.

There were still a few wounded Gens who could not make the long journey home, and that same break in the weather had brought a caravan from Mountain Chapel, headed by Sessly Bron. Swearing balefully in two languages, Slina hurriedly made out papers and tags for all their guests, Zeth and Owen running them around to the various houses as Uel and Abel delayed the inspector lest she find a "Wild Gen" to confiscate.

The inspector became more and more nervous, until at last

she skipped the last four houses and rode away at a full gallop.

It would have been hilarious except for the tax bill she did not forget to present. "I know what spooked her," said Wik. "Gens doing real, useful work!"

Zeth sobered. "As long as it doesn't add to the wer-Gen legends!"

That evening, Maddok and Sessly Bron were sitting at the Veritt kitchen table along with Zeth, Owen, Abel, and Margid. Bron fingered the papers he had been given that afternoon, unable to read the Simelan. "Zeth tells me this paper says you own Sessly and me, Abel."

"A technicality. For tax purposes, I am the owner of all the Gens who live in Fort Freedom. Which reminds me— Owen, give me your papers." In the "assigned to" box, under Slina's scrawl, he wrote Zeth's name, and signed it. "I should have done that as soon as you two got back. Now you're all set, wherever you might go together."

Zeth looked at it and laughed. "Most of the time Owen acts more like *he* owns *me!*"

Just as he said it, a strange feeling came over him—like stepping on a step that wasn't there. Only it went on and on. Owen, turning to retort to his joke, never got the words out. "Zeth—what's wrong?"

When Zeth couldn't answer, Abel said, "It's just turnover. Support him, Owen. The first time can be rough."

Turnover. Zeth had used up half the selyn in his system— the first step down again into the chasm of need. Owen put his arm around Zeth's shoulder, an unspoken promise.

Zeth took two deep breaths, and summoned a brave smile as the room came back into focus. He could certainly manage as well as any other Sime. But then a new sensation spread from his chest into his arms in sharp cramps. One wave of pain followed another, each more severe than the last. *Surely turnover isn't always like this!*

But Abel was on his feet. "Get Jord or Uel!" he directed, and Margid ran out as her husband knelt beside Zeth and Owen. "Jord has such cramps," he said. "Rimon's had them since his injury—but what could be causing them in you, Zeth? No, son, it's not normal turnover."

"Maybe if you balance your fields—" Owen suggested. The two boys were facing one another when Jord arrived. Zlinning them, he said, "That's right, Owen—let him rest on your field, but don't let him draw. Zeth, healing mode. Then—oh, shen!'' He looked around. ''I have to have a Gen to demonstrate.''

''Can I do it?'' Maddok Bron asked instantly.

''Maddok!'' gasped his sister, flaring fear.

''You wanted to learn, Sessly. So do I. If you can't control yourself, you'd better leave. Jord, can I do it?''

''Come on, then,'' said Jord. ''I can't hurt you, doing this.''

Bron stood, his wound giving a twinge of pain, but in a moment he found a comfortable stance and faced Jord, fighting apprehension as the channel held out his hands. ''I'll have to touch you in transfer position,'' said Jord. ''No matter how frightened you are, there will be no selyn flow. Owen has to be perfectly steady for Zeth, but I'm not in pain or need. I'm just demonstrating.''

The Gen put his hands on Jord's arms, tensing as the handling tentacles lashed them together. When the hot, moist laterals touched him, Bron's field took on the same state Abel's did in prayer.

''Zeth,'' said Jord, ''move selyn from your primary system to your secondary, and back again. Keep it up until the pain stops. Like this.'' There was a start from Sessly Bron when Jord's lips touched her brother's, but Maddok Bron held as steady as Owen. Zeth saw immediately how it was done, and took Owen into their transfer position. Instant relief poured through Zeth's ravaged nerves. It felt good—like a massage to his nervous system—but he was too curious to know what had caused the cramping to do more than relieve the spasms, and then return his primary system to normal.

''Thanks, Owen,'' he said, and turned to Jord, finding him and Bron side by side, watching him clinically. ''Jord, Abel said you've had cramps, and Dad. What caused it?''

Jord moved in to zlin Zeth carefully. ''When I'm so sick I can't work,'' he said, ''I get cramps. Now Rimon is so sick he can't work. We've assumed the cramps were part of the sickness, but you're perfectly healthy. . . .''

''He's never worked,'' said Owen, ''not counting the fields.''

''True, but Zeth—when you took first transfer, did it seem to come in two distinct parts?''

''Yes!'' said Zeth and Owen in chorus.

''I'll bet you started using your secondary system then,'' said Jord. ''It's been exercised, then immobilized.''

"Like muscle spasms," Bron observed. "When a man works hard every day, and then cannot work—"

"Exactly!" said Jord. Then, after a pause, "I think."

So Zeth began daily exercise so his system would not go into spasms again, beginning with lessons in drawing selyn and transferring. That experience, though, he would not be allowed to tackle until after his second transfer.

With Rimon still a patient rather than a colleague, the channels' schedule was hectic, but at least there were no other cases requiring constant attention. Slina was rebuilding her pens as fast as the weather would permit, but she could not get enough replacement Gens to allow kills in any but the most extreme emergency.

The Simes from town understood—but most could not face channel's transfer. First the ones without family drifted away . . . and then one morning, six crying children were discovered in one of the houses assigned to the families from town. In the night, the adults had gone.

Abel told the children, "Your parents had to go away, but they loved you so much that they left you here, where you can grow up without worrying whether you'll be Sime or Gen."

Zeth, deep in the gloom of approaching need, thought cynically, *The kids were too much bother to take along in hard times and bad weather. So they abandoned them.* He thought of Jimmy Norton, hardly daring to hope his father wanted him back. Zeth had just begun to realize how lucky he was to be the first child born to a Sime and a Gen.

But Fort Freedom loved all children. By nightfall, Margid Veritt had placed all six where they would truly be loved.

That night Zeth fell into a fitful slumber, and dreamed he was a child again, abandoned by his parents. He knew they were out at the Old Homestead—only he couldn't find it.

Then he saw them. His mother, her flaming hair a halo, her field a shining glory. His father, pale, in need, holding out his arms, tentacles extended, pleading. She moved toward him, graceful, unafraid—but as she touched him, flame leaped, devouring Rimon! Zeth screamed as his father's form blazed. Kadi dropped Rimon, and turned toward Zeth, beckoning—

Heart pounding, he sat up to hug his knees and convince himself it was only a dream. In the other bed, Owen murmured in his sleep, and Zeth zlinned fading anxiety in his friend's field. The uncanny way the Companions responded to Sime emotions, when they had no sense organs to tell them, disturbed him. Even Bron was starting to do it—gleefully, it seemed. Owen and Hank and Trina and the others cared for the channels, but something in Bron's field seemed threatening.

He lay back, hands clasped under his head, massaging his temples with ventral tentacles as he puzzled over exactly what he saw in Bron's field. Pity. Bron didn't hate Simes or want to hurt them . . . he pitied them. That emotion never entered the fields of the Companions—certainly never Owen's. The Gen was deeply asleep again. Zeth let himself be drawn into sleep once more—and drifted into another dream.

This time it was pleasant. Zeth and Owen were riding in the beautiful hills near Owen's home, carefree children, racing their horses and laughing together. Then, in the way dreams have, without transition, they were walking instead of riding, and Zeth was in changeover. The tentacles grew swiftly along his arms, emerging without effort, plunging him into deep need. Owen's nager was sweet with welcome; his hands held Zeth, steadied him—he could feel warmth along his nerves as Owen held him with both hands . . . *both hands!*

The realization screeched up Zeth's spine in a jolt of terror. Dream merged with reality as he woke up screaming, the real Owen before him as the dream Owen had been—

"No! No!" he cried, fighting Owen off as his friend woke up enough to stop trying to restrain Zeth physically and use his field to soothe and calm.

As the terror abated, Zeth felt his Companion's arm—one arm—holding him steady. "It's only a dream, Zeth," Owen said. "It's not real. You're safe. Want to tell me about it?"

Another shudder rippled through Zeth as he remembered his abject terror at the feel of Owen's hands on his arms.

"To tell a dream makes it go away, remember?"

"You were giving me transfer—but you had both arms. I could feel both your hands on me. I don't know why I was so scared, Owen."

Lightly, Owen said, "Well, I always have both arms in *my* dreams, too." But Zeth didn't laugh, so he added, "You're not letting yourself be affected by superstition?"

Slina, after managing to accept transfer from Jord, had headed off to collect on long-owed favors, in the form of Gens. She returned full of stories. The tax collector had spread new rumors all along her route. It was true that the Simes of Fort Freedom could turn Simes into Gens. Hadn't the Freeband Raiders killed off most of their pen Gens? But hadn't the tax assessor found the place full of Gens? Not pen Gens, but conscious people, helping to repair the destruction wrought by the Raiders. Who could such Gens be, but some of the Simes of Fort Freedom turned Gen so they not only would not need to kill, but could provide selyn for the other Simes?

"Do you really think I'm a wer-Gen, Zeth? That I can change my shape, grow another arm at will?" But no matter how Owen tried, he could not coax a smile out of Zeth.

As his second transfer approached, Zeth spent much time at Rimon's bedside, trying to get his father interested in teaching him channeling. But Rimon had no interest in anything, responding even to Zeth or Abel with empty politeness. His burns were not healing; his body had no strength. The channels let him get deep into hard need before they let him take transfer from Hank. Instinct drove him; he drew swiftly enough to give Hank a nerve-burn—but then he closed off before transfer was complete, rejecting Hank and all the other Companions.

And Rimon was no better, the channels talking fearfully of his not feeling pain.

Abel came every day, trying to get Rimon to show some interest. Then he'd pray—and Zeth would zlin once more that dark cloud in his nager. Uel blamed himself when his transfer with Abel did not go well.

Hank said, "I think Abel's approaching crisis again—not next month, but maybe the month after." Zeth caught the implied warning: *I'll be there for you next time, but be prepared to do without me when Abel needs me.*

Zeth began to feel panic anytime Owen was distant enough that he had to zlin for him, and he shivered when he thought that eventually, he, too, would have to do without his Companion occasionally. As Abel went about his business, Zeth marveled at the old man's strength of will. Now Zeth could zlin how frail Abel was, his system precariously balanced—yet his will power gave him twice the energy of anyone else in Fort Freedom. Jord had once said his father lived as much on faith as on selyn; Zeth could now believe it.

Abel's faith, though, was currently facing a test: Maddok Bron's latest revelation.

"We've been partly right all along," he told Abel excitedly one evening. "There *is* a demon threatening each new

Sime, but the Sime is not a demon. Over many generations the words of the Holy Book have been distorted. We say that the sins of the parents are visited upon the child. Misinterpretation. If a Gen parent were simply to give transfer to his Sime child at changeover, the demon would be driven away."

"For a month," said Owen. "It's a natural cycle, not demonic possession."

"Owen," said Bron, "were you not raised in the Church of the Purity?"

"Abel's church here, yes. Not what you teach. I believe in God—probably more than a lot of out-Territory Gens."

"God doesn't punish us for ignorance. You were in a state of grace when you brought Zeth through changeover."

"I wasn't afraid."

"Exactly," said Bron. "God was with you, Owen—but you're not going to claim that if you had not been there, Zeth could have kept *himself* from killing?"

"Perhaps he could have," Abel put in. "Maddok, I witnessed Uel Whelan's changeover. We didn't know about channels, then. Uel thought his only choice was to kill or to die—and he was prepared to die, until Hank persuaded him that he could give him transfer. And did."

"Yes," Bron agreed. "Your Companions. If every Gen were a Companion, the channels could devote themselves to healing."

"There are too many," said Owen, "who *can't* learn to give transfer."

Bron answered, "That is why God called me to Fort Freedom, made me stay to be healed, to see what you have done here—and what I must do for you."

"Pride, Maddok," Abel said softly.

"I am but a vessel for God's will," Bron replied. "All the time I've been here, all I've heard is 'since Rimon came,' but you have said yourself that it was *Kadi* Farris who kept him from killing. A Gen started you on the road away from the kill. Gens keep your channels from killing even now."

"The situation is equitable," Abel replied. "The Companions care for the channels, and the channels for the rest of us."

"True, but you are overlooking the one fact that will explain your failure to disjunct."

Abel was pale, his nager tight against the guilt he refused

to let cloud his judgment. "Tell us this truth you think you have discovered."

"Abel, you are a good man, strong in faith. I can no longer believe that you *are* a demon because you're Sime. But every month you enter a state during which a demon may possess you—and will, if there is no one to prevent it. Once a Sime has been possessed, the weakness is there forever."

"It can be overcome," said Abel. "Rimon disjuncted. Dozens of others have done it—Simes who no longer feel the desire to kill—to kill, as opposed to the need for selyn, Maddok. I don't know if it's possible to explain to a Gen—"

"If he ever once gives transfer," said Owen, "he'll understand. Perhaps the compulsion is not so strong in a Gen, but the desire is."

"You add to my evidence, Owen," said Bron. "If it were not natural for Gens to provide transfer for Simes, those who do so would not feel it to be the privilege your Companions speak of. I pray that God grant me that privilege."

"Your prayers will be easily granted," said Abel. "I zlin the mark of the Companion in your field, Maddok. Zeth?"

"Yes," said Zeth, "but don't encourage him yet. Maddok, most of your selyn production is going to heal your wound. You're not back to full capacity, because your field is still increasing— Oh!" Zeth suddenly realized that he was observing something he had only heard about before.

But Maddok Bron had been studying. "My field is increasing through proximity to Simes who have need of my selyn. That is also God's will. Abel, Gens are not granted this capacity so they can selfishly refuse to use it. You *cannot* drive out the demon alone—but a Gen in a state of grace—"

"Maddok, if you preach any such thing to your congregation, you will be as much a killer as any Freeband Raider," Abel said firmly. "Do you want to be responsible for a parent's being killed by his own child, trying to prove he is in a state of grace?"

"It is the test," Bron answered with equal conviction. "No one should be required to attempt it. Doubt is a good reason *not* to. But I have no doubts. I shall prove the truth of my discovery when I free you of possession."

"When I next approach the crisis, I will not have you near me!" said Abel. He faced Bron squarely across the table. "I commend your good intentions, but your theory is devastating to the salvation of all our Simes. In need, a Sime does have the sensation that he is not in control of his own actions. I doubt you can imagine how tempting it would be to surrender all responsibility to the Gens.''

"That is where it should be," Bron protested. "Why won't you let me help you?''

"Because no man can be responsible for another's salvation! Of all people, the man who has accepted the religious leadership of a community must know that. Maddok, I have sworn an oath, I shall not die a killer. That vow is between God and me—and *I* am responsible for keeping it. When I have achieved it, you will bear witness—but until that time, you will not interfere!''

Not since the day of Owen's mutilation had Zeth seen Abel so angry. He could zlin smoldering fury battling with comprehension of Maddok's total sincerity.

Abel got up and stalked out. Zeth started to follow, worried. Owen put his hand on his arm. "Let him go, Zeth. He'll go to the chapel to pray—and he'll find an answer that satisfies him.''

Indeed, the next morning Abel was his usual controlled self—and the dark cloud was gone from his nager. But Zeth was too deep into need by now to give much thought to anyone else. Zlinning was no longer a novelty; it had become a necessity, as if he dared not use any other senses, lest he lose contact with the selyn fields that promised him life.

Zeth expected to have his second transfer in the chapel, with the people of Fort Freedom to witness. He was not comfortable with the thought, but the ritual was traditional for each new Sime. On his transfer day, though, Uel told him, "Abel thinks it would be better to postpone the witnessing, Zeth. People are too busy.'' But Zeth zlinned clearly that that was not the whole truth. Abel, who was not a channel, feared something might go wrong . . . and the channels concurred?

He could not hold his mind on the question. Some time later, Owen dragged him momentarily duoconscious as Jord was saying, "Take him along and give him transfer, Owen. Be patient—treat it like First Transfer and you'll both be fine.''

By this time, Zeth craved privacy and Owen. They went to the Veritt house, into the insulated room where Abel had coached Marji Carson through changeover. Zeth sat down on the couch, and rested in the warm promise of his Companion's field.

There was no hurry. Need was again a peculiar pleasure now that Owen's attention was fixed on Zeth alone, his "need to give" soothing away all Zeth's nervous jangles.

As he zlinned Owen, he found it happening again: the field pattern of Owen's left arm was there, just as if it had never been cut off. Spurred by a weak echo of his nightmare terror, Zeth forced himself duoconscious—and found his eyes and his Sime senses in disagreement. "Your arm," he whispered.

Owen shrugged. "I still feel it sometimes. Now. It never went away, like your dad said it would. I forgot—you zlinned it last time, didn't you? You kept reaching—well, don't worry." He took off his shirt. "There. You can find your grip whenever you're ready."

It had become habit now to find the rich nerves at the back of Owen's neck. It was as good as Zeth remembered—maybe better. When it was over, he lay back, breathing deeply, letting his body reaccustom itself to full life—

And the world came crashing down.

Mama! Dad! It was real for the first time—raw, and new. Strangled sobs rose in his throat—he could not force a scream past his tears. In one moment of irresponsible curiosity, he had led his friends into the midst of a battle, creating the legend of the wer-Gen, which led to his mother's death. His father would never recover.

In nameless, shuddering fury, he grabbed blindly, his fingers closing on the marble candle holder on the table beside the couch, the lit candle falling to the floor. He felt Owen's alarmed dive to catch it only as a vague movement at the edge of awareness. Something inside him adjusted in a new way. He threw the star-shaped chunk of marble at the nearest wall, fully expecting it to clatter to the floor. Instead, it crashed through the wall and landed with a crack and a clatter in the adjacent bathroom.

At the shock of the noise in the empty house, he found himself staring at the hole in the wall by the light of the candle Owen held. His rage had evaporated.

"Margid's going to be upset," said Owen in a thin attempt at lightness. "You know the rule—no augmenting within the gates."

"Is that what—yes, I did!"

Owen groaned. "Nobody's had time to teach you that!"

"It's not important," said Zeth dully.

"Zeth—what's *wrong?*"

"Mama!" he spat, annoyed at the Gen's denseness. "Mama's dead!" It turned into a sob that caught in his throat. "Owen, she's gone, and Dad is dying, and Abel—!" The rest dissolved into hysterical gasps. His once-secure home was in ruins. The Old Fort, with its volatile mixture of Simes and Gens, was in grave danger of not surviving the winter. But most of all, never again would his mother hold or comfort him, and he understood the emptiness in Rimon's field where Kadi had been. A major part of Rimon Farris had died with Kadi—and what was left would not survive for long.

Owen held Zeth, just as Del Erick had held Owen in the chapel the day of the memorial service. Owen said through his own tears, "I loved Kadi too, Zeth. We're all going to miss her—your father most of all. But we'll pull Rimon through. Jord survived after Willa died—"

"No!" Zeth shook his head vehemently. "You can't zlin him. Owen. It's as if he's dead already. And Abel—Abel's going to disjunct if it kills him—and it will!"

"Come on, Zeth—don't imagine things. Cry for Kadi. Grieve for what's real, not what might be."

On top of all the other agonized knowledge came the realization that Owen, the closest person to him in his life now, would never be able to understand all the things that were real to his Sime senses. Perhaps that was the worst knowledge of all.

Eventually, Zeth calmed down enough to be thankful that he had not been demonstrating transfer in the chapel when his grief overwhelmed him. And when the Veritts came in, he was able to apologize for breaking the marble candle holder, the wall, and the lip of the bathtub. But he couldn't shake off depression and foreboding. Only when he was busy learning to channel could he temporarily forget—but then he would zlin new deterioration in his father or feel in Abel the certainty that bespoke the final make-or-break fulfillment of his vow, and it would all come back. The sudden shock of his mother's death, as painful as it was, was easier to live with than the long, agonizing deterioration his father was undergoing. He could not yet grieve for him, but every time he saw him he felt more certain that was the only appropriate response.

He threw himself into learning the duties of a channel, Owen learning with him. Drawing selyn from Gens was easy—what he found hard was giving transfer. He mastered controlling selyn flow, but Jord and Uel insisted that selyn was not enough to satisfy a Sime in need—he had to give emotional satisfaction. He tried to reproduce the intense pleasure of his transfers with Owen, until Uel said, "All right, Zeth—you're as good as I was in my first months of channeling. We'll schedule the young people for you." Unspoken, Zeth realized, was *those who have never killed*.

Eventually, Zeth would have to witness a kill. But there was an unspoken agreement throughout Fort Freedom that harsh winter that every Sime would refrain from the kill as long as possible. The proximity of Slina's pen Gens had made them, if not people, at least too much like pets to make slaughtering them easy. The snow and freezing rain made rebuilding the pens slow; even Slina's new Gens were kept in the Old Fort, where everyone encountered them daily.

Only a handful of the town Simes were still with them. The spoken agreement was that any one of them could have a kill if he felt he could not stand channel's transfer again. But, for the time being, the unspoken agreement prevailed.

Despite the bad weather, there was considerable travel across the border. The out-Territory Gens accepted the precautions prescribed by the channels and their Sime relatives, and people began talking of this year's turning as a world's turning, toward a whole new way of life.

Glian Lodge came to trade for horses with Del Erick. The two men spent hours haggling—and in a short while became fast friends. Owen was delighted, and began dropping hints that if Eph Norton planned to come to visit his son, he might consider bringing his daughter Sue along.

Maddok Bron hoped to get home in time for Mountain Chapel's own year's turning ceremony, but he overtired himself, and his kidney infection flared up again. His sister stayed with him, soon becoming as much at home among Simes as he was. Sessly Bron was a Gen version of Margid Veritt— quiet, supportive, and often unnoticed until she wasn't around when you expected her.

Zeth's sensitivity passed Uel's, having left both Jord and Marji behind in his first month, but he was still the youngest, least experienced channel. *How can I become the best channel I can be without Dad to teach me?*

One cold, clear morning, Zeth's forebodings were realized. He and Owen were trying to help Marji and Jord convince Rimon to eat. Jord, on the edge of need, was supervising the two younger channels, while Zeth struggled against his personal depression.

Hank and Uel arrived—and at once Uel said, "Jord, I don't want you worn out before your transfer this afternoon. Zeth, take Jord home and see that he lies down."

Knowing perfectly well that he was being sent away because his mood was irritating Rimon as much as Jord's need was, Zeth took Jord's arm and guided him out, Owen following. They passed through the back rooms of the chapel, past the open kitchen door. Sessly, helping to prepare gruel for Slina's Gens, looked up as they passed. "Jord?" She came to the door in concern, wiping her hands on her apron.

He raised a hand, warning her back, and said, "I'm all right. Just tired and in need. I'll have transfer this afternoon, and then if you still want to donate—"

"You know I do," she said firmly. "Take care of him, Zeth," she said with a smile, and turned back to her work.

They headed for the front door, passing Abel Veritt kneeling at his morning's prayers.

It was a beautiful day, the sky brilliant blue, no clouds for a change. The most recent snow was melting in the sun, turning the pathways to ridged mud. Slina was taking advantage of the clear day to get her Gens into the fresh air—a whole group of them were being exercised on the green, their nager more lively than usual because their morning drug dose would be dispensed in the gruel.

As Zeth, Owen, and Jord came down the front steps, Sessly Bron and Mrs. Young came out the side door of the chapel, bringing a huge pot of gruel surrounded by wooden bowls, on a wheeled cart. The Sime woman helped Sessly lift and push the cart over the threshold—but just as they got it out, a rut caught one of the wheels and a stack of bowls fell off into the mud.

"What a mess!" said Mrs. Young. "You go ahead, Sessly. I'll run back and wash these off." She gathered the bowls up and headed back into the chapel.

Zeth paid no attention, for in the morning light he was noticing the unpainted wood that marked the repairs to the wall and nearby houses. The beautiful day only served to throw the problems of Fort Freedom into high relief.

But as they walked on, a surge of the ambient, off beyond the milling pen Gens, caught Zeth's attention. As the flare of intil heightened, he recognized the field of Bekka Trent, the

CHANNEL'S DESTINY   149

out-Territory Sime who was nearing her disjunction crisis.
What had Uel said? She was due for transfer tomorrow, and
he had put her to work—?

No, Margid Veritt had put Bekka to doing laundry, off on
the other side of the Fort, away from the Gens—but here she
came, her small form moving determinedly straight toward
that mob of pen Gens.

The important thing was to get temptation out of her way.
"Risko!" Zeth shouted to Slina's man. "Get those Gens
back! High-intil Sime approaching!"

As Risko and the others herded the Gens out of Bekka's
way, they cleared a direct path between the oncoming Sime
and Sessly Bron. Jord gasped, "Sessly!" and started toward
her under augmentation. Zeth caught up easily, leaving Owen
behind.

Sessly's field registered only surprise and curiosity, not
shock or fear. She and her cart were between Bekka and the
chapel. Bekka pulled up short, dark eyes staring from Sessly
to the chapel. Then her eyes drifted out of focus as she
zlinned the Gen before her.

Zeth came to a stop, catching Jord back. Jord whispered,
"Oh, God, no!" but held steady. They had to keep Sessly
from becoming frightened. The two channels cautiously walked
the last few paces. Just as Owen came up behind them, Wik
came pounding to a breathless halt behind Bekka.

Forcing his voice to be utterly calm, Zeth said, "Sessly, go
in and get Uel Whelan."

She started to obey, but the moment she let go of the cart
handle, Bekka began stalking her. "Stop, Sessly," Zeth said.
"Stand still. I'll take care of it."

How?! was the only thing in his mind, but he forced
himself to think. Uel and Marji were in Rimon's heavily
insulated room; they'd have no idea what was going on. Jord
was in need and flaring fear; he was in no shape to handle a
disjunction crisis. And if Bekka was fixed on Sessly, that was
exactly what Zeth had before him.

He had to make Bekka choose him over Sessly. Healing
mode, then project like a Gen—high field, the need to give.
Bekka wavered, and became duoconscious so she could look
at him, her small heart-shaped face tense with indecision.
"Come on—I'll give you transfer, Bekka. It's what you
really want. You were looking for Abel, weren't you? To
pray with you? It's what you've been praying for. Never to

kill again. No more pain—no more guilt. Come to me, Bekka.''

In a strange clarity of consciousness, Zeth was aware not only of Bekka before him, and Sessly, Jord, Owen, and Wik nearby, but also of other people watching, fascinated. Abel and Uel came out of the chapel, with Mrs. Young and her son Hapen. Uel zlinned the situation, but the more experienced channel dared not interrupt the rapport Zeth was creating. On the other side of the green Slina stood, joined by other Simes who had never seen disjunction before.

Zeth started around the wheeled cart, but not toward Sessly, but around the other end. If he could keep Bekka's attention, Jord could snatch Sessly out of the way—

As if she read his intention, Bekka turned toward Sessly once more. How could Zeth make his field more appealing? He was radiating the desire to serve her—but what the junct Sime craved was not generosity, but fear. Fear was easy enough—all he had to do was stop fighting it. At once Bekka turned, stalking a pace or two toward him. Again she stopped, deliberately resisting. *She doesn't want to respond to fear.* He smiled at her. ''It's all right. You've won, Bekka. You don't want to kill a Gen—you just need selyn. Come here—I'll give it to you.''

Bekka's resistance crumbled. She flung herself on Zeth, pressing her lips desperately to his even before their laterals were properly entwined. He let her draw, feeling her fight for something he wasn't giving, unsatisfied even though selyn flowed into her nerves without resistance—it was resistance she craved. That he could provide, and in a few moments more, Bekka Trent was sobbing in relief. He held her, saying, ''You did it, Bekka. It's all over now—you'll never go through that again.''

People started to move. Wik came up to Zeth and Bekka, saying, ''She ran away from me, Zeth. I'm sorry.''

''It turned out all right,'' said Zeth as Owen joined them. He looked toward Sessly, just as Jord, unshielded by any Companion, started toward her.

In the relief after the crisis, Sessly let go the steely hold she had had on her emotions, and her fear flared. Jord, in need, fought down his response—it took all that was left of his fragile strength, and he collapsed at her feet.

''Jord!'' she gasped, dropping to her knees beside him. ''What happened?'' as Uel and Abel dashed to the fallen channel. Zeth thrust Bekka into Wik's arms and hurried to Jord.

It was the first time Zeth had seen one of Jord's voiding attacks—particularly dangerous when he was in hard need. Uel meshed fields with Jord, and almost savagely forced him to consciousness so they dared move him. Zeth pulled Sessly Bron away, saying, "You can't help him now, Sessly. Your sympathy could cause him to fix on you."

Mrs. Young came up to them, saying, "Come on, Sessly. Help us with the Gens. Let the channels do their work."

In the back of the chapel, they laid Jord down and Uel bent over him. "Get Hank," he said. There was a moment of uncertainty; then Uel said, "Zeth, you'll have to help me," and Abel turned and went for Uel's Companion.

Hank came quickly, alone. Then Zeth was zlinning the way Uel took a grip on Jord's fields and forcefully restrained the leakage of selyn. Jord's secondary system, much higher than his primary system today, had begun the voiding, but by the time they got him into the insulated room, selyn had begun to leak from his primary. No one knew if it was possible, without an actual injury, for a Sime to void to death—but Zeth recalled that the only reason they had never found out in Jord's case was Rimon Farris.

At the surge of apprehension from Zeth, Uel nodded gravely. "Pray you have Rimon's sheer strength, Zeth. Do what I was doing, and see if you can stop the voiding."

Jord's fields were fragmenting, both from the voiding and from the rough treatment Uel had had to use. Zeth swallowed the lump in his throat as Owen placed his hand on Zeth's shoulder, providing secure confidence. He tried to influence Jord's fields, but Jord's resistance took the form of fragmenting further, his fields a tenuous cloud.

Zeth stopped his attempt at pressure. Spreading his laterals above the prone form, he extended his show-field to surround Jord's. After a moment, Jord's field relaxed and began drifting toward normal. Through all of this, Jord was semiconscious, not exactly in pain, but settling deeper and deeper into the agony of hard need. As Zeth managed the fields for him, Jord came down to duoconsciousness. "Sessly?"

"She's fine," said Zeth. "Rest, Jord. Nobody got hurt. And Bekka's through disjunction."

"Thank God," Jord managed, and relief pervaded his nager, speeding his progress in the direction of normalcy.

When Uel judged that Jord was ready, he had Zeth reinforce his containment of Jord's fields while Uel gave him transfer—or rather drove transfer into him, for Jord made no effort to draw. Zeth studied carefully how Uel attempted to give Jord the satisfaction he craved as much as the selyn he needed—but Jord rejected the emotion. His strength, though—what little there ever was of it—had returned. He refused to sleep, resting only a few minutes before getting on his feet again. "I've put enough of a cloud over Bekka's triumph. Come on—there's celebrating to do!"

Although Jord's cheer might stem from pure bravado, there was no pretense in the joy the channels found when they came out. In the chapel proper they found Abel with Bekka, Maddok and Sessly Bron, and Jimmy Norton, who had witnessed the crisis. Bekka's joy was almost matched by Abel's when he saw his son. A ripple of relieved pleasure went through Sessly's nager when Jord walked in, but Maddok Bron's field was a mixture of concern, hope, and resistance to whatever Abel had been telling him.

Jimmy Norton was looking at Bekka worshipfully—and when Zeth entered, the feeling focused on Zeth as well. "I'm going to do what Bekka did," he said. "I'm going to leave the kill behind. Zeth—will you help me?"

"Of course I will. Everyone here will help you."

"We will pray for you, and with you," Abel added.

"On that we all agree," said Maddok Bron. "Jimmy, we'll take you out of the grip of the Devil—"

"Maddok, he will take himself," interrupted Abel. "Your prayers and your encouragement are welcome—but every Sime must make his own commitment to refuse the kill."

Thus it was no surprise to Zeth, when the bell had been rung and everyone was gathered in the chapel, that Abel had a new statement to make. "Like many of you here with us today, Bekka Trent grew up in Gen Territory. She believed that to be Sime was to be cursed—but she had the courage to refuse that curse. To refuse the kill.

"God has blessed Bekka Trent, as He has blessed this community. Never before in history has a community of Gens made friends with a community of Simes. The only way we can continue that friendship is to guarantee their safety among us—to end the kill, forever. When we have done that we can tell the truth—the entire truth—to Simes and Gens alike, to dispel the superstitious fear that brought the Freeband Raiders down on us.''

Abel's voice and his field rang with conviction. "There will be no more equivocation. No more careful wording to hide what is or what must be. Truth will prevail!

"Nine years ago, I made a vow. As God is my witness, I shall not die a killer. I gave no thought to the wording of that vow. In nine years, I have killed eleven times—and yet I have said I am not forsworn. I still live. I live for the day when no Sime's need will be a need to kill. To bring that day about, there must be a new vow. I do not ask it of any of you today—but I pray that one day each and every one of you will vow it, before God, as I do now. It does not matter whether you have killed never, or once, or a hundred times. What matters is a future in which everyone, Sime and Gen, is in control of his own destiny. To that end, I make a new vow:

"As God is my witness, I shall never kill again!''

Chapter 10

Carried away with Abel Veritt's joyous dedication, Zeth was amazed to feel utter horror from Owen. Incredulously, he realized that Owen didn't think Abel could keep his vow. If only he could zlin! Bekka Trent's feeling that morning was *nothing* toward Abel's. He whispered to his Companion, "He's really going to do it, Owen. You can't feel—"

"Yes I can!" Owen returned in an agonized hiss. "He'll die, Zeth!"

But the despair that had gripped Zeth since his second transfer was gone now—the sorrow he sensed in all the Companions merely made him pity their inability to share what all the Simes in the chapel knew that day—all except Jord, whose field also showed worry and sadness, probably because he didn't trust himself to join in his father's vow.

But Zeth could join in. He might not feel the personal presence of God the way Abel Veritt apparently did, but his vow was no less heartfelt: *I will never kill. Never!*

As they left the chapel, Zeth caught traces of community feeling even from the town Simes. As he and Owen stepped outside, Slina came over to them, her little girl at her side.

"I seen what you done this morning, Zeth," she said. "For a minute I thought it was your father out there, pushin' my men around. Born leader."

Before Zeth could assimilate that, Slina was off on another topic. "Zeth, your dad don't kill—you don't kill—the old man there, he'd do anything not to kill—an' you're all good people. You folks are the only reason there's still a town here. You bailed me out more times than I can think—"

"And you've always helped us, too, Slina," said Zeth.

"Yeah, well, you don't return favors, you don't get none. Shidoni. I'm too old to change now. But change is comin'.

154

An' my kid—'' She pulled the little girl forward. "My Mona, she—oh, shen it, Zeth, I want her to be better off than me!"

The child studied Zeth solemnly with piercing black eyes, disturbingly familiar. Slina squatted down to talk to the girl, pushing a lock of black hair back off her forehead. "This here's Zeth Farris—you remember him? Well, he's a channel now. Mona, you know what changeover is?"

"Yeah," said the girl. "You grow up—turn Sime."

"That's right. Well, when that happens, you come to Zeth, so you don't kill."

"You're not goin' away, Ma!"

"No, honey—just my usual trips. Now quit that!" as tears ran down the girl's cheeks. "You promise me!"

Mona looked up at Zeth, and then back at her mother. "I promise, Ma," she said, throwing her arms about Slina's neck. "I'm gonna be just like Zeth!" Slina stood, picking her up, and with an embarrassed shrug headed back to the temporary quarters of her pen, saying, "Well, maybe so, but no matter what, Zeth will take care of you."

The afternoon was spent trying to straighten out the transfer schedule, which had started late because of the problems with Rimon. Bekka's disjunction, Jord's problems, and the ceremony in the chapel had thrown them even later, but at least Jord was at work again now, hours early—and Zeth, his gloom dispelled, also rejoined the schedule. He found it slightly annoying, though, that three Simes scheduled for him told him with varying degrees of diplomacy that as long as Jord was unexpectedly available they'd "really rather . . ."

It was not a new story. Everybody used to clamor for Rimon, but now that he was not functioning, the choice of all the older Simes was Jord. Zeth could see the pattern: the younger Simes, those who had never killed, had little preference among Uel, Marji, or Zeth. But those who killed occasionally, and even those who had disjuncted, preferred something Jord could give them that the others could not.

Still, Zeth was busy. When he was done he stopped to see his father again. Rimon had fallen into a coma-like sleep, completely unnatural for a Sime. Abel said, "He used to get like this before he disjuncted," the gloom in his nager contrasting with the guarded hope of the channels.

Zeth and Owen had begun work before dawn that morning, and it was hours after dark when they got back to the Veritt house. Owen barely managed to eat supper without falling asleep. Zeth put him to bed, and slept for a few hours, waking after midnight, wanting a cup of tea.

Zeth went down the hall, and was about to enter the main room when he suddenly realized there were two people in it: Sessly Bron and Jord Veritt. She was seated in Abel's big armchair; he was sitting on the rug at her feet, his head resting against her knees. Her hand was on his shoulder, and he had placed his hand over it. They were sitting very, very still, completely absorbed in one another. And Sessly was low-field.

". . . and if he dies trying to disjunct," Jord was saying, "who will hold Fort Freedom together? I can't. I never could, and now as a channel, I'm too busy. I'm not even a very good channel," he added bitterly.

"Of course you are!" said Sessly. "I couldn't have donated to anyone else, Jord. Not after what you did today—to save my life."

"You should never have been in danger from me! I'm a channel—I'm supposed to give life, not take it."

"Jord, you refused to—"

"You don't understand, Sessly. I didn't kill today—but I'll come into crisis again, and then I'll—"

"No!" she said, leaning down, her arm across his chest, holding him tightly. "Never again, Jord. We'll keep the demon off."

"It feels like a demon," Jord said. "I used to believe in demons—but—oh, it would be so easy . . . !"

"Believe it!" she whispered fiercely. "Let me help you!"

"No," he said flatly, but Sessly obviously felt what Zeth could zlin: there was no conviction whatsoever in the word.

Grasping control of his show-field, hoping that Jord was too involved in his own thoughts to notice him, Zeth retreated silently to the room he shared with Owen. There he wrapped himself in a blanket and sat down, getting madder by the minute. If Jord were tempted to abdicate responsibility for his actions, how could other juncts resist Maddok Bron's claims? No one would ever disjunct again. His frustration grew until Owen turned restlessly, mumbling in his sleep. Then Zeth turned his mind to ways to disprove the theory. *But who will listen to me?*

One eager listener was Jimmy Norton. In fact, the next day Jimmy sought Zeth out, promising to break the habits he had learned among the Freeband Raiders. He had been wasting selyn augmenting, making a nuisance of himself. Ever since Fort Freedom had been built there had been a firm rule: no augmenting within the gates. Bowling over Gens or children in a fit of high spirits was not to be tolerated.

But after Bekka's disjunction, Jimmy was a different person. "Zeth, I want transfer from you from now on."

"Jimmy, we've got you scheduled for Jord, because—"

"I know why, and I don't *want* that! Please, Zeth, help make it safe for me to be around my father or my sister without three other people to grab me if I try to kill one of them!" He blinked back tears. "I'm never going to kill again. I swore that with Mr. Veritt. I want to be like you, Zeth. Oh, God, how I wish—" He broke off, setting his jaw firmly. "It's my responsibility. Bekka decided not to kill—I zlinned it all. If she can do it, I can do it."

"I'll do everything I can to help you, Jimmy," said Zeth, thinking, *If a Freeband Raider can disjunct by his own will, that should prove there is no demon.*

Even with Jimmy Norton on his schedule, Zeth's simulation of killbliss did not improve, creating great difficulties in juggling the schedule. He could handle the sheer numbers of transfers his father had, but he could not satisfy all his father's clients.

"You're afraid of the kill," said Owen after another session in which the complaint had been raised against Zeth. "Why are you so frightened? You won't be tempted to kill. Even if you were, you don't think I'd let you?"

"I don't require you to keep the demons away," Zeth snapped.

"Come on, Zeth—you know that's superstition. It's like Abel said: you take care of other Simes, and I take care of you. It all works out equally between Simes and Gens."

"No, Owen. It leaves Gens running things because they control the channels. I don't want you controlling me!"

"I'm not—"

"Oh, yeah? Don't tell me you don't know what you're doing right now, trying to calm me down when I don't *want* to calm down! I want to *think*. Why don't you just run along and see Sue Norton? I'm going to visit my father."

The Nortons were back again, along with Glian Lodge, all staying with Del Erick. Del, however, was in Rimon's sickroom, high-field—the visit of his Gen guests was timed for that—and therefore no irritation to Rimon. Zeth had noticed

how carefully Del timed his visits, and how faithfully he
came, despite Rimon's indifference.

"You should have zlinned Glian when Jana cut those
horses out for him!" he was telling Rimon proudly. "He said
he's never seen a girl ride like that. Of course she explained
to him just how she selected the best stock." He chuckled.
"He said he'd like to replace his wrangler with Jana." He
looked up. "Hi, Zeth. Where's Owen?"

"Over at your house. I don't have to have a watchdog
every minute!"

"Hey," said Del, "nobody said you did. I was just asking
about my son. What's wrong, Zeth?"

Rimon seemed not to have noticed either Del's conversation or Zeth's entrance. Anni Steers was sitting on the other
side of the bed, her attention focused on her knitting so as to
be as unobtrusive as possible. Zeth recalled that she was
pregnant again—and Uel teasing Hank about how he had
found time to accomplish that feat. It never seemed to bother
Uel to rely on Hank—in fact, now that he thought about it,
even the way people referred to them was different. Rimon
and Kadi. Zeth and Owen. Marji and Trina. Always the
channel first—except Hank and Uel.

The silence stretched until Zeth blurted, "I'm tired of
Owen pushing me around."

"Does he?" asked Del. "Just to exercise power?"

"No," Zeth admitted. "He thinks it's for my own good."

"Maybe he's a little tactless? Should I talk to him, Zeth? I
can't fully understand the relationship between a channel and
his Companion, but often an outsider can help when someone
too closely involved can't."

But Zeth couldn't explain. Owen *wasn't* tactless. He was
just supremely confident . . . and Zeth wasn't. He found
himself saying exactly that to Del.

"And why do you think that is?" Del asked.

"Because Owen has faced death," Zeth realized, "and I
haven't. I thought I had when I was trapped in the stable at
Mountain Chapel but I didn't really come close to dying,
because of Owen."

Del smiled. "And so you resent Owen's ability to take care
of you. I can remember Rimon and Kadi arguing over the
same problem." He looked hopefully toward Rimon, his field
ringing with expectancy, but Zeth's father did not respond.

"Dad's getting worse," said Zeth.

"It's chronic need. Get one good transfer into him—"

"Who's going to do it?" Zeth demanded. "Owen's his only match!"

After a pause, Del said, "If you can face that, Zeth—if you can give up Owen, just once, you'll conquer the feeling that he's controlling you."

Zeth considered, automatically blending his nager into the room to ease his father's aching fields while at the same time choking down the panic Del's suggestion brought. Then, in desperation, he said, "*I* could match him now!"

In a very sad, quiet tone, Del said, "Rimon—*needs*—killbliss. Kadi could let him have that."

"Well, Owen doesn't have it to give. But I could learn. I've got to learn!" He hoped he hid from Del the irrational panic that accompanied that resolve.

That evening, Zeth tackled Jord, convincing him to let Zeth watch him giving transfer to a junct. Dan Whelan, Uel's father, volunteered since he was Jord's last client of the day. "I guess," he said nervously, "this is the only way you can learn. And if it saves Rimon—"

"Come on, Dan," prompted Jord. Zeth went hyperconscious, watching as Jord's show-field rose to entice Dan into transfer contact. Zeth concentrated, letting the fields soak through his system. Dan's draw was a savage ripping away of selyn, shallow and slow compared to the channels, but Jord put up a mock resistance laced with pain and fear. Dan reveled in pain which became its own pleasure, mocking the pleasure Zeth knew with Owen.

No! Without conscious intent, Zeth was duoconscious, his showfield dominating the room, damping down every shred of that mounting bliss he could not face. Dan Whelan wrenched away from Jord in a thudding agony of shen.

"Out!" Jord shouted at Zeth, and moved to grasp the older man's tentacles. When Zeth didn't move, Jord growled, "Out before I shen you!"

"I'm sorry," he whispered as he groped for the door. Afterwards, Uel found him on the steps of the chapel.

"Zeth, you'll freeze to death out here. Come on inside. I have an idea."

Reluctantly, Zeth went with him, knowing that Owen had put him up to this. And sure enough, Hank and Owen were waiting with Jord in the chapel. Both Jord and Zeth apologized, and Uel said, "None of us is qualified to teach Zeth. But we've got to improvise until Rimon gets better."

He went on to suggest how Zeth could participate in a junct's transfer without overcontrolling Jord, by emptying his secondary system into Uel's so that he couldn't grab the fields. It took all day to set it up, Zeth and Uel giving transfers without accepting donations, in order to empty their systems. Even so, Zeth's "small" amount of selyn nearly staggered Uel.

Margid Veritt was the next volunteer, over Jord's objection. "You're too deep into need, Mother. Dan was early—"

"There's no point in delaying then, is there?" she asked, and Zeth found his own throat tightening at the shrill tremor in her usually low-pitched voice. He could not seem to grow used to the trembling anxiety of need in the people who had been strong adults to him all his life.

Selyn flowed, and Margid's field erupted with pleasure as Jord provided resistance. Desire peaked into pain, reveling in pain, sadistic pleasure, pain *as* pleasure—

The point where Zeth had shenned out was reached and passed, as he hung on, determined not to hurt Margid. He shared the pain/pleasure killbliss growing in her and kindling something horrifying in himself; the knowledge of what it meant to be Sime. He *wanted* pain—he *craved* the ultimate agony of seared Gen nerves dying under his tentacles!

Roaring to a peak of satisfaction, Margid exulted. Then a new agony closed round like a black cloud—*guilt*. Zeth flinched away from it, ripped down into hypoconsciousness, the fields disappearing and the candle-lit killroom emerging. His hands were clamped about the joined arms of Jord and Margid, his tentacles lashing them all together. His convulsive grip flashed real pain through them all.

The next thing he knew he was on the floor, Owen flinging himself across the room and Uel dashing to Margid's side, while Jord bent over his own bruised arms.

Jord said, "You weren't supposed to touch us."

"I didn't know I had." He put his hand around Owen's neck and let the Gen help him up, then moved to Jord's side. He found where Jord's fields were disturbed and, using what little selyn there was in his secondary system, projected a soothing effect. Wik, acting as Jord's Companion today, did the same on the other side as Zeth instructed him, and soon Jord was feeling better.

"Jord," said Uel, finishing with Margid, "this just proves what I was saying. None of us can teach Zeth anymore. He's got to teach himself, now."

Zeth went to Margid, apologizing. "But I think I did learn something," he offered. *If I ever have the courage to use it! And if it doesn't destroy me—as it has you.*

For as he watched the woman who had been a second mother to him leave the transfer room, he was trying desperately to recapture the feeling he had always had for her. He felt again that hideous compulsion to derive pleasure from Gen pain. Her satisfied expression woke revulsion in him. And he couldn't make himself zlin Owen at all.

Each time Zeth tried to produce killbliss his own fear drove him out of rapport. Although Jord actually respected Zeth for the inability, Zeth faced the fact that his efforts to learn were destroying what channeling ability he did have. Furthermore, he had hurt Margid. He could feel her shame whenever she looked at him.

One morning, Zeth was trying to get several people acutely in need of a junct-satisfying transfer off his schedule and onto Jord's. The schedule was kept on a chalkboard in the back hall of the chapel, and Zeth stood with chalk in his fingers and an eraser in his tentacles, raising a cloud of white dust and creating more problems than he was solving.

Bekka Trent came in, watched him for a few minutes, and said, "Zeth, why are you wasting a channel's time on that? There are three people waiting for you."

"I'm coming," he muttered, continuing to scribble.

After a moment, Bekka said sharply, "Zeth! Here, let me take care of the schedule. You go do your work."

"You don't know how to match people—"

"Well, *tell* me." She stretched on tiptoe to lift the board down from its hook. "Why did you change Risko?"

"He's used to choice kills from Slina's pen and he's voluntarily not killing now, to help us through the winter. He deserves better than I can give him, Bekka."

"Better!" She shuddered. "No—I understand. But if you move him to the afternoon—" To Zeth's amazement, Bekka soon created order from the chaos on the board.

By the time Zeth had finished the morning's work, Bekka had arranged a schedule that used the four channels more efficiently than Zeth had seen since he had begun working. Marji, who still tired easily, said to Zeth, "Thank you for putting Bekka in charge. I thought I was going to drop!'' The schedule didn't last long, however. Just as Zeth and Owen were headed to their next appointment, Trina Morgan came running up. "Zeth—your father's calling for you!"

Zeth had to force himself not to augment as he dashed to the chapel, Owen right behind him. Rimon was thrashing on his bed, calling out, "Zeth! No, Zeth—NO!" His field was chaotic agony, and all Marji's efforts to restrain him served at most to keep him from flinging himself off the bed.

Zeth tried to mesh fields, knowing that Rimon was not hearing anything.

"Zeth, I didn't mean it! I didn't know it was you!" The words made no sense, but Zeth continued calming Rimon with his field, hoping recognition would bring his father out of the nightmare. Eventually his hysteria subsided, but Rimon sank from sharp anguish into bleak despair . . . and from there into the coma-like sleep that had claimed him lately.

Marji's round brown eyes were worried. "When he started calling for you, I thought maybe it was a good sign, but—"

"He's worried about you, Zeth," said Owen. "I think it *is* a good sign." But Owen couldn't know that Rimon had not shown the slightest recognition of Zeth's presence.

When they emerged from the sickroom, Bekka had rearranged the schedule, and they were able to go right on to another appointment without a conference. By the end of the day, the channels were wondering what they had ever done without Bekka, and she had found a full-time occupation.

The winter became a constant sequence of storms, and Fort Freedom battled snow and temperatures far below freezing. Maddok and Sessly Bron finally managed to go home between storms. Like his sister, Bron insisted on donating selyn before he left. It was clearly a part of his new belief that Gens had the obligation to give transfer, though it didn't go over well with his congregation.

Zeth heard the news about three weeks before year's turning. By now Zeth and Owen were automatically included in the council sessions around the kitchen table. This one was called when Glian Lodge, Eph Norton, and Lon Carson appeared one day, blown in on a storm swooping out of the west. The other channels were busy; Zeth, to his deep chagrin, was the one who could most easily be spared from the schedule.

Abel managed to be there, pale and drawn. Zeth wondered if with his more powerful field, had he only been able to use what he'd learned with Margid, he might have given Abel a normal transfer. Seeing his gaze, Abel whispered, "I'm all right, Zeth. Soon you will do for me what you did for Bekka."

The out-Territory Gens had brought coins to cover the tax money Fort Freedom had had to pay—but otherwise what they brought was bad news. "The ranches are in trouble," said Glian Lodge. "I lost three top hands in the battle, and others lost more. Two of the ranchers killed got no kids old enough to take over. Their wives are thinking of selling out . . . and this is no time to bring new people into our area. I don't even want to hire men on when we don't know how they'll accept these, uh, trips across the border."

"You mean they might set spies on us," Eph said angrily. "Tell them about the horses, Glian."

Lodge grimaced. "Remember those prime horses I bought from your pa, Owen? Damn government agent confiscated 'em!"

"What?" asked Zeth. "But why?"

"The ownership marks showed they're from Sime Territory— but so what? Lots of people raid across the border for horses. I bought a couple a few years back that probably came from the same herd. But now the Border Patrol's roused, and they came along and took the horses as 'evidence' for an 'investigation.' I dunno what's gonna happen in the spring."

"I'm afraid I know how the government was alerted," said Lon Carson. "Maddok Bron caused a rift in the church when he started preaching that everybody had to give transfer to prove they're in a state of grace. Those of us from Fort Freedom are willing to learn—but you can imagine how most people feel. The elders didn't have quite enough votes to kick Bron out—but only because removing the minister takes a two-thirds majority. Half the town has either packed up and left, or will as soon as the weather permits."

Abel sighed. "Why didn't I think to discuss practical aspects of his theory with Maddok? I was so angry at his foolishness . . . and wrath is a sin."

"Listen," said Carson, "he's coming back here the end of the month—says he's got to give a real transfer. So you can talk with him then, Abel—"

"No!" Abel's vehemence startled Zeth, but the old Sime calmed at once. "No, not until spring. He's not fully recovered from his wound, and should not attempt such a difficult journey in the middle of winter.

Zeth zlinned the apprehension under the old man's surface calm and felt a fierce protectiveness. *If Bron so much as lays a finger on Abel, I'll—*

Carson was saying, "I don't think there's any more stopping him than there is stopping you when you feel God's will, Abel. So we got real trouble. We thought we were going to be able to help Fort Freedom out. Now half our workers are planning to leave at spring thaw, and I wouldn't be surprised if it was someone from Mountain Chapel alerted the Border Patrol."

So the Freeband Raiders' strike had decimated all three communities. The fragments left, Zeth saw clearly, could not survive independently. "Simes could work your fields much more efficiently than Gens," he suggested.

"And how do we explain *that* to the Border Patrol?" Glian asked, his voice heavy with sarcasm.

"Now wait a minute," said Eph. "I sure would like to bring Jimmy home, once he's . . . all right again. But, Zeth, just for being here talking to you, we're all liable to be executed and our property confiscated. I just don't know—"

"What we've done here," said Zeth, "is change the law. A little bit, anyway. We still haven't managed to get Gens recognized as people, but eventually, we'll do that, too."

Abel put a hand over Zeth's. "It's good to plan for the future, Zeth—but right now we have to help one another survive this winter. I'm afraid," he added to the Gens, "you'll have to curtail your visits. The worst of the winter is yet to come. No one will travel much until spring—and then we'll have a single courier again. If you are too badly harassed, you are welcome here. Is there anything we can give you to help you through the winter?"

There was a flurry of letter writing. Eph insisted on donating before he left, "To help support my son," and Lon Carson donated as well. Glian shrugged, said, "Don't look as if it hurts none," and also gave selyn. Then he went with Zeth and Owen over to the house Del Erick was using for the duration. There they found Jana struggling with a recalcitrant flue in the kitchen stove.

"I hate cooking!" she declared when they had the stovepipe drawing properly and the smoke cleared away.

Glian Lodge laughed. "You keep on handling horses the

way you do, and you'll never have to cook. Maybe in the spring you can come visit me, Jana.''

''Sure—I'd like to go out-Territory before I change over. Zeth and Owen have. Boys always get to do the good things.''

Jana's cooking certainly wasn't good enough to tempt a Sime, and even Owen's hearty appetite rebelled after half a plate of her stew. Del arrived home from checking his stock while they were still at the table.

Zeth noticed how normal the family gathering seemed: two Simes, two Gens, and a child, all talking and laughing together comfortably. What he had been used to all his life—until the world had turned inside out. It wasn't right that families should be illegal—on *either* side of the border. At least it wasn't wholly forbidden here—

What if we moved the border?

At Zeth's surge of excitement, Del smiled at him, but Glian Lodge was at that moment holding forth on some of the technicalities of ranching. Zeth subsided into shivers—and had time to wonder why he should feel cold and locate the source: Jana. She had moved her chair close to the stove, and was huddled up in a big sweater. He zlinned her—then got up and went over to her, Owen following.

He bent down, taking her freezing hands in his, and said softly, ''I'm afraid you're not going out-Territory, after all, Jana.''

She looked up at him out of the blue eyes that were her only claim to beauty. ''But I don't feel bad,'' she said. ''I'm just cold.''

Although he had never zlinned a changeover victim before, Zeth said confidently, ''Owen can tell you how cold *I* got.''

Del came over. ''Changeover? Zeth, I can't zlin the slightest sign—but then, your father can always tell hours before the first symptoms.''

Lodge's first response was ''Oh, the poor kid.'' When that drew odd looks, he grinned sheepishly. ''I guess you don't really mind, huh?'' Luckily, his field was too low to bother any of them.

''I'll see her through it, Del,'' said Zeth. ''Would you please let Bekka know where Owen and I are? There goes the schedule again!''

Bringing Owen's sister through changeover was the most pleasant duty Zeth had yet performed as a channel. Her breakout came late the next afternoon, and as he gave her transfer he felt as he had not felt in weeks—competent, fulfilled.

When it was over, Jana kissed both Zeth and her brother, then sat back and examined her new tentacles dispassionately. "But I'm not a channel," she said.

"We can't all be," Owen reminded her. "Congratulations. Now you can *really* help Pa with the horses!"

She thought a moment. "Yeah, I guess that's what I wanted all along," she said with a smile.

In the excitement of Jana's changeover party—a much appreciated excuse for a happy celebration—Zeth forgot all about moving the border.

From the emotional high of his first First Transfer, Zeth sank into worry about his father's strange hallucinations. Over and over he would call for Zeth—but never recognize his son when he came. Del solved the mystery when Zeth described one of the attacks to him. "It's not you, Zeth—it's the Zeth you were named for. Rimon's cousin—the Sime he killed in first Need. He's in chronic need just like before Kadi established, and he's reliving his First Kill." He sighed. "I wish I knew if it helps to visit him. He doesn't even look at me anymore."

"He knows you're there," Zeth half lied. Rimon's field responded to the ambient . . . but Zeth doubted that Rimon recognized anyone these days.

Nor could Zeth go to Abel with his troubles. The old man was declining toward crisis, and when he was capable of a few hours of alertness, he was most likely to spend them with Jimmy Norton, telling him how he had broken his ties with the Freeband Raiders, encouraging the boy to disjunct. As Abel fully intended to do.

Zeth reached turnover and began the grueling slide into need himself. Owen began dogging Zeth's steps, even going to the ridiculous length of dragging himself out of bed when Zeth had had enough sleep. Soon Owen's temper frayed from lack of sleep, making Zeth even more edgy.

The last straw was the arrival, in the brief interval between storms three days before Zeth's third transfer, of Maddok and Sessly Bron. When Abel forbid Bron his house, the Gen waylaid him in the chapel, the one place Abel made the effort to go these days. Abel's shouting brought Zeth, Owen, Marji, Trina, and Bekka running in from the back of the chapel.

". . . agent of the Devil, tempting me to kill!" Abel was raging when Zeth flung the door open.

Bron's field was pure temptation, ringing with the "need to give" of a Companion—but way too low from his last donation. He had spent the interval away from Simes, and was in no manner ready to face a disjunction draw such as Zeth had experienced with Bekka. He only thought he was.

"Owen—Trina—" directed Zeth softly. "Shield Abel. Marji—"

"Abel, God has sent me to dispossess you of the murderous spirit holding you in thrall," Bron insisted, holding his ground.

"Well, you can just do it for someone else!" Zeth said, grasping Bron's arm as firmly as he grasped the fields. "Shen you, you shidoni-doomed fool, I'd like to toss you—"

"Zeth!" protested Owen. Zeth's anger was grating harshly on Abel's ragged nerves. Where had he found the strength to move at all?

Marji took Bron's other arm, their fields, too, sheltering Abel. The Companions were working on him—but the reason his anger melted so quickly was that he had no strength to sustain it.

"Marji, you and Trina take Abel home. I'll be right there," said Zeth, worried by a discordant thread in the old man's mood, a steely determination stronger than the frail body.

Zeth half dragged Bron into the back hall of the chapel. He slammed the connecting door to the chapel and tugged Bron toward Bekka's schedule board. "Bekka, who's on the schedule? Find me one of the town Simes—someone badly in need of a choice kill."

"Zeth!" Owen gasped in utter horror.

It was Bron Zeth had intended to frighten—but he simply said, "You see? *Your* demon, Zeth. Even you are susceptible, when your Companion is not protecting you."

Demons aside, the man's words were too close to the truth. What was a channel doing trying to provoke real fear in an untrained Gen? In sick disgust at his own feelings, he snapped, "I'll be with Abel," and plunged back into and through the chapel, the quickest way to Abel's house. Behind him, Bron also returned to the chapel—but he knelt down and remained there.

Zeth, Owen on his heels, caught up to Abel and the two women on the front porch of his house. The old Sime was protesting that he could walk—but it was obvious he could not.

Margid Veritt opened the door. Zeth felt cold fear grip her—she knew Abel too well to hope that he would accept a kill this time. They put him on the couch. Taking a deep breath to steady himself into healing mode, Zeth remembered when his father had given Abel the first Sime-Sime transfer ever—right in this very room. Then he had no more time to think. He moved in to zlin Abel closely. He wasn't even on the transfer schedule yet, and Zeth was hoping that he was not yet near hard need, that they could keep him resting for a day or two with a Companion at his side, to put him in the best possible condition to attempt transfer—but as soon as Zeth zlinned him, that hope died. He was not only deep into need, but his system was in turmoil, fragmenting much the way Jord's did during a voiding fit. But he wasn't exactly voiding. He seemed to be consuming selyn, as if he were augmenting, although he lay still, at peace physically and emotionally. Zeth had never seen anything like it before. *In all my vast experience*, he thought helplessly. "Get Jord and Uel," he ordered, and never noticed who went.

Zeth extended his show-field to support Abel, drawing his field back to normal consumption rate. The moment he let go, Abel's field went back to augmentation mode, consuming and consuming from his pitifully small store of selyn.

Duoconscious, Zeth saw that Abel's eyes were half closed, his lips moving in prayer, but otherwise he showed no indication of being conscious.

Zeth became aware of Jord and Uel, and looked up. "What should I do?"

Uel fought down his emotions, forcing himself into the channel's professional stance, and said, "What you're doing. I don't know of anything else."

Hank and Jord were little help. They were too close to Abel. No matter what Zeth did, the augmentation would not stop. Abel was far past ordinary hard need and into attrition. Now there was only one thing to do: get selyn into him, even if he suffered nerve-burn. The room was full of people, but not one suggested going for a Gen.

Zeth took Abel in transfer position. Astonishingly, he was conscious and cooperating—but his field was not. When Zeth tried driving selyn into Abel's system, he met the old reflexive rebellion. By exerting all his power, he could just hold the fields balanced, but Abel was locked against the selyn flow, and his heart wavered under the strain. Zeth had to let himself take the shen backflow as the fields collapsed.

Leaning back against Owen, he gathered strength and tried again—and again—but each time the result was the same. Though he could feel Abel's will accepting the transfer, his body would not.

Clammy with sweat, he let Owen's field soothe him while he racked his brains for an idea. He had been using his very best imitation of Genfear, enticing Abel with the promise of killbliss. Perhaps Jord . . . ?

But when Jord moved forward, Abel twisted away, curling himself into fetal position, rejecting them all.

"Wait!" said Zeth, motioning Jord back and gripping the fields around Abel again so that all the old man would sense would be Zeth's Gen field. He said, "Owen, pretend you're going to give me transfer!"

Owen nodded, closed his eyes, and instantly the strong bond between them activated. Zeth resisted the temptation to melt into Owen's control and remained in healing mode, taking his texture from Owen now, instead of doing his rotten imitation of fear. He offered *that* field to Abel, and the Sime responded, coming willingly back into transfer grip.

And then something shifted, leaving Zeth gasping in duoconsciousness. The searing tension of need was gone. Abel had not taken transfer, but he was not dead. He was euphoric. "Get Maddok Bron."

"No!" Zeth cried as if wounded.

Abel found the strength to move his head in a negative. "He must be shown the truth. God has granted my prayers." He closed his eyes, resting for a moment. Then he opened them, saying, "God bless you, son." His blissful peace indeed felt like a blessing.

When Bron entered, Abel let go of Zeth's left arm and held his hand out to the Gen. "Come, Maddok," he said. "See that there is no demon."

Bron knelt, taking Abel's hand in both of his, looking at the bulging ronaplin glands and dripping wrist orifices with understanding. Then he met Abel's eyes and saw what Zeth and everyone else perceived—peace beyond need. Zeth had never seen death by attrition, but he knew it was never like this. And so did Bron.

Abel smiled; his eyes crinkled with joy. "You see? God

would not let me die forsworn, my friend. Forgive my angry words.''

"I forgive you. But, now you must let me—''

Zeth, holding his show-field in Owen's pattern, felt the moment when Bron also began to entice Abel. Suddenly, he was at war with the Gen for Abel's attention. It lasted only a moment. Abel released Bron's arm and pulled away from his grip, seeking Zeth's tentacles.

"I choose my channel.''

Zeth bent to make lip contact, expecting now that Abel would draw smoothly to completion. But no sooner had selyn begun to flow than the old reflex clamped down, catching Zeth wholly unprepared. He was shenned out of the contact again, reeling back into Owen's grip.

When his senses cleared, Jord was holding Bron back and Abel was saying, "No, Maddok. I will not risk losing what I have gained. Your prayers must guide you now. Help the channels, Maddok, and let them help you. But most of all, help those who have killed to find out what it is to have no need to kill. It is in ourselves—but it is not in me any longer. Witness, Maddok.''

His laterals, dripping selyn-conducting fluids and trembling of their own eager accord, caressed the minister's fingers as purest joy engulfed Abel's field. The room rang with triumph, echoed and reechoed in every Sime field, and penetrating the Gen nager.

And then it was gone. Abel was dead. And somehow, Fort Freedom must continue.

Chapter 11

Abel Veritt had left his affairs in perfect order, and he had left his community a legacy of ritual to get them through any crisis. The one thing Zeth could not cope with though, was that Abel's will left Fort Freedom's Gens to Zeth, not Rimon. It was a mere technicality—but Zeth could not bring himself to have Slina complete the paperwork.

The year's turning ceremony, only a few days away, became the memorial service. Jord Veritt, who always carved the names of martyrs into the Monument in the chapel, began bringing it up to date. Sessly Bron spent hours watching him work—and one day Zeth, hoping that Jord had worked off his emotions in physical labor and could go back to the overcrowded schedule, found Sessly holding Jord while he shook with guilt and sorrow. The last name on the Monument—Abel's—was incomplete, the last letter he had been working on shaky.

Sessly frowned at Zeth over Jord's shoulder, and continued with what she was saying to him. "You'll do it, too, Jord—but you won't die. You're young, and you're a channel. I'll help you. I know you can do it."

Zeth went quietly away—and within the hour, Jord resumed his duties as a channel, without comment.

Zeth was too deep into need to feel true grief—he wondered distantly whether he would collapse again as he had when his mother's death hit him after his second transfer. His need nightmares took the form of reliving Abel's death—but they ended in that transcendent joy Abel had known when he found his desire to kill gone. Zeth would wake, clinging to the ecstatic feeling, only to have it burned off by encroaching need.

His fear of the kill was not nearly so strong—knowing that

171

Abel had overcome it made it less the unconquerable creature that he dared not let touch him, lest he be forever contaminated. As a consequence, he began to approach Uel's ability to simulate killbliss.

His distaste at being around Margid also disappeared—but he didn't know how to let her know it. An apology would hurt her again, when she had enough grief to bear.

Then on the day he was to have transfer, Zeth woke hours before dawn. He zlinned the house, and found Margid alone in the kitchen. Determined to try to make amends, he got up and went out to the kitchen. She was seated at the table, staring at the china tea container. When Zeth entered, she said, "I was just about to make tea."

Pouring for Zeth and herself, she sat down, putting the tea container back on the table. "Abel brought me this from Summer Fair," she said, "the year he registered the deed on Fort Freedom. I was pregnant with Hope, we had very few people here, and the town Simes hated us. We could barely scrape together the taxes—and he spent money we couldn't afford to bring me something beautiful."

She gave Zeth a sad smile. "It was so ugly here. Oh, the hills were just as beautiful as now, but the Fort was a mud hole. The houses were unpainted—it was dreary, and so were we. I tried to accept Abel's teaching that I was still human in spite of being Sime—but I couldn't accept that anyone could really love me. Abel . . . well, he never was very good at saying *that* with words, no matter how eloquently he spoke about anything else."

She extended her handling tentacles, protecting the delicate container as she turned it over and over. "Then he brought me this . . . totally frivolous object. A way of saying, if you appreciate beauty, you're human." She sighed, got up, and emptied the tea into the wooden box. Then she carefully washed the china container, dried it, and replaced it on the shelf where it had always stood.

As Margid stood staring at the container, Zeth came to her, putting his arms around her. She turned, buried her face against his shoulder, and sobbed. "Oh, God, Zeth, I loved him so. What am I going to do?"

"You'll go on," he said numbly, wondering himself. "We all have to. It's what Abel always did, isn't it?" And he held her until she had let out her grief.

It was fortunate that Abel's family found other outlets for

their grief, for the memorial service could not be the healing time that Abel had always made it. When the snow clogged the passes once more, so Maddok Bron could not get home to conduct his own year's turning ceremony, everyone assumed that he would conduct the one in Fort Freedom. Bron himself certainly assumed it—until he let slip that he had not given up his demon theory.

It was Owen to whom he said it, obviously thinking a fellow Gen would understand. Zeth and Owen had had transfer that morning, and shared their own grief. Then Owen went to the chapel to pray—and encountered Bron.

Zeth was in Rimon's room, trying to get his father to understand that Abel was dead. If he would only grieve, and realize how much now depended on him, perhaps he would recover. But although Rimon's field made its automatic response to Zeth's, he remained suspended in emotionlessness. Owen entered, closed the door, and leaned against it. Even low-field, he projected a burning frustration too strong for Zeth to block.

"What's wrong?" asked Zeth.

"Maddok Bron," Owen replied. "Zeth, we can't let him conduct the year's turning. He's going to preach about demons again! Why did you ever let him give transfer?"

"You think I should have let him run around high-field, tempting the juncts?" Actually, that had not been Zeth's motivation at all. After Abel's death, by way of a combined apology for his threats in the chapel hallway and confirming lesson on what transfer *really* was, he had carefully chosen one of their nonjunct Simes and let Bron give transfer. The strictly supervised session had gone very well. Bron had not bothered Zeth again, and he had thought the problem solved.

Owen sighed. "No—but you should just have taken his field down. Now he's ready to start exorcising demons."

"How did he get back onto that again? Surely even a Gen could see that Abel died at peace."

Ignoring the implied slight, Owen said, "Oh, he saw that, all right. He agrees Abel is a martyr—but remember Abel wouldn't attempt transfer with Bron. Now Bron thinks Abel was still afraid of his demon, and had to die to dispossess himself of it! How many people are capable of making that sacrifice!"

"If it weren't so serious, it'd be ridiculous," said Zeth.

"Zeth—it's sacrilege!" objected Owen, and Zeth recalled his friend's deep faith.

"It's desecration of Abel's memory," Zeth agreed. "Stay with Dad, Owen—I'll put a stop to this."

Enlisting Uel's help, Zeth confronted Bron. There was no swaying him. "You know I'm right, Zeth. I saw even you almost succumb, remember? If Owen hadn't been there when you were in need, and worried and angry at the same time—"

"And I suppose," said Hank Steers, who had accompanied Uel, "that you have never regretted words spoken in anger? I'm Gen, too, and I certainly know *I* have!"

"I make no claim to perfection, Hank," Bron replied. "I simply act in accord with what God has revealed to me."

"Well, you're not going to do it at Abel's memorial service!" Zeth said, tears choking his voice.

"We won't have it," Uel took over. "Abel's wife, his son, his granddaughter will be there. All the people to whom he's been a father. You will not deny everything he stood for."

"Then I will not conduct the service," Bron said firmly. "I cannot speak other than the truth."

That left them with no one to conduct the service. Dan Whelan suggested that Hank should be the speaker, but Hank demurred, saying, "I'd just burst into tears and my field would have every Sime in the building in hysterics."

Then Whelan looked to Owen. To Zeth's surprise, Owen said, "I think I could do it." He flashed Zeth a tight smile, and Zeth thought, *I should have volunteered.* But that form of leadership was not for him, just as it had not been for his father.

The ceremony was simple and quiet, a candlelit ritual spanning midnight on the longest night of the year. Owen made no attempt to reproduce Abel's year's turning ceremony. Instead, he spoke of the love he had had for Abel, and why. He told of Abel's inspired decisions—how Owen had been made Zeth's punishment for disobedience, and how the tension thus set up between them had led to his becoming responsible for his own life despite his handicap.

"Abel Veritt was a man so close to God that such inspirations were everyday occurrences. His steps were guided so that he could guide the steps of others—of Rimon Farris, for example. Abel knew him for what he was before Rimon did. Impossible as it might have seemed a year ago, we are now friends with out-Territory Gens. Zeth went to them for help when his home was in danger, and because some instinct drove him to seek me for his changeover. That couldn't have happened without the bond Abel had forged between us.

"We no longer have Abel to guide us—but his spirit will be with us always. If we mourn now, we mourn for ourselves—for what we have lost with Abel's death. But let us not mourn for Abel Veritt. He taught us that our prayers are always answered, as was his most fervent prayer. All who were there will bear witness for the rest of their lives that Abel Veritt did not die a killer! More—I, a Gen, bear witness before you now that Abel Veritt died having left behind the *need to kill!*"

After that, Zeth felt certain that no one could accept Maddok Bron's claims—but apparently there were those, especially among the older, semi-junct Simes left without a religious leader, who found it comforting not to be held responsible for killing. As his parents had always done, Zeth avoided the theological arguments. He got enough of it secondhand from Owen, who was appalled at the growing response to Bron's teachings.

Furthermore, the junct Simes from town were coming up on their third and fourth transfers without killing—but those who had elected to stay had developed enough respect for Fort Freedom to shun the kill while guests there. They talked longingly of rebuilding their community—but when they came to the channels it would be "Oh, I can manage one more time."

When Uel, Jord, and Marji consulted Zeth, he replied, "But what can we do? Force them to kill?"

"I don't know," said Jord, "but we'll have a cascade if one of them goes into disjunction crisis and sets off a bunch of the others."

"What would your father do?" asked Marji.

Zeth shrugged, and Uel answered, "Probably give them all the best transfers we can, and hope."

The channels were constantly on the run, their Companions with them, but when Owen would try to make him eat or rest, or use his field to affect Zeth's emotions, Zeth would rebel. "Sometimes I think you really *do* think you're warding off demons!"

"I'm only trying to make you take care of yourself," Owen would reply patiently, and Zeth would quell an angry retort. The fact was, only Bekka's artistic schedule juggling kept the Gens safe and the Simes satisfied in the close proximity dictated by the unremitting winter.

The river that marked the border near Del Erick's property froze over for the first time in years—and in weather that in any other year would have kept people huddling in their homes, but was "mild" by this year's standards, Glian Lodge crossed the frozen river along with Eph Norton and his daughter Sue. "To see if we could do it," they explained. "The Border Patrol won't be watching that route and it'll be good for the rest of the winter."

Owen wanted to spend time with his uncle, and as Zeth dimly understood, with Sue Norton. But only when Owen was too tired to work with Zeth could he leave the grueling schedule. Watching Owen stumble off toward his father's house as Wik joined Zeth in a quick-march to the Deevan house at dawn one day, Zeth determined that one of the buildings that had to have top priority in the spring was a center for channels' functions, such as the New Homestead had been. Then the channels wouldn't have to drag their Companions out in all sorts of beastly weather, going to people's homes.

When Owen came down with a cold, Zeth mentioned his thoughts at one of the "council sessions," still held around the Veritt kitchen table.

There was immediate agreement. Zeth realized that he had been accepted as spokesman for the channels, so he continued, "I wish we could find a way now to centralize our work. Every house is full of people, though. We really can't ask people to crowd in the way they did for those few days after the battle, just so we can take a house and—"

"Zeth." Strangely enough, it was Slina who provided the solution. "Why don't you think what Abel would advise?"

"Huh?"

"Right now, he could be here, he'd be tellin' you—use the chapel. Abel'd never've stood for that big insulated room standin' empty all day, if it'd make it easier on people."

Owen sneezed, and that settled it.

Centralizing the channels' duties made life much easier. Zeth and Owen had time to spend with Del upon occasion, and Owen to be with Sue. He got over his cold quickly. One midnight, Owen was with Sue when Rimon had another of his hallucinatory seizures—the worst ever. Zeth, a week past turnover, had had to practically force Owen to leave him, and now Owen cursed himself for going as he met Zeth at the back of the chapel, where the other channels would not let Zeth into Rimon's room without his Companion's protection. Del, much closer to need than Zeth, had gone right in, and Zeth was seething.

Hank and Uel had been with Rimon, who was approaching hard need again, but Bekka had had to pull them out, and so they had left Trina, who had been working all day, to sleep in the room. The practice of alternating channels working with him with Companions sitting with him had become part of Bekka's routine.

Trina had fallen so deeply asleep that she hadn't wakened until Rimon was out of bed and in the middle of the floor, where he had fallen, crying out for Zeth. By the time his son was allowed in, Uel had the attack under control, and he and Del were lifting Rimon onto the bed.

Zeth had been hoping that Rimon's getting out of bed was a sign of returning strength—but the moment he came into the room he had the shock of seeing, for the first time in months, his father's hideously burned legs. The wounds, which had showed blackened muscle oozing blood when Zeth had first seen them, now dripped pus and were lined with a webbing of yellow infected tissue. Here and there he could see glistening bone. The skin stretched tightly over the rest of his badly swollen legs appeared dry, and hung loosely ready to fall off around the spreading area of the wounds. The room stank with putrefaction.

Del carefully laid Rimon down, and helped Marji arrange clean bedclothes so they would not irritate him. "Uel, you've got to *do* something!"

"What else can we do? We can't get transfer into him—"

"When he was just through changeover, nobody could get him to kill, either. Shen it, he's fixated on that memory of killing his cousin! Try some of the techniques his father used on him then."

"We can't make him kill someone—" Uel began.

Hank put a hand on his arm. "Tell us, Del. Maybe we can rouse his intil so one of us can give him a good transfer."

Rimon's field started vibrating again—Uel meshed and tried to stop the fluctuations, but it took Zeth's strength to bring them into line, leaving him dizzy, leaning on Owen. Del winced, saying, "That's an old symptom. Turnover used to bring it on—before Kadi. Why don't you rouse one of

Slina's Gens to panic? I know that's cruel, but if it brings Rimon to intil and you can intercept—"

Uel clenched his jaw muscles, the idea clearly abhorrent to him. "Zeth," he said finally, "he's your father—"

"Try it," said Zeth. "He's dying, Uel. We have to try *something!" He won't kill. He can't. And by next time I'll learn to give a completely satisfactory transfer—even if it means witnessing an actual kill!*

Bekka was off duty, so the channels had to struggle with the schedule themselves until she showed up at dawn. Zeth stayed on duty, helping Marji while Owen napped. Night duty was normally light—most of the Gens were asleep then, and the Simes took the rest they required. At dawn Jord came to relieve Marji, Owen joined Zeth, and the day's routine began.

Bekka started on the day's slate. Uel, Zeth, and Jord were all to be free that afternoon to try to get transfer into Rimon. Del, who had been scheduled for late that evening, was so shaken by the events of the night that they decided to move up his transfer. As Jord was up for transfer himself just before Rimon, that meant taking Del off Jord's list and putting him on Zeth's.

Already people were filing into the chapel, which was carefully divided with heavy hangings. This morning Zeth, Uel, and Jord would take donations from Gens; the dispensing for Simes would begin just before noon. A long line of Gens waited for Zeth, shorter lines for Uel and Jord.

Everything proceeded normally. By the time the first edgy Simes were seated in the Sime waiting area outside the cubicle where Zeth was working, they were finishing with the last donations. It looked as if they'd have all three channels free to work on Rimon.

To avoid having high-field Gens passing by the waiting Simes, the Gen line came into Zeth's working area from the opposite side. Most of them went out toward the back door, passing the Simes only when they were low-field. As Zeth worked, he became aware of a glare of impatience on the Sime side of the hangings. *Not again!* he thought as he recognized Jimmy Norton's nager. They did not yet have him on a normal four-week cycle. At first, with constant augmentation, he had driven himself into feeling need within a week of any transfer—except that it was turnover he perceived as hard need, and he reacted from that point on with the dangerous instincts of a Freeband Raider.

Since Bekka's disjunction, Jimmy had been trying very hard, and had gone from ten days last time up to fifteen now—but that was still only half a normal cycle. He had to do better, even if he never managed a full four weeks. He still insisted that he would take transfer from no one but Zeth—and Zeth couldn't help wondering if the lack of junct satisfaction was hindering Jimmy's progress.

One of the Gens left, and Jimmy took the opportunity when the hangings opened to slip in to Zeth. "I'm in need," he said agitatedly. "I've gone much longer this time—"

"Yes, you have," Zeth assured him, trying to be encouraging. "Half again as long as last time. But you're not really in—"

"I am!" Jimmy insisted.

"It's all right," Zeth soothed, as Owen's nager also went to work on Jimmy. "I'll give you transfer as soon as I finish with the donations—right after Del. You can wait that long, can't you? Of course you can, when you know you'll have transfer in say—half an hour? Every hour, every minute you can add will make it that much easier next time."

The hangings cut selyn fields, but not sound. From the Gen side. Hapen Young came in, saying, "It's my fault, Zeth. I was scheduled to donate, and Jimmy came along. He was just fine before he came in here. Maybe I should stay high-field and—"

"Oh, no you don't!" said Zeth. Hapen and Jimmy had become good friends, but after the nerve-burn Hapen had suffered in the raid, even though he now seemed steady and unafraid, the channels had decided he should donate for several more months before trying an actual transfer. So Jimmy was settled on the bench outside, and as soon as he had donated, Hapen sat down beside him, to keep him company until his promised transfer.

Zeth began dispensing with Del. He tried earnestly to give Owen's father a satisfying transfer, but as usual, he could not produce that pain/bliss even the semi-juncts craved. Del insisted he was perfectly comfortable, but it was due more to the way Owen soothed him than to anything Zeth had done.

Hank and Uel headed in to check up on Rimon before beginning their dispensing schedule. "I'll go with you," said Del. "My field won't irritate Rimon now."

"It didn't this morning, either," said Uel. "I wish it *had* triggered his need—we might have gotten transfer into him then."

Just then a high-field Gen approached, and Zeth turned, recognizing Eph Norton even through the hangings. As a deliberate encouragement to Jimmy, Zeth left the curtain open on the Sime side while he let Norton in—so father and son could see one another. Jimmy managed to smile at Norton, proudly taking control of himself. Zeth was pleased to see it. Then he closed the curtains as Norton said, "I'm sorry I'm late. Sue was pretty upset at the way you left last night, Owen."

"It was an emergency."

"I know—I tried to explain that to her. But girls at that age—" He shrugged. "I wish her mother were alive."

Norton's donation was quickly taken, but when Zeth opened the curtains to call Jimmy in, he found Jord approaching. "Zeth, I'm—I'm really feeling bad," said the other channel. "If I don't get some rest before my transfer—"

Zlinning the appalling ache of need in Jord's system, Zeth said, "Come on in and give me what you're carrying in your secondary system."

When the imbalance was relieved, Jord sat resting as Zeth opened the curtains once again. Eph Norton had stopped to talk to his son, who was trying to show his best side to his father. That motivation, and the inbred courtesy of someone raised to standards similar to those of Fort Freedom, suddenly plunged them all into trouble.

By now, the women in the chapel kitchen were getting ready to feed Slina's Gens. Sessly Bron walked out of the kitchen toward the back door, carrying a snow shovel. At once, Jimmy Norton got up, saying, "Let me help you, Miss Bron."

Eph Norton looked around, saying, "No, Jimmy, you're in need. I'll do it." He reached to push his son back down, as Jimmy raised his hand to ward off his father's touch. Their hands met—and Jimmy went hyperconscious, his tentacles lashing about his father's hand. Norton stared at their united hands, not comprehending. Hapen Young tried to influence Jimmy, but his field was as low as Norton's.

"Owen!" Zeth said, but his Companion was already in motion. Zeth moved to shield Jord, who had come up behind

Zeth, his channel's sense of duty outweighing his physical condition.

Just as Owen reached the Nortons, Eph looked up from his son's grip to his face, and saw the raw need in his eyes. His field flared a combination of revulsion and sympathy, throwing Jimmy into killmode. He struggled to fight it, Owen's field helping, but the situation merely stabilized. Owen could not bring Jimmy down to duoconsciousness, and so he did exactly what a high-field, experienced Companion ought to do—he placed his own hand over the joined hands of the participants—

The moment he touched them, Owen recognized killmode—the sign of disjunction crisis. He looked to Zeth, no words necessary—but Zeth realized, *I can't seduce him away, anymore than Owen can! I can't produce pain and terror!*

"Jord!" he said. "You'll have to—"

Jord pushed past him, his own discomfort forgotten—and at that moment Slina came in the back door, prodding before her the undrugged Gen they planned to use to provoke Rimon to take transfer. She zlinned the scene. Sessly was also watching, the shovel still clutched in her hands. As Jord approached the Nortons, Jimmy, sensing another Sime in need, turned with a snarl, gripping his father even tighter.

Zeth zlinned at once what was wrong—Jord's show-field couldn't mask his need—his secondary system was empty! *I've got to do it! I've got to!* But he remained frozen. When Zeth didn't take action, Sessly did: she threw the shovel between the two faced-off Simes. It had no effect—both Jimmy and Jord were hyperconscious; they didn't hear the noise, and the passing of an inanimate object was no shock at all.

The clatter startled Slina's Gen. He flared fear, stumbled back and tangled himself in his lead chain, cutting his ankle and sending a shrieking pain through the nager. Jord, already swamped in Jimmy's killmode, flipped over. Zeth had never zlinned it before—genuine unrepentant killmode possessing both Simes at the same time the pen Gen flared irrational terror and Eph Norton woke to perfectly rational but no less enticing fear.

One or both Simes were going to kill. Instantly, Zeth saw the only choice: even if Jord killed the pen Gen, Jimmy could not be allowed to kill his father! He flung himself at Jimmy, letting his own field resonate to the pain and terror of the pen

Gen. His show-field was infinitely stronger than Eph Norton's. Jimmy dropped his father and lunged at Zeth, who met him with the first killmode transfer he had ever given, riding on the ambience of the room.

Jord began stalking the pen Gen, who cowered back against Slina. She gave the Gen a vicious shove in Jord's direction, just as Zeth fell back to duoconsciousness with Jimmy gasping in his arms. Sessly cried, "No! You can't make him kill!" and leaped to intervene, grasping Jord's arms and forcing herself against him.

The door to Rimon's room flung open, and Uel came running, Hank behind him—too late to do anything but witness Sessly pressing her lips to Jord's, shock and surprise at the pleasure of first-time transfer ringing through her field. No fear—determination turning to ecstasy.

It's all right! Incredulous relief swelled Zeth's heart. *Nobody killed—and now I know how to save Dad's life!*

But at that very instant, through the open door of Rimon's room came a flare of killmode that paralyzed every Sime in the chapel except the two who had just dropped hypoconscious after transfer. Zeth was the first to recover, as Del's voice rang, "Rimon—no!" and Owen started to run through the crowd.

Zeth leaped past Owen, over and around the other Simes and Gens frozen in tableau, zlinning the struggle in the sickroom, Del trying to hold Rimon down as his killmode was triggered by potent fields uncut by the curtains which had been flung aside by the curious.

Then Rimon was grasping Del, calling, "Zeth—help me! Zeth!"—and Del's fear flared as he saw Rimon fixed on him. He struggled to free himself as Rimon, with the strength of desperation, dragged him into kill position, drawing and drawing as pain scorched through Del's nerves, burning with the voracious, unfulfilled need—

In his desperate struggle to break the contact, Del thrust Rimon's arms away—and Zeth's nerves vibrated to the screech of shock as Del's fingers clenched over the delicate nerves. But it was a deathgrip. As Zeth flung himself into the room, Del was falling, limp, from Rimon's grip.

And Rimon was in agony. "Kadi!" he screamed, thrashing in pain, still in hard need, for Del's selyn could not begin to fill his capacity. Moreover, his injured laterals began to void selyn—the precious little in his system draining away as his son dashed to his side, shoving Del's body away to grasp Rimon in transfer grip. He forcefully entwined their laterals, for Rimon's were out of control, nerve-injured. Rimon continued to call out for Kadi in an agony of need, pain, and guilt.

Finally, Zeth secured his grip on Rimon, and found the fifth transfer point. Rimon drew—the aching void of his need filling and filling—but never reaching fulfillment. It was not the absence of a satisfactory emotion—Zeth was giving exactly what he had just learned, but there was no satisfying Rimon now. As fast as Zeth poured selyn into him, it leaked— then poured—away through his injured nerves.

On the periphery of his awareness, he noticed Owen come in, and fall to his knees in horror over Del's body. *Del's body! Dad killed!*

That agony hit Zeth just at the moment when Rimon had drained his secondary system and was ripping away at the natural barrier, making Zeth flinch away in self-preservation as his father's life ebbed away beneath his tentacles.

No—I won't kill. Ever!

He willed his system to flip over into primary mode and let his father drain and drain him. But there came a point of searing crescendo when he could hold it no longer, even to save his father's life, and Fort Freedom's dream. His body convulsed, ripping loose the contact points just as pain ceased in blackness.

Chapter 12

Zeth became slowly aware of Sime tentacles twining about his arms, pulling . . . a ripe, insistent Gen nager throbbed expectantly before him, and suddenly the tentacles forced his laterals out and into contact with the Gen—*Owen!*

At first, selyn came through no volition of his own, trickling deep into his systems, dispelling the numbness of attrition and wakening him to a savage draw as he sought the shrieking delight of killbliss.

The speed slacked off short of pain, Owen's way of saying, *No, I won't let you kill.* Momentarily, he succumbed to his instinct to draw against that imposed discipline, and felt Owen's pain blossom. *No! I won't kill!* He surrendered control, and the flow came to an indrawn pause that relieved the screeching ache. When selyn came again, it was at his normal speed, flowing without effort. It ceased without his stopping, though he was relieved of every trace of need.

Hypoconscious, he stared up into Owen's worried blue eyes. Uel knelt behind Owen, holding Zeth's hands so his laterals could make contact at the back of Owen's neck. When he found Zeth conscious, he let go—and Zeth's hands fell limply. Owen caught his left arm, but his right hit the floor, nerve-burn surging through him.

Uel said, "Someone get the fosebine."

It was Jord who brought it, by which time Zeth was beginning to remember—and despair. He didn't have to ask about his father; if Uel and Jord were with him, Rimon was dead; they wouldn't leave a critical channel in Marji's care.

He's better off dead, Zeth thought. *Maybe we all would be. Thank God Abel didn't live to see Rimon kill.*

No one said anything to Zeth except "You're all right" and "Here, drink this." Maybe they thought he didn't know what had happened, and would be better off sleeping before he faced it. *I've been making such judgments for other people for weeks now. What right did I have?* The dream Fort Freedom had stood for was shattered. The numbness was wearing off the other people in the room. They must have worked as a team to save his life without giving a thought to the implications of what Rimon had done . . . but now they had pulled Zeth through, and they were beginning to think.

Sorrow built like a slow tide. Hank let tears slide down his cheeks—less painful than trying to hold them back. Owen held his field steady, braced, not allowing grief to penetrate as he worked on Zeth, but it was a duty, not his usual spontaneous outpouring of help.

As the fosebine drew him toward sleep, Zeth realized that things could never be the same between him and Owen, either. *My father killed his father.*

Zeth woke in the room he shared with Owen in the Veritt house. As he wasn't disoriented, they had moved him sleeping, not unconscious. What woke him was Sessly Bron replacing the covers he had tossed off. She smiled at him. "Hello, Zeth. Feeling better?"

Jord Veritt, who had been sitting on Owen's neatly made bed, came over to zlin him, and Zeth automatically zlinned back.

Jord's fields were in a healthy configuration for the first time in Zeth's experience. He looked years younger, too, his eyes beginning to emerge from their perpetual hollows, glowing with serenity. Zeth had completely forgotten Sessly's intercepting Jord. *I'd never have allowed it—never! And look what she's done for him.*

Jord said, "Yes, you *are* better, Zeth. Another dose of fosebine should stave off that headache." As soon as the soothing effects of the medicine were flowing through Zeth's system he asked, "Do you want to talk, Zeth? Should I get Owen?"

"It doesn't matter," Zeth said flatly, and Jord frowned.

"Zeth . . . you do remember what happened?"

"Dad killed Del. There's no such thing as a Sime who won't kill, given enough provocation. Dad was never any different from you, Jord—Mama kept him from killing."

Sessly said, "That's no reason to despair, Zeth. God has

showed us the way. No one will be allowed to kill anymore. With Owen's help, you'll use your blessed gift of healing.''

"I can't!" he protested.

"Zeth," Jord said firmly, "you could *not* have saved your father's life. You risked your own, trying, but that injury was fatal. Grieve, Zeth—but don't blame yourself.''

Jord understands, Zeth realized. *Simes can't be blamed for being Sime.* Tears of weakness slid down his face.

Uel arrived a while later, to spell Jord—or rather to rest there while Jord went back to work. The pattern formed quickly—Zeth really required only fosebine and sleep, but just in case, one of the channels remained with him.

Until Owen came. Then they were left alone. It was after midnight, and Owen was groggy, his eyes red with weeping, his field hollow with emotional exhaustion. He sat on the edge of Zeth's bed, saying, "I should have been here earlier, but I couldn't leave Jana to make all the arrangements . . . and I had to pray—''

"Owen, I'm so sorry!" Zeth blurted "It's my fault everyone was in the chapel that way, and—''

"And it's my fault you almost died!" Owen said bitterly. "When I saw Pa lying there, and you trying to revive Rimon— Oh, God, Zeth, I had to try to help Pa, though I knew he was dead. Uel dragged me away—I would have let you *die*, Zeth!''

"If you had, it wouldn't matter much.''

"Zeth!''

"Maddok Bron is right. Simes must be protected. Not from demons—just from the fact of being Sime. It's up to you, Owen. If my father could kill, I can—unless you stop me.''

"No! Zeth, I've never tried to control you, and I'm not going to start now. Your father was right. I'm not fit to be a Companion. Even if I'd had my wits together, I couldn't have helped you. With only one arm, I couldn't force your laterals to extend. I couldn't lift your arms into position—Uel had to do it. If we'd been alone, Zeth, you'd have died.''

Zeth sighed. "That won't happen again. You can handle anything I'll ever need, Owen.''

Margid brought soup for Zeth and a full meal for Owen. "Eat, and then I want you both asleep," she told them firmly. "There'll be plenty of time to talk in the morning.'' And because it was too painful for either of them to continue, they obeyed her.

The next day Zeth progressed on shaky legs as far as the main room. A stream of visitors began with Dan Whelan, who tried delicately to find out if Zeth had any special wishes for the memorial service for his father. Zeth didn't want to think about how Rimon had died—so he just said dully, "Whatever you think is appropriate."

Maddok Bron came—and the sincere sympathy in the man's field was almost more than Zeth could bear. Bron said gently, "Your father was not responsible for his last act, Zeth. For all the good he did over many years, he is certainly now reunited with your mother in heaven. I'll pray for his soul, and for that of Del Erick. They were good men."

But despite his cautious words to Zeth, Bron apparently used Rimon's death as proof of his demon theory, for Dan returned later that day to reassure Zeth that Bron would not conduct the service. Zeth nodded, not really caring—what if a Sime's instincts were personified as demons? They were just as deadly either way.

A while later, Owen came in with his sister. Owen seemed angry, and Jana was trying to calm him down. "Go splash cold water on your face," she told him, "and then come back. You can't help Zeth if you're all upset."

Zeth didn't ask, but Jana pulled up a chair and started in just as if he had, "It's that Sue Norton. I knew no good would come of Owen getting involved with an out-Territory girl! If there's anything Owen shouldn't have to worry about, it's that woman trying to take him away from you!"

That pulled Zeth out of his lethargy. "What happened?" he asked, thinking, *There's no other Gen who can handle my need—without Owen I'd kill someone!*

Owen came back in, answering his question. "It's over between us, that's all," he said. "Sue's *never* understood what it means to be a Companion. She thinks it's some sort of obligation—she had the nerve to tell me I was being disrespectful to the m-memory of my father"—he paused to brush angry tears away—"if I k-kept on as your Companion, Zeth." Tears coursed down his cheeks.

Jana took her brother's hand, wrapping handling tentacles about it, her own tears flowing. The two, Zeth's best friends ever since he could remember, were cut off from him by one fact. *My father killed their father.* Neither of them made the accusation, but it hung in the air until Zeth felt compelled to say it aloud. "My father killed your father. I'd give my life to change that—but I don't know how."

Startled, they both looked up at him. He felt the tensions release in them—and then Jana reached for his hand. "Oh, God, Zeth—it's as awful for you to live with as it is for us! They were both like fathers to all of us. Maybe if we can think, they came here together . . . and they died together—"

Jana's words were echoed by Dan Whelan two days later, at the service for Rimon Farris and Del Erick. He spoke of the loss not only of the first channel, but also of his closest friend—and the support Del had given Fort Freedom over many years. Zeth only half listened. He didn't really want to be here, listening to Dan try to avoid the real meaning of Rimon's death. He had grieved with Owen and Jana over Del, but something seemed to stop him from grieving for his father, as if Rimon had betrayed him and he could not mourn.

As the choir began to sing, Dan lit the lamps surrounding the monument to the martyrs. Zeth hadn't realized Jord had found time to carve a new name. There had been space for only one more. Del's would be the last name on the original monument.

And then Zeth saw what Jord had put on that last line. There were two names, side by side:

DEL ERICK—RIMON FARRIS

Suddenly grief poured through Zeth. His loss was real. Rimon was no longer wasting away in the back room of the chapel. He was dead, and with him the hopes of the community to which he had brought such change. *If only I'd mastered junct transfer sooner . . . !* Zeth sobbed. He was not alone. Owen and Jana put their arms around him, and the choir struggled through their hymn with choking voices.

When the emotion began to wane, Dan Whelan stepped back to the podium. "All who founded our new way of life are gone now: Kadi Farris, Abel Veritt, and now Rimon Farris and Del Erick. But Fort Freedom continues. They left us a legacy—their beliefs, their teachings, their practices. Even more, they left us their children. Abel's son Jord, his granddaughter Marji—both channels. Del's son Owen, a Companion. His daughter Jana—one of the new generation of Simes who have never killed.

"But more than any of the others, the fate of our community depends on one young channel who has been called upon to endure more and work harder than anyone might reasonably—or unreasonably—expect, and who has never failed us. He is Rimon and Kadi's son—''

Zeth listened with growing horror. *But I have failed.* He waited for the rejection of the congregation. Surely they could see he was the most dangerous of all the channels, the one with the highest capacity. He could be controlled by only one person in the community—and if something happened to Owen—

But the ambient nager did not deny as Dan said, "God has taken our leaders into His peace. They worked and suffered and died to start us on the right path. Now as we continue, let us thank God for our new leader, Zeth Farris!"

The wave of gratitude nearly drowned Zeth. He cried out in dismay, "No! No—you're wrong. I can't do it!" And he bolted from the chapel, Owen dashing after him, while everyone else sat in stunned bewilderment.

There was no place to run. Ice crunched under his feet in the dry cold. He half thought of the Old Homestead, but there were people staying there.

Patches came bounding up to Zeth, tail wagging. He yipped, pacing Zeth for a few strides, and then drew ahead, making for the Veritt home. Zeth followed him into the room he shared with Owen, where he sank to the floor and buried his face in the dog's shaggy fur.

All he could think about was the day when Owen lost his arm. *Owen should have been the channel. Then he could be their leader! Oh, Patches!*

There was no accusation in Owen's field when he opened the door. Zeth looked up, and Patches licked his face. Owen held out his hand, his field pure kindness. It wasn't right that Owen should be so good to him!

"Owen," he said wretchedly, "I killed my father."

"No you didn't, Zeth," said Owen, pulling Zeth up onto the bed. "He died of a lateral injury, which *my* father inflicted. Certainly Jord and Uel told you—"

"They didn't *feel* it! He was actively drawing for the first time since Mama died. I knew the only way to save him was to get enough selyn into him to support him till we could stop the leakage . . . so when my secondary system was empty, I let him draw from my primary. There was enough there to keep him going the few minutes it'd have taken . . . but I couldn't *control*, Owen! When it got low—"

"Low! Zeth, you almost died!"

"Oh, no," Zeth said bitterly. "I saved my own life—and let Dad die. I wanted to refuse to kill. I wanted to give Dad the selyn he needed to live . . . and I aborted out! Just because it hurt, I couldn't save my own father's life!"

"Zeth, how could anyone voluntarily give away *all* their selyn? A reflex—perfectly natural and unavoidable . . ."

"Reflex? Natural and unavoidable? Isn't that why Simes kill Gens, Owen? Simes are killers unless Gens stop them."

"What about Abel?" Owen asked.

"Yes . . . Abel," Zeth said in despair. "He showed us, didn't he? There's one way not to kill—and that's to die. That's what I didn't have the strength for. He'd really be proud of me, wouldn't he, Owen?"

"Not right now, he wouldn't. You've forgotten the difference between responsibility and blame."

"But I *can't* be blamed! I'm Sime—and you've got the responsibility for me."

Nothing else Owen might say would budge Zeth. Having worn himself out emotionally, he fell asleep. An hour later Owen woke him. "Come on, Zeth, there's a council meeting."

"Tell Uel," Zeth said dully, "I'm not channeling anymore."

"Don't be ridiculous," said Owen, flicking Zeth wide awake with his indignation. "Get up and wash your face, and come on out to the kitchen!"

"Whatever you say, Owen," Zeth replied. Owen's field flickered with annoyance, but he quelled it for the moment.

Zeth joined the group at the table: Dan Whelan, Slina, Eph Norton, Maddok Bron, and Owen. Dan started with an apology. "Zeth—I forget how young you are. It's the worst time of your life, and I loaded all of us onto you."

"You're not alone, Zeth," said Maddok. "You'll have help and counsel—but until the channels can be relieved of—"

"No you don't!" Slina inserted. "Ain't none of my people nor me gonna kill them poor folk you're preachin' at. Flamin' superstitious, *vicious* teachings! Rimon would—!" She choked off, swallowing back her grief.

"No, Slina," Zeth said. "Maddok is right."

"Thank God!" Bron murmured, but Zeth continued.

"I don't believe in demons—but need is as much of a

demon as anyone would care to face, and the fact is my father was wrong. It's not possible for a Sime not to kill. The Gens have to do it for us.''

Eph Norton said, ''I couldn't do it for my son—but you did, Zeth. You saved my life, and you kept Jimmy on the path—''

''On the path toward an empty promise!'' Zeth flashed. ''Over ten years my father didn't kill—but only because my mother kept him from it. Jord—who knows? Maybe Sessly can do it for him now. Willa did—his wife, years back,'' he added for those who didn't know. ''But when she died, he had to kill again. Dan, do you think your son could prevent himself from killing? Uel's never been tested, has he?''

''Zeth, you're upset,'' said Owen. ''I should never have let you come out here—''

''*Let* me? You *made* me!''

''I'm sorry,'' Owen apologized to everyone.

Slina said, ''Zeth, you got every right to grieve. It's no time for us to be worryin' you with our problems. Owen, take him and get him to rest till tomorrow.''

''No more!'' said Zeth. ''No more channeling—I can't hold people's lives in my hands like that ever again!'' He gasped as a spasm rang sharply through his whole body, followed by another. ''Oh, no!'' he groaned, doubling over, clutching his middle. *It's only been a couple of days since I worked!* Another cramp hit, and he gritted his teeth—but Owen had already recognized what was happening.

''That's what happens to any channel when he stops working—God's way of telling you that you're responsible for *using* His gifts.''

''Shen you—don't preach at me!'' Zeth grated. He turned to Maddok. ''Help me—please?''

Bron held out his hands willingly, his field instantly assuming the soothing attitude of prayer. Zeth balanced his fields, leaning back finally with a sigh of relief. ''Thank you.''

Owen's field rang with shock and rejection—and Zeth remembered that Bron could not possibly match him if he tried to draw. Suppose he had lost control? ''I shouldn't have done that,'' he apologized to Bron.

''My sister provided transfer for a channel,'' Bron reminded him. ''Zeth, if you ever need me—''

''You don't understand,'' Zeth said sadly. The energy of his momentary anger had drained away. ''I'm sorry, Owen.

I'll do whatever you want me to. You're my only match here.''

So Zeth went back to work. As the days passed, he found it easier and easier to leave decisions up to Owen as his old—dangerous, he thought—habits died. His job was easier now, for Jord's health had improved, Marji's capacity was increasing, and Zeth's new skill at junct transfers meant less juggling of Bekka's slate. Sessly was quickly learning to be a Companion, and she and her brother encouraged other Gens who had been donating for some time to try transfer.

The Brons were not stupid—they saw the channels as having the function of matching Simes and Gens for transfer, as well as healing. Though the channels would not cooperate, they figured out a pretty fair rule-of-thumb matching system, and soon there were transfers going on all over Fort Freedom. Zeth shook his head in dismay at some of the matches, wondering how they avoided disaster.

Changeovers were left up to the channels, but out-Territory there were three that grueling winter. In Mountain Chapel, one child was successfully given First Transfer by Maddok Bron—but when the second one occurred, neither he nor Sessly was there, and the girl killed her mother before being shot dead by her father. He then left town, weather notwithstanding. Word reached the ranches, and the next victim was shot before breakout.

The result was that one day five children from the ranches turned up at Fort Freedom, having crossed the frozen river. The channels treated them for frostbite and listened to their story. All of establishment or changeover age, they were determined that they wouldn't chance killing—but neither were they willing to be murdered when they knew about Fort Freedom. Therefore they had come to stay until nature declared which they would be. Two of them turned out to be already Gen; the other three showed no sign one way or the other, and Fort Freedom willingly found room for them.

Most Simes who succumbed to the Brons' matchmaking service were the older semi-juncts who had been heavily dependent on Abel Veritt's strength of character to keep them from despair. When no new spiritual leader rose from among their own, they turned to Bron—and believed that the Gens who served them were, indeed, warding off demons.

Not surprisingly, Dan Whelan, Margid Veritt, and the others who had been closest to Zeth all his life rejected anything but channel's transfer. At least over the years these Simes had moved apart in their cycle of crisis, and would not all face the overpowering need to kill in the same month or two. But Slina and the other Simes from town also refused to have anything to do with Bron's program. Zeth knew they were offended by his religious tenets as they had never been by Abel's, but he didn't understand how they could resist real Gen transfer. He almost wished they would succumb—it might avoid another cascade.

Maddok Bron kept trying to persuade Zeth to see his religious point of view. All Zeth could say was "It doesn't matter—demons or need, it's all the same thing." Even though he now felt that Abel Veritt had died futilely, he was certain that Abel had been right about that. "It is in us," he had always said.

Owen insisted, "Abel died to prove that every man is responsible for his own salvation. I can't be responsible for yours, Zeth."

"I don't believe in that kind of salvation."

"That doesn't matter—the point is the very lesson Abel made *you* teach *me!* You weren't to blame for my losing my arm, but you were *responsible,* remember? And so Abel made you responsible for me until I rebelled. Come on now—it's time for you to rebel against me!"

But Owen's arguments did no good—at least for Zeth. Dan Whelan, though, asked Owen to speak at the services in the chapel—and Zeth was surprised at the way people listened, and seemed to be comforted. Soon there was a rivalry going when Maddok Bron was in town. Then there would be two services, and Zeth noticed people beginning to count the attendance at Bron's versus Owen's. Some people attended both, but there was a growing schism between the two factions.

There was also a growing rivalry between Bron and Owen for Zeth. Bron had learned a great deal about the work of channels and Companions, mostly from Jord, who now planned to marry Sessly in the spring. Soon Bron was working his own cycle into phase with Zeth's, and hanging around Simes in need to encourage his capacity to grow. Owen wasn't blind to Bron's intentions and Zeth found the only amusement in his life in watching the two Gens compete for his attention. Zeth wasn't worried—Bron could not possibly realize how great the difference was between him and Owen, and Owen could always handle Zeth. So Zeth relaxed and enjoyed—and maybe encouraged a little.

Finally the harsh winter ended. Slina's shipment of Gens arrived just as the roof was going onto her new pens. The town Simes who had gritted their way through the winter allowed themselves kills, and the worst tension went out of the community.

The thaws dissolved the route across the frozen river and turned the other trails to mud. Travel time across the border began to approach the day's journey of last summer, although it was a long, hard, muddy ride. Visitors from out-Territory voiced concern about the government investigation. "Oh, we'll handle it," said Eph Norton on one of his frequent visits. "They'll probably have Commander Whitby, from the local garrison, conduct it. He has no patience for paperwork—he just wants to go out and shoot Simes, and then go back to the garrison and get drunk."

"Since there won't be any Simes on your side of the border, it shouldn't be much of an investigation," said Dan.

"A hearing, probably, and it'll be dropped. Glian figures he'll never get his horses back, but if we don't make a fuss, and if we slip enough money under the table, it'll all blow over. I never thought I'd be *grateful* for that bunch of slobs in the garrison! We've been protesting for years that they were no protection against the Simes—who'd ever have thought one day we wouldn't *want* protection!"

It was tax time again, on both sides of the border. The out-Territory Gens went home, to avoid the fiasco of the previous quarter, and Norton also wanted the three ranchers' children to return. "They take a family census. A kid that age ain't accounted for, they assume he's dead or turned Sime and escaped—and he better not be there the next year!"

Maddok Bron said, "There are now enough of us who can give transfer to handle any changeover that might occur."

"Unless it's a channel," said Zeth

"The solution is obvious," said Bron. "Zeth, you must let me give you transfer this month—then I'll be qualified to serve at any changeover, channel's or no."

Zeth saw Owen tense, but he would not give Zeth the satisfaction of zlinning his jealousy. When he deliberately removed his attention from Zeth, he also removed his shield against the annoyance of turnover. The onslaught of that sinking feeling prodded Zeth to say, "Well, I don't know,

Maddok. I can't promise today—but if you stick close to me for the next two weeks, if your field becomes high enough—''

"You just do that, Maddok," said Owen. "That way I'm free to go out-Territory again. Eph, I'll help you take those kids home—and do some teaching about changeover, too. Now that the weather's broken, it's possible to get a changeover victim to Fort Freedom in plenty of time—if the poor kid hasn't tried to hide his first symptoms out of fear."

Zeth fought down panic. Bron's field enveloped him in triumphant promise—but the man could never reach his capacity by the end of the month. Still he refused to ask Owen to stay.

As Zeth didn't apologize, neither did Owen. He simply packed and traded rooms with Maddok. It was strange to have a different Gen nager in Zeth's room. Awake, Bron was adequate protection against encroaching need, and when he knelt to pray, the calm, meditative state soothed Zeth almost to the point of considering Owen's absence with equanimity. But the moment Bron fell asleep, his field would have kept any of the other channels comfortable, but not Zeth. What likelihood was there that an out-Territory child would change over into a channel of Zeth's power? Virtually none. *If Owen makes any move to apologize in the morning,* Zeth promised himself, *I'll ask him to stay, and tell Bron he can handle any channel he's likely to encounter.*

But Owen didn't apologize. Zeth stood back, waiting on the chapel steps, refusing the urgings of his waning field to run to his friend and beg him to stay.

Owen came over to him, leading Flash. When Zeth remained silent, Owen said, "I'll be back in ten days, Zeth."

"Fine," Zeth forced himself to say casually. "See you then. Have a good time."

Zeth felt Owen bite back a retort—then he mounted up, kicked Flash in the ribs, and was gone.

Zeth's need nightmares inevitably took the form of searching madly for Owen, never being able to find him. It was a week before Maddok even started to wake up in response to Zeth's discomfort, unless he woke up shouting. Still, Bron never tried, as Owen did, to provoke Zeth to make his own decisions. He was content to order Zeth around, and Zeth was content to obey.

The tenth day, though, relief flooded Zeth every time he remembered, *Owen will be back today!* But he wasn't. The day passed, and the night as well, with no sign of Owen. Zeth fought down panic. *I can survive one month without Owen. I can take a healing-mode transfer from Bron and balance my fields and then I'll be in good enough shape to go out-Territory and bring Owen home*. Never did he let himself fear that Owen was not to be brought home. *He's not dead. I'd know*.

That afternoon, a mud-covered figure rode through the gates of Fort Freedom, radiating alarm. Eph Norton—announcing as he slid down from his horse, "It's not an investigation—it's a takeover! Owen's been arrested!"

Zeth's panic spiked so high that Bron put his arms about him, as if to hold him from attack—but there was nothing to attack. *Where is he? Who's got him?*

Only when Norton had collapsed into a chair in the Veritt kitchen, a cup of tea in his hands and Margid busy making him a meal, did the story come out.

"They send out soldiers from the garrison to collect the taxes in the spring—but two or three together, not twenty or thirty! They come onto my place demanding tax money. I had it, but then they wanted a head count—and Owen happened to be there. Yesterday—no, day before. He was headed back here. Damn—if he'd've left just an hour earlier—I couldn't pass him off as a hired hand, him with only one arm, so I said he was my nephew—but seems they'd met Owen before and he claimed to live in Mountain Chapel. They decided to search the house, sayin' they heard we was harboring Simes, sellin' 'em Gens! I been hangin' these damn tags over my gun by the door, so's I'll remember to put 'em on before I ride over here. They found 'em, and then they ransacked the house, found my papers in Simelan—searched Owen and found his tags and papers, and that was enough to arrest him."

Norton's eyes met Zeth's. "Nothin' I could do, unless *I* wanted to be arrested along with him. They told me to stay put, they were gonna send out more troops to put us under martial law. We all knew what that meant! My men took out the guard they left on my place easy enough, and I rode right out here. By now, I figure they got reinforcements headin' for my place, and all the others, too."

"And maybe in Mountain Chapel," said Bron. "The law says they can execute Sime collaborators or Genrunners, and

Whitby would love some action to show he's doing his job! Zeth—''

"I came to you for help, and you gave it. You don't think we'll refuse to help in return?''

"I'm goin','' said Slina. "None of my people're gonna miss this.''

"We can be ready to ride by sundown,'' said Dan.

Zeth was ready to go right that minute—but preparations had to be made to cover his absence, and the absence of Uel and Marji and their Companions. Most of the Simes would go, so most of the channels had to go as well. Marji, raised in Mountain Chapel's traditions, was astonished that she should be expected to go on a military campaign while Jord, a man, was to be left behind—but Jord was the least stable channel and therefore best not exposed to battle.

Zeth felt Sessly's resentment that Jord should be called unstable while he was in her care, but he also felt her relief that he would not have to risk his life in battle—and that kept her silent. Not that the channels were supposed to fight; they were the medical team. Zeth chafed as Dan deployed the people of Fort Freedom, the channels and Companions at the rear of the line of march. Zeth's inclination was to lead the charge—but of course he knew intellectually that Fort Freedom could not allow him to take such a risk.

Slina left one of her old faithful hands, Flieg, in charge of the new pens. The town Simes formed a separate line. There was no time to practice together, so it seemed best to leave each to its own tactic and leadership in battle.

They decided to head straight for Mountain Chapel, where they could pick up additional manpower to liberate the ranches. Slogging their way across the highest pass, they met another messenger on his way to Fort Freedom: Lon Carson. He was on foot and exhausted.

"I had to sneak out,'' he explained. "They sent a whole troop of men in, confiscated our weapons and set up martial law. Now there's only about twenty men guarding the town— but they have guns and we don't. The troops from the garrison are trying to keep everyone put while they round up reinforcements. Then they plan prejudged trials, and mass executions for Genrunning.''

"Twenty men,'' said Slina. "Dan, Zeth, you let me and my men go in there and clean 'em out for you.''

"We want to avoid killing—'' began Bron.

Slina gave him a look that said her opinion of him had just dropped several notches below its previous rock-bottom position. "That's the idea," she said with exaggerated patience. "My people are professionals. They can handle Wild Gens without hurtin' 'em, so's no one's provoked to a kill. Put 'em up for sale later."

"Slina's right," said Dan Whelan. "All right—you bring your people around us—"

Zeth chafed at not being in on the action. *It's just the first step in rescuing Owen*, he reminded himself. *He's not in Mountain Chapel.*

The Gens took the easier but longer wagon trail toward Mountain Chapel, Simes and the Companions riding with channels the shorter but narrower way that Zeth had first come to the town. As the sun rose, both troops approached the bridge. Glinting flashes told them spyglasses were turned on them—Simes and Gens, meeting and joining to progress inexorably in the direction of the town.

The Gen troops headed out to defend the bridge. Slina and her party rode forward, whips at the ready. Shots rang out—but none reached its mark. In the second volley, when the Simes were upon them, one townswoman went down, dead, caught full in the face. Otherwise, flesh wounds, but nothing serious—and the Simes were riding straight over the soldiers. On the other side of the bridge they turned, cracked their whips, and began herding the terrified Gen soldiers back across the bridge.

In the town, people came running out, cheering. Half the soldiers dropped their guns in panic, and the others' were quickly wrenched out of their hands.

Slina dismounted, coiling her whip, and strode briskly toward the captives. "Prime Wild Gens," she said in English. "Keb, Bree, Taris—you take 'em on back to my pen—tell Flieg to tag 'em and make out papers. And tell him to sell the two that give you the most trouble on the way back as Choice Kills, to pay the taxes on the rest!"

The tensed alarm in the captives put an edge on Zeth's need, and he almost objected until he recalled that Slina's pen was the only structure that could possibly contain the prisoners—and her threat would assure they went docilely with their escort. *None must get away to warn the others!*

Beside him, Bron called, "Take those uniforms, and let

them travel in their underwear, Slina. They won't give you any trouble.''

Slina squinted back at him, zlinning him oddly, and then issued the orders.

Soon the soldiers were on their way back to Fort Freedom. In the town, the people were liberating their guns from where the soldiers had put them, inside the chapel—but no one seemed certain of their next move. ''Now what do we do? There'll be more troops on the way here, tomorrow at the latest, with orders to hold executions!'' said Lon Carson in the Brons' main room.

''Not if this were Sime Territory,'' said Zeth. It seemed so obvious he couldn't imagine why Bron was staring at him. ''I saw it months ago—before Abel died. There aren't enough people in any of our communities to survive alone now. We've got to unify.''

Maddok said, ''Zeth, I'm calling everyone into the chapel. Your idea will have to be considered.''

After everyone had been calmed by prayer, Bron announced, ''We're not safe here anymore. We have to help the ranchers oust the military from their property—but that isn't enough. Once word gets out, we'll be the target of the whole territorial army. Fortunately, Zeth Farris has a suggestion.''

Zeth made his way to the lectern and faced the over-crowded chapel, noting the way the Simes had arranged themselves to protect those in need. It was the first time he had faced them thus, but he knew this was the only way he'd get to Owen in time, and so he found his voice.

''We are four communities united in a mutual struggle for survival—ranchers, Mountain Chapel, Fort Freedom, and Freedom Township. A law which decrees a parent must be executed for saving a child's life is an abomination of the human spirit. If we are to continue as human beings, we must remove the border that divides us. If we move it so that your communities lie in-Territory, it will not be illegal for you to love your parents—or your children.''

''I'm for that!'' cried a Gen. Another spoke up, ''But how can we?'' A Sime called, ''If we can do it, we'll have autonomous control of the new land for a decade. We can write our own laws!'' And a portly man from the back added the clincher, ''We won't have to pay taxes on *both* sides of the border anymore!''

Enthusiasm for Zeth's idea was growing. Eph Norton expressed it for them all. "Hell—we got nothin' to lose. If we *don't* move the border, our government's gonna execute every last one of us." He pointed to Jimmy, sitting across the aisle with other Simes. "I got a boy there can't be my son under Gen law. He hasn't killed five months. There's nothing wrong with him now. No reason he shouldn't inherit the ranch I built!"

Soon a plan was formulated: they'd ride out and take the Gen garrison. Zeth breathed a sigh of relief. *That's where Owen is!*

Had it been up to Zeth, everyone would have gone straight out to their horses. However, there was an immense amount of preparation first. Horses had to be shod and shells loaded, and men discussed how best to deploy the new, fast-loading guns with the older type. Women packed food and medical supplies. Meanwhile, arguments erupted as to exactly *where* they meant to move the border.

The arguments, the preparations—all seemed to Zeth a deliberate waste of time. "The reinforcements will reach the garrison while we're fooling around here!" he protested. "They'll have a full force."

"And if we're unprepared," said Cord Ashley, one of the secular leaders of Mountain Chapel, "they'll put us to rout. I've served in the army, son. It'll take them time to gather their men—and we have to decide exactly what we're going to do. What we *can* do."

Bron agreed. "We have no right to try to take other communities into Sime Territory—perhaps one day we'll encourage others, but we must not force them."

"Look at it practically," said Ashley. "What we take we gotta hold. Chances are, if we attempt to hold only land that's ours anyway, they'll think twice about trying to move the border back—'specially if the Sime government will help us hold it?"

He looked questioningly at Zeth, but it was Slina who answered. "Rimon an' Abel an' me—we been playin' games with the government the past ten years—an' I ain't forgot how it's done. You worry 'bout takin' the land, and we'll worry 'bout holdin' it."

Bron assured Cord, "You can trust Slina to know the ins and outs of Sime Government. And you just saw the way the people she commands handle themselves in battle."

Finally they got to what interested Zeth: the garrison. It lay in a plateau beneath a cliff that made a natural barrier across that section of Gen Territory. "If we can take the garrison," said Ashley, "that cliff makes a natural border. There are only two passes through it, three days' ride apart. It won't take many people to guard those passes. We put the border there, we can defend it! Now—how do we take the fort?"

Bron had an answer obvious to the Gens—a solution no Sime would think of. Find twenty men, Sime and Gen, wʰo fit the uniforms they had taken from the captured soldiers. Send them in as returning troops. By the time they were close enough for Gens to realize that they didn't recognize them, they'd be close enough to charge the gate while the force from Fort Freedom and Mountain Chapel swept down out of the hills. Those who entered the fort would also be armed with a Gen innovation, powder kegs with fuses.

Maddok Bron had further plans. "As a safety measure, and to be certain the Simes fighting with us can tell which Gens are which in the heat of battle, the channels ought to take down the fields of all *our* Gens—even those staying behind. You'll have to have that selyn for healing, Zeth."

Much as he itched to be off, Zeth had to agree. As a large number of Mountain Chapel Gens had never donated before, the three channels had to work slowly the next few hours. By the time they were finished, it was finally time to ride for the garrison.

They rode through the night, reaching the hills overlooking the garrison at midmorning. Scouts moved forward—Zeth was called up front, as he was the most sensitive of them all. Eagerly, he ran to the top of the rocks and peered over. Small bands of soldiers were leaving the fort on horseback, scattering in all directions. "What the bloodyshen hell is going *on?*" demanded Slina, now dressed in a Gen officer's uniform that hung shapelessly on her spare frame.

"I can't tell," Zeth whispered back, and extended his laterals. All he could read was a bustle of Gen activity spiked with anger, dismay, annoyance, and apprehension. What he did *not* read kept him frozen in icy horror until Slina shook him.

"Owen's not there!" he gasped. "Slina—he's dead!"

"He ain't there don't mean he's dead. I'd stake Owen against them lorshes any day." Zeth remembered his mother saying the same thing, and took heart. Maybe he'd escaped.

Quickly, before the Gen soldiers stumbled on the massed

attack force, their little troop of counterfeit soldiers broke up
into small groups and infiltrated the others. Without appear-
ing to be bucking the tide, they worked their way toward the
fort—and when they were close enough, the charge began.

Gen fear and astonishment permeated the plateau as the
force of Simes and Gens appeared. Shots rang out, horns
sounded, and the troops wheeled their horses and galloped
back toward the gates, which were moving ponderously shut.
Zeth could zlin Gens manning the walls, and saw puffs of
smoke as they began firing. But some of their planted soldiers
were inside by the time the gates closed.

Knowing Owen was not in the garrison made it easier for
Zeth to do what he was supposed to: set up a field hospital
outside range of those firing from the fort walls. Jimmy
Norton, assigned to help Zeth, led up a pack horse and began
unloading medical supplies as Hank and Uel set up the stan-
dard to mark the location of the channels for the Gens.
Ironically, the flag they flew was one of the brand-new vivid
green pennants from Slina's pens.

Already wounded were being brought in—mostly Gen soldiers who hadn't made it back inside the fort.

Then, even through the raging battle, Zeth caught the pain
of the inevitable—the first kill. It came from inside the
fort—one of the town Simes, then. Within seconds there was
another—and then a roar of shock as the garrison exploded,
shards of wood flying high into the air on a roiling black
cloud. They'd blown the powder depot! With it went one side
of the wall. Zeth could barely zlin through the shrieking Gen
pain as men were torn to pieces or burned. Instantly, every
Sime past turnover was shocked to intil, and the high-field
Gen soldiers were plucked up and killed on every side.

Soldiers came billowing out of the fort, on horseback and
on foot, their only chance now to attack swiftly and powerfully.
At close range, their shots connected, and the hospital was
suddenly busier than Zeth had yet seen. He worked, not
allowing himself to think or he would sink into total despair.
The kill raged around and through him, his heritage, his
destiny. There was no way out. Owen was gone.

He worked numbly, glad now for the selyn the Mountain
Chapel Gens had donated. He could heal a few more before
he killed. Maddok, praying as he worked, was a rock Zeth
could lean on—provided he didn't lean too hard.

Simultaneously, Zeth became aware of two facts. The first

was the fighting arrowing steadily toward the hospital. Bron said, "Dear God! They think the banner marks the command post!"

At the same time, a familiar nager approached from another direction, flickering as it moved between the rocky outcroppings. *Owen!*

Maddok started for the banner—obviously to tear it down. Zeth grabbed him. "No! Owen has to see it to find me!"

Bron stared at him as if Zeth had gone out of his head. "Owen's not here, Zeth—but I am—"

"No—he's coming. There!" He pointed to where Owen's bright hair could be seen shining in the sun as he dashed between two rocks, making his way down to the plateau. "And," added Zeth, "all the Gens have to be able to see where the channels are!

A few soldiers were driving directly toward the pennant. Zeth grabbed the ambient fields and sent up a shattering call for help. Nearby Simes fought loose and converged on the station to protect the channels. Mrs. Young, Hapen's mother, grasped one of the Gen soldiers who had made it almost to Zeth's feet, and killed. Zeth knew that he himself was poised to kill right now—that he *would* kill, without compunction, to save himself, or Owen, or anyone he loved.

As Owen's nager continued to work toward him, zigzagging to avoid the fighting, Zeth pulled his concentration down to healing one of the Mountain Chapel Gens. He had to let his own need pour through his nerves to get the Gen cells to produce more selyn, to heal themselves. He tried not to be aware of the long time Owen was taking, not to notice when the distant Gen's attention flicked to some battle scene before him. Slowly, the bleeding under his hands stopped. He gave Jimmy Norton a grim smile. "Bandage it," he instructed, and started to turn to the next patient when he saw and zlinned Owen, not a hundred paces away, caught on the opposite side of a mass of fighting.

Owen was watching Eph Norton and two burly soldiers. The soldiers closed on Norton, bayonets jabbing. Owen threw himself into the fight, knocking one of the Gens down while Norton rammed the butt of his gun into the other's jaw.

Zeth hardly felt the pain amid the scrambled ambient nager, and only realized he himself was in motion when Jimmy zipped past him at the highest level of augmentation.

The first soldier was on his feet again, slashing with his

sword while Norton parried with the clumsier gun. Jimmy leaped to his father's defense, flinging the sword from the soldier's hand with one blow to his wrist, and then even as the man was screaming in pain, grasped him in killmode. On a wave of augmentation, Zeth leaped on Jimmy, hauling him back with all his strength, shenning him out of the attack in pain that put Zeth helplessly into killmode himself.

Jimmy fell unconscious, and Zeth groped toward Owen—just as another soldier charged Zeth with his bayonet. Augmenting again, Zeth grasped the gun barrel, intending to fling it away—but he had forgotten the relative weights of Sime and Gen. The man stood rock solid until Zeth got his grip, and then he flung Zeth's lighter body right up into the air—and toward another man waiting with a sword to spit him!

Zeth twisted in midair to land on his feet—but as the soldier slashed at him he automatically grasped the man's right wrist with his left hand, twisting until he dropped the weapon. The soldier sought to throw a punch with his left hand, and Zeth grabbed that as well—and was holding the soldier in kill position while he flared horror.

Owen ran toward Zeth, trying to leap between them, but another soldier caught him in the stomach with his gun butt. It reached Zeth as the most exquisite flash of pain he had ever experienced. He was in killmode, the face before him already forming the rictus of fear as he reached for lip contact.

Owen, unable to move or even breathe, snatched his hunting knife from his boot and flung it straight into the back of the man Zeth held. The Gen died in Zeth's arms before he could kill—the nager going flat and tasteless though still replete with selyn.

In a rage of denied killbliss, Zeth turned as another Gen field, high, warm, welcoming, closed on him. Pure predator, Zeth grasped and drew. He sought to slake his wakened yearning in true killbliss. But this Gen was giving—giving— He speeded his draw, already close to depleting the Gen field. He could still kill—drain—burn— Fierce joy spread through him as the Gen felt pain, then fear, and began to struggle.

Something in Zeth shifted. The searing need for Gen pain was gone. Though need was still there, he was filled with the joy of release.

Something slammed him duoconscious. The Gen fell away from his loosened grasp. In agonized protest, his dual system went into spasm. And then blackness closed over him.

Zeth came to, struggling to breathe, Owen's full weight crushing him. He was on his back on the battlefield, his hands pinned between their two bodies, against Owen's bare chest—this time Owen hadn't waited for help to give transfer when Zeth was unconscious. He'd torn open his shirt to let Zeth's laterals find contact. Somehow, it had worked; after the last trickle of termination, Owen lifted his head, smiling in relief to find Zeth looking at him. He climbed to his knees, his field ringing with triumph at overcoming his handicap. Zeth breathed deeply and managed, "Thanks."

The battle was skirling away from them now. Zeth knew he had tried to kill, but couldn't remember clearly why he hadn't. He sat up, ignoring the bruised feeling through his system. Uel was bending over Maddok, who was unconscious and very pale. The other channel looked up at once. "He'll live, Zeth. It's just a burn. I zlinned the whole thing, but I couldn't reach you. You shenned yourself, thank God."

"No—Owen—"

"It wasn't me. You dropped Maddok before I could touch you. Then you started convulsing like Rimon used to—just about scared me to— Anyway, you're both all right."

"Zeth?" The voice was querulous, plaintive. Jimmy Norton. Zeth shoved himself to his feet. Jimmy was clinging to his father for support—but there was no nageric link between them. It was Zeth Jimmy was reaching toward—and Zeth held out his arms to him, feeling in his nager the sweet, clean ease of tension that meant disjunction. The transfer wiped out Zeth's pain as totally as it did Jimmy's need—and afterward he hugged the boy, saying, "It's over, Jimmy. You made it. No more need to kill."

Eph Norton, his field glowing with joy and gratitude, took his son from Zeth's arms. "He insisted it had to be you, Zeth. You did it—you made Jimmy my son again!"

But Jimmy Norton was not the only Sime who needed a transfer. As the battle wound down, the channels were faced with lines of people determined not to succumb to the kill in the weakness of relief. Owen tugged at Zeth. "Jana needs you—hurry!"

Owen's sister was trembling with need, brought on partly by selyn loss from a sword wound in her thigh, and partly by the same augmentation every Sime in the battle had indulged in—to win. The Gen soldiers were all dead or captured and a strange hush had fallen. Zeth told Jana, "You came through just fine. You resisted, Jana."

In response, she flung herself on him, and when it was over, she clung to Zeth, sobbing, "I wanted to kill. I only murdered a few of them. Sissy Brandon, though—Zeth, she never killed before! Never! And I saw her—"

"We'll have to help her, Jana," Zeth began.

"No, no—she's dead! I think she let them cut her down after—"

"No, Jana—it was war." Even so, their casualties were light. No one close to Zeth had died, and he chose to take that as an omen of better times.

The evening passed in a blur—transfers, post-reactions, and caring for the wounded. Just before sundown, they carried the last of the wounded into the fort, where the men's living quarters, on the side opposite the hole in the wall, were turned into an infirmary. Zeth had no time to think until well after midnight, when he was making a final check through the barracks before trying to find a place for himself—and particularly Owen—to get some rest. Finally it occurred to him to ask his Companion, "How did you escape? We came to rescue you, you know."

Owen had tied the torn ends of his shirt together, but his Gen tags with Slina's dagger-like emblem flashed in the candlelight. He had repossessed the tags along with his knife. "I wasn't going to let those fools make me miss my transfer," he explained. "I just pretended to be helpless. None of those soldiers were very bright, especially Commander Whitby. He came to question me this morning. By then I had them convinced I couldn't even button my shirt without help—so when I paced around behind him, pretending I might tell him something, he never thought I'd pick up the washstand and bash him over the head. Then I took his keys, and off I went! The so-called guards never even saw me sneak out the gate. I was halfway up the mountain before they started sending out search parties."

"They never saw you leave? You *are* trying to earn the title 'wer-Gen,' aren't you?"

By this time they had reached a knot of people, Simes and Gens, clustered around the bunk where Maddok Bron was recovering from transfer burn. As they had plenty of fosebine, his headache was only a dull throb. Dan Whelan, Eph Norton, Hank and Uel, Slina, and Cord Ashley were all deep in plans.

". . . as a decoy," Slina was saying as Zeth and Owen came up. "Not one trooper escaped today. When the others come back, the Simes here'll zlin 'em. We get some folks in uniform up on the walls, and those Gens'll just ride right into the trap, nice as you please!"

"But half the wall is down!" Cord Ashley protested. "It'll take days—"

"Shen," Slina laughed, "bunch of my Simes are out hauling logs now. We'll have that wall back by sunrise—just has to look the same from the outside." Replete with selyn from a guiltless kill that day, Slina was hypoconscious and in a jolly mood. Now she looked up and saw Zeth. "Well," she said heartily, "your plan sure worked!"

My plan? But just then Jana came up from the other side. "Please, Slina, speak more softly. The wounded Gens must sleep."

"Sure thing, kid," said Slina in a whisper far more penetrating than her speaking voice. "Well, Zeth, what next?"

Jana remained behind Slina, looking expectantly at Zeth, as did everyone else. "Slina, you'll handle the legal problems. Maddok, I'm afraid the Simes who killed today will be coming to you for comfort."

"I think I can manage that," Bron said evenly. "I will tell them what we are fighting is no demon—but you overcame killust today, Zeth. I was wrong. My pride could have gotten me killed—and made you a killer. I couldn't stop you. You did it yourself. I've been thanking God for your strength since I woke up."

He felt inside his shirt, searching for something.

"I just wish I understood what happened," said Zeth. "*I* didn't kill, but others, even those who had never killed—"

"Zeth," said Uel, "you zlinned just like Abel Veritt before he died."

Zeth remembered the feeling Abel had given them all. He had gone beyond the kill. "But Abel *died*. He couldn't accept selyn."

"You're a channel, Zeth," said Owen.

"But Abel *wasn't*. Why should—?" Suddenly it all fell into place. "Owen—I remember now what Abel and I had in common. We were both *almost killed*! Marji almost killed Abel at her changeover. And Dad almost killed me. You have to die to be free of the kill!"

A weight lifted from his spirit. He barely heard Uel say, "Then I'll do it, too," as Hank's nager flared real fear.

Jana said, "Do it to me, Zeth. I don't ever want to be tempted again."

"No," said Owen. "You're not a channel, Jana. I'm not allowing any experiments on my sister!"

"That's right, Jana," said Bron. "Let the channels decide what's best." He was holding his papers and tags. Putting the tags around his neck, like Owen's, he said, "Zeth, only someone who is beyond the kill has the right to make such decisions." He held out his papers to Zeth. "You're my channel now. I choose you."

Dan Whelan and the others all looked at Zeth, echoing Bron's trust. It was the same excruciating feeling he had known in the chapel at his father's eulogy. But now it was bearable.

Abel had chosen him to hold the papers of the Gens of Fort Freedom, and he had not been able to accept. Now, his hand closed firmly over Bron's papers. "Abel once told me the truth of our predicament in Fort Freedom. Fear is our real enemy, not the people it possesses.

"So many of our—family—have died fighting that fear. But so long as we can live together, they didn't die in vain." He looked up at Owen, then around the circle of familiar faces and back to Bron. "I'll do my part to see that Fort Freedom continues, if you'll all do yours."

The wave of affirmation drove him duoconscious, and there were tears behind his eyes as he added, "I can do it because I know now that Abel Veritt did not die forsworn, nor was his faith in the future unjustified." Zeth held the papers aloft, accepting without reservation the triumphant knowledge: "Fort Freedom lives—forever!"